The
Forgotten Pages:

Stories Born, Forgotten, and Finally Told

Brett C. Persson

The Forgotten Pages:
Stories Born, Forgotten, and Finally Told

Third Printing

X

@BrettCPersson

www.brettcpersson.com

Nudous Publishing, LLC

www.nudouspublishing.com
info@nudouspublishing.com

Paperback ISBN: 978-1-964793-66-5

This is a work of fiction. Names, characters, places, businesses, events, and incidents are either the product of the author's imagination or are used fictitiously. Any resemblance to actual persons, living or dead, or actual events is purely coincidental.

Note from the Author

Before you dive into these stories, I want to offer a moment of care.

The Forgotten Pages was born from the shadows, those parts of life we often hide, bury, or try to forget. These stories explore addiction, loss, grief, violence, homelessness, trauma, and moments of deep emotional and spiritual struggle. Some pages are hard. Some may bring back memories you weren't planning to revisit.

But within the brokenness, I've tried to leave space for light, for the quiet strength of survival, the stubborn flicker of hope, and the beauty that sometimes rises from ruin.

If you've lived through some of these things yourself, please take care while reading. And if you haven't, I hope this book helps you understand those who have.

Thank you for being here, and for turning the page.

—Brett C. Persson

Trigger Warning

This collection explores real and raw human experiences: addiction, trauma, loss, grief, and personal struggle. Some stories contain depictions of substance abuse, violence, and emotional distress. While hope and healing thread through these pages, readers should proceed with care.

Table of Contents

One Step at a Time 2

The Quiet That Stayed 18

What the River Left Behind 26

The Fall of the Body Politic 38

Lifeline..52

Room 7A...70

Whispers of the Neon God..82

Not Even a Whisper in the Silence................................98

Just One More Day.. 118

Dead Cold Winter.. 126

I Learned to Drink My Coffee Black in Rehab................ 154

Known Destiny.. 172

Laid to Ashes 202

Eldkula II.. 236

Relapse 264

The Lineage.. 286

Smoke Over Hollowpoint 318

The Car Wreck.. 382

We Live by the River 386

Echoes of an Empty Bottle 408

Killer of Giants.. 420

It was just after 7:00 a.m. on a Wednesday morning when Jonny was pulled from a restless sleep by the sharp, ringing sound of the phone. He sat up slowly, groaning, his head pounding from the night before. But he didn't reach for the phone. Instead, his hand searched the cluttered desk beside his bed until it landed on a half-empty bottle of Jack Daniels. That was the only thing he cared about right now.

He unscrewed the cap and took a long swig straight from the bottle, not even thinking about grabbing a glass. Mornings didn't mean much to Jonny anymore; any time was the right time for a drink, especially after a night like last night. Whatever had happened was still a blur, and maybe that was for the best.

With the bottle resting between his legs, Jonny dug around until he found his crumpled soft pack of Marlboro Reds. He pulled one out with his lips and fumbled through his pockets until he found his lighter. It took a few tries, his hand still unsteady, but finally, the flame caught the end of the cigarette. The tip lit up bright red as he took a deep drag, the paper crackling quietly. He held the smoke in for a moment, then let it out slowly through his nose and mouth. He took another swig from the bottle, letting the burn settle into his gut.

His face told the story of a man who had clearly taken a beating. A fresh, crusted-over cut stretched about three inches above his left eye, and his nose was crooked, swollen, and obviously broken. He hadn't shaved in days, and the rough stubble only added to his worn-down appearance. A sour, heavy smell clung to him, not just the usual stench of sweat and whiskey but something darker. It was the smell of blood and something close to death.

His black hair was a mess, matted down in places and streaked with dried blood on the right side of his scalp. He didn't need a mirror to know he looked awful. He could feel it in every aching part of his body. And still, he took another drag, another drink, like it was the only thing holding him together.

The phone stopped ringing after a while, leaving a thick silence behind. Jonny didn't care who it was. Nobody called him with good news anymore. If it wasn't someone asking for money, it was someone telling him something he didn't want to hear. Either way, he wasn't in the mood.

He leaned back against the wall, letting his head thump lightly against the drywall. It hurt more than he expected. A sharp flash of pain ran from the base of his skull down to his spine. He winced and took another drink to chase the sting away.

Outside, the sun was already climbing, casting pale light through the half-closed blinds. Dust danced in the beams, making the air in the room look heavy like it hadn't been cleaned in months because it hadn't. Empty bottles cluttered the floor like forgotten memories, and cigarette butts overflowed in a cracked ashtray on the nightstand. A stained T-shirt hung from the back of a chair, stiff with dried sweat. The room smelled like stale smoke, alcohol, and something sour, like regret that had been left out too long.

Jonny finally stood up, legs shaky, joints stiff. He walked barefoot across the cold wooden floor, wincing with each step. His ribs ached with a deep, bruised throb, and he felt the sting of a pulled muscle in his side. The fight from last night was coming back to him in pieces, yelling, fists, flashing lights. He wasn't sure who had hit first, but he was pretty sure he didn't win.

He made it to the bathroom and flicked on the light. The mirror was cracked, but it was enough to show him what he needed to see. His face was a mess. Blood had dried at the edges of the cut above his eye, and the skin around his nose was purple and swollen. He touched it gently and flinched.

"Damn," he muttered, shaking his head.

He turned on the faucet and splashed cold water on his face. It stung, but it helped wake him up a little. He reached for the towel, then thought better of it; it was crusty and smelled worse than he did. Instead, he just wiped his face with the bottom of his shirt and stumbled back into the bedroom.

The phone started ringing again.

This time, he looked at it.

The screen lit up with a name he hadn't seen in over a year.

Maya.

His stomach turned. She was the last person he wanted to talk to, and maybe the only person he still cared about.

He stood there for a long moment, staring at the screen as it rang. Then, finally, he picked up the bottle and took another drink.

Jonny stared at the screen like it might burn a hole through his hand.

Maya.

He hadn't seen her in over a year since the night she packed up her things and walked out without looking back. He remembered her standing in the doorway, holding her purse, tears in her eyes. He'd said something cruel. She'd said nothing at all.

Now, for some reason, she was calling.

He let it ring one more time before pressing the green button and raising the phone to his ear.

"…Yeah?" His voice came out rough, coated with whiskey and smoke.

There was a pause. Then her voice was soft but sharp like it always was when she was angry and trying not to be.

"Jonny?"

He swallowed. "Yeah. It's me."

Another pause.

"You sound like shit."

"Thanks. You always had a way with words," he said, rubbing his eyes.

She ignored that. "I wouldn't be calling if it wasn't important."

Jonny sat back down on the edge of the bed, cigarette still burning in the ashtray beside him. "Then say it."

Maya's breath came through the line, shaking. "It's your brother. He's in the hospital."

That hit harder than the bottle ever could. Jonny sat up straighter, blood draining from his face.

"What happened?"

"There was an accident. A bad one. He's alive, but… you should come. I'm at St. Luke's. They're not sure if he is going to make it."

Jonny stood without realizing it, the floor tilting slightly under his bare feet. His brother. The last piece of family he hadn't managed to drive away. The one person who still believed in him even when he didn't deserve it.

"I'll be there," Jonny said, voice low.

Maya sighed. "You sure? Last time—"

"I said I'll be there," he cut in, firmer now.

She didn't argue. "Room 317. Don't take too long."

Then the line went dead.

Jonny stood in the silence that followed, the phone still in his hand. For a long time, he didn't move. Then he looked around the room at the mess, the stink, the wreck of his life, and finally tossed the bottle across the room. It hit the wall with a dull thud and rolled to a stop under the dresser.

He stubbed out his cigarette, found a half-clean shirt, and pulled it over his head, wincing at the pain in his side. His head was still spinning, but it didn't matter.

For the first time in a long time, he had somewhere to be.

Jonny stumbled around his room, kicking through dirty clothes and empty bottles as he looked for his jeans. He found them crumpled near the foot of the bed, one leg still inside out. As he bent down to grab them, a sharp pain ripped through his side, nearly dropping him to the floor. He cursed under his breath, gritting his teeth until it passed.

Pulling the jeans on took more effort than it should've. His hands were shaky, and his head felt like it was full of wet cement. He swayed on his feet, pressing one hand against the wall for balance.

His mouth was dry, bitter, and sour like something had died in it. He grabbed a lukewarm water bottle from the nightstand, twisted the cap off, and poured what little was left into his mouth. It wasn't enough. His body craved more alcohol, more poison, but he forced himself not to reach for the bottle he'd just thrown. That part of him wanted to forget the phone call had ever happened. But a deeper part, buried beneath the bruises, the rot, the years of bad decisions, he couldn't.

He made it to the bathroom and stared at his reflection again. This time, he really looked. He didn't see a man anymore; he saw a ghost with sunken eyes, a busted nose, and skin pale with patches of dried blood. He grabbed a towel and scrubbed at his face like he could wipe away everything he'd become.

Then came the worst part.

The shakes.

His hands twitched, then trembled, then jerked uncontrollably. Cold sweat broke out on his forehead. His stomach turned, bile rising in his throat. He dropped to his knees and threw up in the sink, dry heaving until there was nothing left but spit and regret.

He sat on the floor for a while, back against the tub, arms resting on his knees. His breathing was heavy. His whole body throbbed. He felt like he was falling apart from the inside out, but he had to go.

He forced himself to stand. Found some Advil and swallowed three without water. He brushed his teeth, spit blood from a split gum, and rinsed his mouth until the sink ran pink. He ran cold water through his hair, towel-dried it, and dug through his drawers for something clean to wear. Eventually, he settled on a hoodie that didn't smell too bad and a pair of worn sneakers with busted laces. He looked like hell, but he didn't care.

He made it to the door, opened it, and stepped outside. The sunlight hit him like a punch to the face. He squinted against the glare, shoved his hands in his pockets, and started walking toward the bus stop three blocks down.

It was going to be a long ride to the hospital. But this time, he was going.

The walk to the bus stop felt longer than three blocks. Jonny moved like his joints were rusted, every step jarring something loose inside him. His ribs ached with each breath, and the sun was too bright, too loud, and it seemed to burn straight through his hoodie.

He kept his hood up and his head down, hoping no one would look too closely. But people always looked. That was the thing about being broken in public: there was no hiding it, no matter how much you tried.

He reached the stop and sat on the metal bench, already sweating through his clothes despite the chill in the air. His hands were still trembling. His mouth was dry again. He wanted a drink so bad it made his teeth hurt. But the bottle was blocks away now. All he had was the ache in his chest and the sharp pulse behind his eyes.

A woman and her daughter stood a few feet away, waiting for the same bus. The girl, maybe six or seven, kept glancing at Jonny. Her eyes were big and curious. The mother held her hand a little tighter and pulled her closer, not saying anything, just giving Jonny a sideways glance like he was something to be avoided, and he couldn't blame her.

The bus hissed to a stop in front of them. Jonny stood slowly, joints popping, and stepped on behind the others. He dropped a few crumpled bills into the fare box and made his way to the back, trying not to draw attention to himself. But the smell of sweat, smoke, and whatever else clung to him like a second skin and he was sure people noticed.

He slumped into a seat and stared out the window. The city moved past strip malls, traffic lights, and kids waiting for school buses. Life kept going like it always did. It didn't matter if someone was dying in a hospital bed or another guy was falling apart trying to get there.

He closed his eyes and leaned his head against the glass. The cold felt good.

Voices murmured around him. A couple of teenagers were laughing a few rows up. A man across the aisle from him coughed, deep and wet. Somewhere near the front, an old gospel song played quietly through someone's headphones.

Jonny felt like he was underwater, everything muffled and slow. His body was there, but his mind kept drifting. He saw his brother's face, smiling through childhood memories of bike rides, fishing trips, and the way they used to be before everything turned sour.

He didn't know what he was walking into at that hospital. Maybe a goodbye. Maybe worse.

All he knew was he couldn't screw this up. Not this time.

The bus hit a pothole, and Jonny jolted upright. His side flared with pain again. He gritted his teeth and sat forward. He could see the hospital now, rising above the next intersection like some pale monument.

He pulled the cord.

The bus slowed to a stop.

Jonny stood, wiped his hands on his jeans, and stepped off.

The bus pulled away behind him with a groan of exhaust and brakes, but Jonny didn't move right away. He just stood there on the sidewalk, staring at the hospital. The building was tall and colorless, all glass and concrete, like a place where feelings didn't belong. Only facts. Charts. Machines.

He shoved his hands into the pockets of his hoodie and took a shaky breath. Then he crossed the street and walked through the sliding doors.

The smell hit him first, antiseptic and cold, like bleach and sorrow. It was too clean. Too quiet. His footsteps echoed on the tile floor as he stepped inside. People moved around him, nurses, orderlies, and visitors, but no one looked his way. Everyone had their own problems. Their own people to worry about.

Jonny walked up to the front desk. "Room 317," he mumbled.

The woman behind the counter didn't ask questions. Just pointed toward the elevators. He nodded and moved that way, his stomach twisting tighter with every step.

By the time the elevator doors slid open, he was sweating again. He stepped in, hit the button for the third floor, and leaned against the wall. His reflection stared back at him in the polished metal, dark circles under his eyes, busted lip, hoodie pulled low like he had something to hide.

Maybe he did.

The elevator chimed. The doors opened.

He stepped out and walked the long hallway, counting the room numbers. 309… 311… 313… 315…

Then he saw her.

Maya.

She was sitting on a plastic chair outside Room 317, arms crossed, legs tucked up under her like she was trying to make herself smaller. Her dark hair was tied back in a messy knot. Her eyes were red. When she looked up and saw him, she didn't smile.

"Jonny."

He stopped a few feet away. "Maya."

"You look…" she started, then stopped herself. "Rough."

He nodded. "I feel worse."

A silence passed between them, heavy with everything they hadn't said in over a year.

"Is he…?" Jonny asked, his voice barely above a whisper.

Maya stood and walked toward him. "He's awake. But he's weak. He is more stable than he was earlier. I don't know how much time you'll have."

Jonny looked at the door, heart pounding in his chest like a warning. "What happened?"

"Car wreck. A drunk driver ran a red light." She glanced down. "Jonny… he's still not doing good. It's going to be a long recovery."

He nodded again, jaw clenched. "You stayed with him?"

"I didn't want him to be alone. I tried calling you for hours last night."

That hit Jonny harder than anything else. Because he knew what it meant to be alone.

Maya reached for the door handle and then looked back at him. "You sure you're okay to go in?"

"No," he said. "But I'm going anyway."

She stepped aside, and he opened the door.

The room was dim, the only light coming from a small lamp near the bed. Machines beeped softly. His brother, Mark, looked smaller than Jonny remembered, pale and bruised, with tubes in his nose and an IV in his arm. But his eyes were open. And when he saw Jonny, they lit up just a little.

"Hey, big brother," Mark said, voice hoarse. Jonny stood frozen in the doorway.

"Hey," he finally said, stepping inside. "You look like hell."

Mark gave the faintest smile. "Takes one to know one."

Jonny walked to the side of the bed, pulled up a chair, and sat down. He didn't know what to say. He just reached out and put a hand on his brother's arm, and for the first time in what felt like years... he didn't feel completely empty.

For a long moment, neither of them spoke. The beeping of the heart monitor filled the silence, steady but too slow for Jonny's liking. Mark looked tired, beyond tired, but there was something in his eyes that hadn't faded. That quiet strength Jonny had always envied.

Jonny finally broke the silence. "I should've been here sooner."

Mark let out a faint breath that might've been a laugh. "Yeah, well... better late than never."

Jonny looked down at his hands, scarred and stained. "You were always the one holding things together. Me? I was the one breaking everything."

"You're still here," Mark said softly. "That means something."

Jonny shook his head. "I've messed up everything, Mark. I lost Maya. I lost myself. I drink just to forget who I am."

Mark shifted slightly in bed, wincing. "You ever think maybe it's time to stop forgetting and start fixing?"

Jonny looked at him, and for a second, he hated how calm Mark sounded. He didn't understand how hard it was, but then again, Mark was lying in a hospital bed, ribs broken, lungs barely working. And yet, he was still fighting.

"I don't know if I can," Jonny said.

"You don't have to fix everything today," Mark said. "Just start with one thing. One step. Come see me again tomorrow. That's it. One step."

Jonny nodded slowly, eyes stinging. "Okay."

Mark smiled weakly. "And maybe… shave. You look like a washed-up mountain man."

Jonny let out a quiet laugh, half sob, half chuckle. "Deal."

He sat there a little while longer, just holding Mark's hand, feeling the warmth and the weight of it. He didn't realize how badly he needed this, to feel like someone still saw something good in him.

Eventually, a nurse came in to check Mark's vitals. Jonny stood and backed away, giving her space. Mark looked at him, tired but still smiling.

"Come back tomorrow," he said again.

"I will," Jonny promised. "Sober." It felt strange saying it, but it felt right.

As Jonny left the room, Maya was still waiting in the hall. She looked up at him, her expression softer now.

"He was happy to see you," she said.

Jonny nodded. "I was happy to see him."

They stood there for a moment, uncertain. Then Maya asked, "Do you need a ride?"

Jonny looked toward the elevator, then back at her. "Yeah. I think I do."

She turned and walked beside him, quiet and steady, like maybe, just maybe, not everything was broken beyond repair.

And for the first time in a long time, Jonny felt like he had a reason to try.

Epilogue

It had been six weeks since the hospital.

Jonny stood outside the small church basement; hands stuffed into the pockets of his worn hoodie. The cigarette tucked behind his ear was more habit than temptation now. He hadn't lit one in over a week. The bottle? That had been harder to walk away from, but he hadn't touched a drop in twenty-three days.

The folding chair beneath him creaked as he sat down, joining the small circle of people around him. They all looked different, some old, some young, but their eyes shared the same weight. The kind of weight Jonny had carried for years without realizing how heavy it had gotten.

A woman named Cheryl opened the meeting with a soft voice and a kind smile. "Tonight, we're sharing what brought us through the door. You don't have to speak unless you want to."

Jonny looked at the floor, thumb rubbing the edge of his coffee cup.

What had brought him here?

A busted face. A phone call. A dying brother who had more strength in his broken body than Jonny had ever shown in his whole life.

When it came to his turn, Jonny cleared his throat. "My name's Jonny," he said, voice scratchy but steady. "And… I've been lost for a long time. Still am, honestly. But someone I love gave me a reason to stop running."

He paused, eyes finding the floor again. "I don't know who I'm supposed to be. But I know who I don't want to be anymore."

The room was quiet, holding his words like something sacred.

After the meeting, Maya waited outside in her car, the engine idling, with the windows down. She leaned out and gave him a small wave.

"You stayed the whole time, that's good," she said as he climbed in.

"Yeah," Jonny replied. "Felt like I needed to, and I wanted to."

She nodded, pulling away from the curb. "I'm proud of you."

Jonny didn't answer right away. He looked out the window as the city passed by, quieter now, less angry somehow.

"I'm not proud of myself yet," he finally said. "But I'm getting there."

Maya smiled and reached over, resting her hand on his, and for the first time in what felt like forever, Jonny believed he might make it.

One step at a time.

The trees stood like silent guards around him, tall and still under the pale morning light. A cool mist clung to the ground, curling around his boots as he stepped over a fallen log. The forest didn't ask who he was or why he had come. It didn't care what he had done or what he had lost. Out here, the world didn't speak unless you listened hard enough.

He'd been out for five days now. Maybe six. He wasn't keeping track.

His camp was simple: a rolled-up sleeping bag, a worn backpack, and a fire pit made from stones he'd gathered on the first day. The food was basic. Canned beans. Dried meat. A few protein bars were shoved in the side pouch of his pack. He had no real plan, just a quiet urge to disappear for a while. Maybe forever.

Each morning, he hiked with no set direction, just letting his legs carry him deeper into the woods. His only company was the wind through the leaves and the occasional chirp of a bird brave enough to sing.

He liked the silence. It was the only thing that didn't lie to him.

In his chest, the weight hadn't lifted. It sat there like a stone, grief, guilt, something heavier than sadness but quieter than rage. He hadn't cried. Not once. Not when he left. Not when he buried the photo under a stack of rocks near the creek. Not even when he looked at her handwriting one last time before tossing the letter into the fire.

He wasn't trying to find himself. He wasn't on some healing journey. He just didn't want to be around people anymore.

At least in the woods, nothing expected him to smile.

That morning, as the sun began to break through the trees, he slung his pack over his shoulder and started walking again. The air smelled like wet earth and pine. Birds fluttered overhead, but he barely looked up. His boots crunched softly over dry leaves and moss-covered roots.

Then, about a mile in, he spotted a trail of hoofprints near the streambed. Fresh. Light. A deer.

He stopped. Something in him stirred, not hunger, not instinct, but something quieter. Curiosity, maybe, or possibly it was wonder. He crouched beside the prints and followed their path with his eyes. They curved gently along the edge of the water and disappeared into a patch of tall grass.

He stood again, slung his pack off his shoulder, and left it by a tree.

Then he moved forward, carefully and slowly. Something was waiting just ahead.

The ground softened as he neared the stream, damp with early morning dew. He moved quietly, each step deliberate, like he was back on patrol, heel first, then toe. The forest around him stayed still, the silence broken only by birdsong and the soft rustle of leaves overhead.

Then he saw her.

A doe stood at the water's edge, drinking. Her coat was a soft blend of brown and gray, her body slender and graceful. Sunlight filtered through the trees and lit her back like she was something out of a dream. She hadn't seen him yet, or didn't care that he was there if she had.

He crouched low behind a tree, watching her. His hand rested near the knife at his belt, not because he needed it, but because he always did. Old instincts never faded completely. He had spent too long surviving not to think like a hunter. He could take her down. A clean shot. Quick. Quiet. She'd feed him for days. But as he stared at her, he felt something he hadn't expected: hesitation.

He didn't need to kill her. Not today. There was still food in his pack. The thought of taking her life just felt... wrong. Not because he couldn't, but because he didn't want to.

He let go of the knife handle and stood slowly. His eyes stayed fixed on the deer as if trying to understand why she held his attention so tightly. She wasn't just another animal in the woods. There was something different about her, something calm. Something unafraid.

He stepped forward.

Then another step.

The deer didn't move.

He was closer now, no more than ten yards away. Her ribs rose and fell in a slow rhythm as she drank. His boots pressed into the moss without a sound.

Six yards.

She was still there.

Three.

Then her head lifted. Her ears twitched, and her eyes, deep, dark, and wide, locked with his. He froze, breath held, heart thumping. This was it. The moment she'd bolt. The forest would explode with movement, and she'd vanish in a whisper.

But she didn't run.

She stared at him.

And nodded.

Once.

Twice.

Then she turned back to the stream and continued to drink.

His mouth went dry. He blinked, unsure if what he saw was real, but it was. She had seen him. She knew, and she stayed.

He stepped forward again. Slowly. Carefully. The deer remained still. Soon, he was only a few feet away. Close enough to see the gentle flick of her tail. Close enough to reach out his hand.

His fingers trembled as he raised his arm.

She'd run now. She had to.

But she didn't.

His hand came to rest on her head. Her fur was soft and warm beneath his touch. She turned slightly, lifting her gaze to meet his. Then, without fear, she leaned in and licked his hand.

A tear slipped from the corner of his right eye. It slid down his cheek without shame or warning.

He didn't know why, at that moment, something had broken inside him. Maybe it was the quiet. Maybe it was her trust. Maybe it was the simple truth that even after everything, after the pain, the loss, the silence, he could still feel something.

And at that moment, he did.

Joy.

It was small and sudden, but it was real.

He stood there, hand resting on her head, heart slower now. He could breathe again, not because anything had been fixed, but because something inside him had shifted. He didn't feel healed, but he no longer felt lost.

The deer stepped back, pausing for one final look. Then she turned and trotted down the riverbank, graceful and quiet, until she vanished into the trees.

He stayed by the stream, watching the spot where she had stood, letting the silence settle around him. It wasn't empty now; it was full of meaning.

He let out a slow breath and turned away.

The walk back to camp was quiet but no longer heavy. The silence didn't press in on him like it had before. It simply was natural, calm, and alive. The trees, once tall and distant, now felt familiar, as if they had been watching him all along.

He noticed things he hadn't noticed before. A squirrel was darting up a pine tree. The call of a bird overhead. The rich scent of earth where mushrooms grew beneath the roots. The sun was breaking through the canopy in soft, golden beams.

The weight he had carried for so long hadn't vanished. But it no longer crushed him.

By the time he reached camp, the fire pit was just a ring of cold stones. His pack leaned where he'd left it, and a small bird had perched on the top strap, pecking at the fabric. It flew off when he approached.

He didn't sit down right away. Instead, he walked to the pile of stones near the edge of the clearing, the place where he had buried the photograph. He crouched and brushed away a few pine needles. The top rock was smooth and round. For a moment, he ran his fingers over it, then left it where it was.

He didn't need to dig it back up. He knew what it showed: her face, smiling beneath the summer sun. He could see it now without the photo. That was enough.

He stood again, slung his pack over one shoulder, and looked up at the sky. Blue, open, cloudless.

He could stay another night.

But he didn't want to.

For the first time since he arrived, he felt the pull of something beyond the forest. Not the rush to return to the noise of the world, but a quiet whisper telling him it was time.

Not everything had to be fixed, but it didn't have to stay broken either.

The path out of the woods wasn't marked, but he didn't need a trail. His feet knew where to go. He walked with a steady pace, no longer rushing toward or away from anything. The weight he had carried still lingered, but it felt different now, less like a burden, more like a part of him he no longer needed to fight.

Every now and then, he glanced over his shoulder, not because he was afraid, just to remember.

The image of the deer stayed with him, not just her eyes or the way she let him near, but the moment she trusted him, touched him, gave him something he didn't know he needed.

He hadn't spoken a word aloud since she left. He didn't have to. The silence was no longer empty. It was full of meaning. It was his.

By the time the trees began to thin and the forest floor turned to gravel, he felt it settle inside him, a calm he thought he'd lost for good. Not joy exactly. Not peace either. But something close.

A quiet that stayed.

He reached the edge of the clearing where he'd parked his old truck, its green paint faded and chipped, half-covered in dust and pine needles. The keys were still in his pocket. The engine would start. It always did, even when everything else had failed.

He stood there for a moment, hand resting on the driver's side door, eyes sweeping back toward the forest. It would be easy to turn around, to stay. No one was waiting for him. No one even knew he was gone.

But he wasn't the same man who had come here.

He didn't need to run anymore.

He opened the door, slid into the seat, and started the engine. The sound broke the stillness, but the quiet inside him didn't leave; it remained, a steady rhythm under his ribs, like a heartbeat that had finally found its pace.

As the truck rumbled down the gravel road, back toward a world that hadn't changed, he felt something stir deep within his chest.

Not a promise. Not a plan.

Just a simple truth, he was still here.

What the River Left Behind

The sun was just beginning to rise, casting streaks of pale gold across the foggy surface of the river. For most of the night, a heavy mist had settled over the water like a blanket, hiding the world beneath it. Now, as the fog slowly lifted, a man lay still on the mossy riverbank, half-buried in the cold morning silence.

Franklin stirred, his body aching with every breath. He didn't move right away; he couldn't. The pain was too sharp, like knives twisting inside his ribs. His clothes were damp from the mist and stained dark with dried blood. For a long moment, he stared at the gray sky, trying to remember where he was or how he had gotten there.

His stomach growled loudly, reminding him that he hadn't eaten in two days. Hunger clawed at him, but the pain in his chest made even the thought of sitting up feel impossible. Still, he knew lying there wouldn't keep him alive. If he didn't move, he'd die out here. Simple as that.

With a deep, shaky breath, Franklin rolled to one side. His ribs screamed in protest, and he let out a low grunt, clenching his teeth to keep from crying out. Something in his chest felt like it was tearing with every motion. He wasn't sure how many ribs he had broken, four, maybe five, but each one burned like fire. His left arm was worse. It dangled uselessly at his side, the shoulder clearly dislocated or worse, twisted at a wrong angle.

He tried pulling himself up using only his right arm, every movement sending lightning bolts of pain through his body. His vision blurred for a moment, and he had to pause, breathing shallowly to keep from passing out.

The river whispered nearby, the current moving gently along the bend. The world around him was quiet except for the soft sound of water and the occasional cry of a distant bird. It was peaceful, in a strange way, but Franklin had no time for peace. Not today.

He spotted a long, weathered, and smooth branch nearby. Crawling toward it, he grabbed the stick and used it as a makeshift walking stick. Slowly, carefully, he rose to his feet. A warm wetness spread down his side; his chest wound had started bleeding again. He swayed unsteadily but forced himself to stay upright.

"There you go," he muttered under his breath, more to himself than anything else. "One foot in front of the other."

The riverbank stretched ahead, winding along the trees. Somewhere along that path, there had to be something: food, shelter, a sign of life. Franklin didn't know what he would find, but he knew he had to keep moving. Giving up now just wasn't an option.

He took his first step, leaning heavily on the branch. The pain was there, sharp, raw, but so was the will to survive. He had made it through worse situations before. Whatever had happened here, whatever had brought him to this quiet, broken place, he wasn't ready for it to be the end.

Each step down the riverbank felt like walking on broken glass, but Franklin kept going. The weight of his injuries made every movement a battle. He focused on the path in front of him, scanning for anything useful, berries, footprints, even broken branches. But with every step, the memories clawed their way back into his mind, whether he wanted them to or not.

He remembered the roar of the explosion first. It had been just after sunset, the sky still glowing orange behind the trees. Franklin and Cole had been moving fast through the woods, trying to make it to the drop point before nightfall. They had been warned there might be trouble, something about the deal going sideways, but neither of them expected an ambush.

Franklin saw the flash before he heard the bang. Then the world tilted.

The blast had knocked him straight off his feet and thrown him into the river. He hit the water hard, his chest slamming against a rock as the current dragged him under. His arm got twisted in the fall. Everything after that was a blur, dark water, broken light, Cole's voice yelling his name, and then… nothing.

The river must have carried him downstream, away from the ambush, away from the blood and the gunfire. It saved his life, but it didn't leave him in good shape.

Franklin blinked hard, trying to shake the images. He didn't know if Cole had made it. He didn't know who had set them up or why. He just knew someone wanted him dead, and whoever it was, they'd nearly finished the job.

His stomach growled again, louder this time. Pain mixed with hunger churning inside him. He reached for a low-hanging branch to steady himself, taking a moment to catch his breath.

He had to survive. If not for himself, then for answers. For Cole. For the truth behind what had gone wrong.

Franklin kept moving, following the river's curve. He didn't know where it would lead, but anything was better than going back. Back meant bullets. Back meant betrayal. Forward, at least, meant a chance.

A small voice inside him whispered doubt. What if Cole were gone? What if there was nothing left to find?

He shoved the thought away and kept moving; that was all he had right now.

The sun had climbed higher now, burning off the last wisps of fog along the river. The air was still cool, but Franklin could already feel sweat on his neck. His shirt clung to him, damp with river water, blood, and the weight of survival.

His legs felt like old brittle wood, stiff, unsteady, and untrustworthy. Still, he kept going, one slow step after another, leaning hard on the makeshift walking stick. Every so often, he stopped to scan the brush for food. His stomach cramped with hunger, and his tongue felt dry as dust.

About twenty yards ahead, something caught his eye, a splash of red in the green. He hobbled toward it, hope rising in his chest.

Berries.

They were small and dark red, clustered low on a bush nestled between a pair of trees. He hesitated for a moment, squinting at them. His survival training kicked in. Not all berries are friends. But these… these looked familiar. He remembered something like them from his time in the service. They weren't sweet, but they weren't deadly either.

He reached out with his good hand, careful not to crush the fruit, and picked a few. They were slightly sour and gritty between his teeth, but he didn't care. They were food.

Franklin ate slowly, pacing himself even though his body screamed to devour everything. When he finished, he sat against the trunk of a tree to rest. The pain was still there, steady, unrelenting, but the food settled his stomach just enough to clear his mind.

From where he sat, he could see a stretch of riverbank further down, where the sand piled higher, and the trees thinned out. He squinted. Something about that spot seemed promising. Maybe there'd be turtle nests. He remembered digging for turtle eggs during a training exercise years ago. It was slow work, but if he could find just a few…

He pulled himself back up with the stick and started moving again.

When he reached the sandy stretch, he knelt slowly, painfully, and began to scan the ground. After about ten minutes, he spotted a small mound of disturbed sand. Carefully, using a flat rock, he scraped away at it.

A few inches down, he found what he'd been hoping for— smooth, white eggs, no bigger than golf balls. He whispered a breath of thanks and gathered them gently into his shirt.

He wouldn't eat them raw. Not unless he had no choice. If he could just find dry wood and spark a fire, he could roast them. But that would take time. Energy. Maybe even draw attention.

Still, it was a risk he'd take.

Franklin leaned against a tree and looked up at the sky, watching the wind move through the leaves. He was still bleeding. He was still broken. But now, for the first time in two days, he wouldn't be starving.

And that right now, was enough.

By midday, Franklin was running on sheer will. The berries had taken the edge off his hunger, and the turtle eggs, still tucked in his shirt, were his next hope. But his body was giving out. His legs trembled with each step. His vision blurred more often now, and the bleeding hadn't stopped completely.

Just when he thought he couldn't take another step, he spotted something through the trees.

Smoke.

A thin gray ribbon curled upward into the blue sky, just beyond a patch of tall grass and wild underbrush. Franklin froze, blinking to make sure he wasn't imagining it. But it was real, steady, twisting smoke.

His heart kicked up.

Where there was smoke, there was fire. And where there was fire... maybe help.

He turned toward it, moving as quickly as he could without falling. As he pushed through the trees, the forest opened to a small clearing. That's when he saw it... a cabin.

The cabin was old, weather-beaten, and leaning slightly to one side. The roof sagged in the middle, and the logs were dark with age, but it stood solid against the wind. Smoke puffed from a crooked metal chimney. Someone was inside.

Franklin's eyes drifted to the right of the cabin. Just a few feet from the front steps was an open patch of grass. Three handmade grave markers stood there, simple wood planks, carved by hand, their surfaces worn and cracked by years of weather. No names, just markers.

He stared at them, feeling a chill crawl up his spine. He wasn't sure why, but they hit him harder than he expected. Whoever lived here had lost something, maybe everything.

The front door creaked open.

A man stepped out, holding a rusted old rifle in one hand. He was tall but hunched with age, his beard white and wild, his clothes layered and patched in a dozen places. His eyes were sharp, though, clear and cautious. He looked like someone who hadn't seen another person in years and wasn't sure if he wanted to now.

Franklin raised his hand slowly, keeping the walking stick steady under his arm.

"I'm not here to cause trouble," he said, his voice hoarse and dry. "I just... I need help."

The old man didn't lower the rifle, but he didn't raise it either. "You bleeding?" the man asked, squinting.

Franklin nodded. "Chest. Arm's busted too."

The man stared at him for a long moment, then gave a slow grunt. He lowered the rifle just enough to show he wasn't planning to shoot. "Get over here, then. Slowly."

Franklin limped forward, careful not to make any sudden moves. As he got closer, the old man gave him a better look, deep lines etched into his face, hands rough and scarred from manual labor. His eyes were tired. Not just from age, but from time. Time alone. Time spent burying people.

The old man stepped aside and opened the cabin door wider. "You can rest here," he said. "I ain't got much, but there's a fire and a bit of broth left. You look like hell."

Franklin smiled weakly. "I feel worse."

The man didn't smile back. "Don't get used to talking too much. I don't care for company." But he let him in anyway.

Inside the cabin, the warmth hit Franklin like a wall. The fire crackled in a stone-lined hearth, its orange glow casting shadows across the single-room interior. The place smelled of woodsmoke, old leather, and dried herbs. Everything inside was simple: hand-made furniture, shelves lined with jars, a tin kettle steaming over the fire. But it was clean and orderly, the way someone lives when they've had a lot of time and nothing to distract them.

The old man motioned toward a cot in the corner. "Sit. Or lie down. You're about to hurt worse than you already do."

Franklin removed the eggs from within his shirt and handed them to the old man. He then eased himself down with a grunt, cradling his limp arm. "Name's Franklin."

The man set the eggs down on the counter. He began digging through the cabinet. "Didn't ask."

He came back with a worn canvas bag and knelt beside Franklin, opening it to reveal a rough first aid kit, bandages, crude splints, old scissors, and even a bottle of something that looked suspiciously like homemade alcohol.

"You ever done this before?" Franklin asked, nodding at his arm.

The old man gave him a sideways glance. "Only about two dozen times. Once on myself." He pulled out a length of cloth and tore it in half. "This is going to suck."

Franklin gave a dry laugh. "Good. I was starting to worry this might be fun."

The man poured some of the alcohol into a chipped cup and handed it over. "Drink that. All of it."

Franklin did, and it burned all the way down. His chest wound throbbed in time with his heartbeat, and his broken ribs flared with every breath. But that arm, hanging like dead weight, was the worst. The muscles around the shoulder had gone stiff and swollen. He knew what was coming.

The man positioned Franklin's body just right, bracing his back against the wooden wall. Then he leaned in, taking hold of the shoulder with one hand, the wrist with the other.

"Bite down on something," he said. "You scream, it's fine. Just don't move."

Franklin nodded and shoved a folded piece of cloth into his mouth. His knuckles went white around the edge of the cot, and then it happened.

The old man pulled, twisted, and shoved the shoulder back into place in one fast, brutal motion.

The sound alone made Franklin's stomach twist, a sickening pop followed by a jolt of fire that raced through his body like lightning. His vision went white. His heart thudded in his ears. The world narrowed to a single moment of blinding, gut-wrenching pain. He didn't scream or pass out, but he had gotten close to both.

The old man began wrapping his shoulder in a crude sling. "Still alive?" the man asked.

Franklin nodded, sweat pouring from his face. "Barely."

"Then we did it right." He stood slowly, wiping his hands on a cloth. "Takes grit to stay awake through that. Most folks pass clean out."

Franklin swallowed thickly. "I've had worse. Not much, though. Feels better now."

The man raised an eyebrow, then finally gave the faintest hint of a smile. "You're lucky the river didn't take you."

"It did, just not far," Franklin said, leaning back and catching his breath. "But it seems it brought me far enough, brought me where I was supposed to be."

The man didn't answer. He just tossed another log onto the fire and sat down across from him.

For the first time in what felt like forever, Franklin wasn't just surviving, he was healing. Not quickly, not painlessly, but slowly, he was getting better; he could feel it. And for now, that was enough.

Franklin stayed in the cabin for ten more days.

Each morning, he woke to the sound of the fire crackling and the old man moving around, stirring a pot or splitting wood with hands that still worked with steady precision. The pain in Franklin's ribs faded slowly, and his arm, though still sore, was no longer limp. The old man had even helped fashion a better sling out of deer hide and cloth.

They didn't talk much, not at first. The silence between them was the kind that didn't need to be filled. It was the kind of silence men shared when they'd both seen things that didn't need retelling.

On one of the nights, though, as they sat around the fire, Franklin finally asked, "The graves out front. Family?"

The old man stared into the flames for a long time before answering. "Wife. Son. Daughter."

Franklin lowered his gaze. "I'm sorry."

The man gave a short nod. "Long time ago now."

A moment passed, and then the old man added, almost too quietly to hear, "I used to hope someone would come. A traveler, maybe. Or someone lost. But no one ever did. Not until you."

Franklin didn't know what to say, so he just nodded. Sometimes, just being there was enough.

By the morning of the twentieth day, Franklin was strong enough to travel. He had cleaned up, wrapped what food he could carry in a satchel the old man gave him, and tied the walking stick to his back. The man handed him a crude hand-drawn map, marked with a trail that would lead to a road about thirty miles east.

"Follow the river another couple of miles, then head uphill when the bend forks left, and you'll see the devil's fork, can't miss it, then just keep following the map. I'll lead you out."

Franklin took the map and slid it into his pocket. "You sure you're going to be okay out here?"

The old man shrugged. "I was okay before you came. I'll be okay when you're gone."

Franklin offered his hand.

The man looked at it for a second, then took it in a firm shake. "You keep fighting," he said. "You've got more in you. I can see it."

Franklin smiled. "Thanks for everything. For saving me."

The old man just nodded. "Ain't about saving. Sometimes it's just about not letting someone die alone."

Franklin stepped off the porch, the morning sun warming his face as he walked past the three wooden grave markers. He paused for a moment, brushing his fingers across the top of one.

"I'll remember this place," he whispered. "I'll remember all of it." Then he turned toward the trees, toward the river, and kept walking.

The old man stood on the porch and watched until Franklin disappeared into the woods, the smoke from the chimney rising steadily behind him.

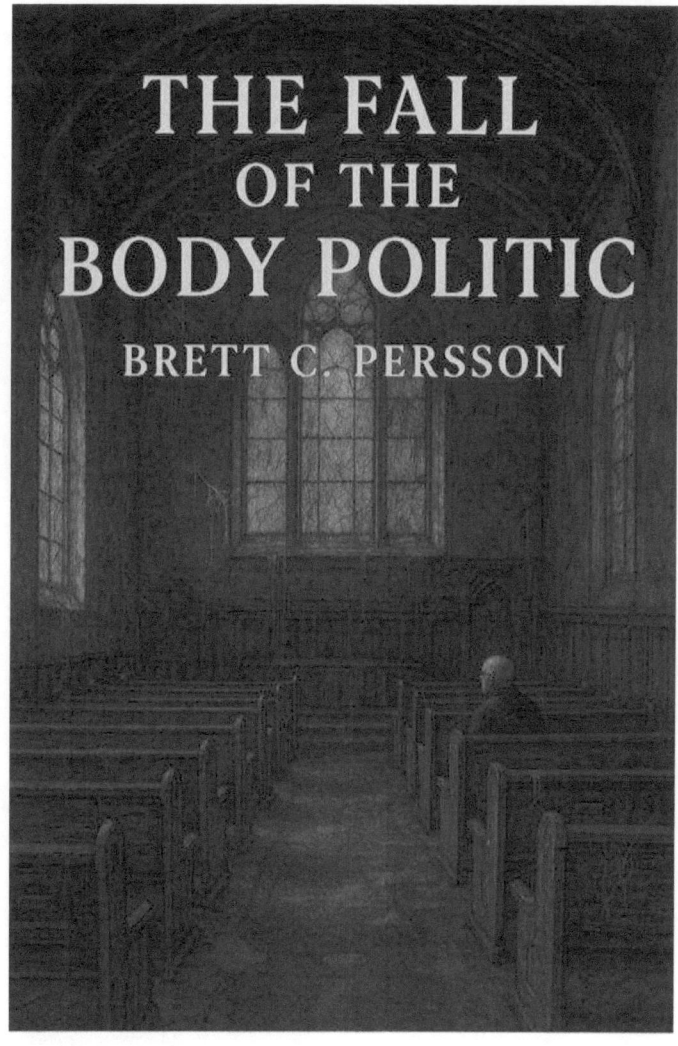

I.

St. Luke's Church used to be the heart of the town, a place where people sang together, prayed together, and believed things could get better. But now, it feels more like a tomb than a church.

The wooden pews are covered in dust, some of them cracked or splintered. The stained-glass windows, once bright and colorful, are now faded and cracked, with spiderwebs in the corners. Rain drips slowly through holes in the ceiling, landing in puddles on the moldy carpet. The whole place smells like old wood and something rotting.

Reverend Thomas Carter sits alone in the front pew, staring up at the broken windows. He's been the pastor here for decades, but it no longer feels like a blessing. He used to preach to full pews, with voices singing hymns that echoed with hope. Now, the silence is heavy, and those memories feel like ghosts haunting him.

He remembers when the church brought people together, including families, neighbors, and kids, who would run through the aisles. Now, those same people don't come around. Most have left, lost faith, or just given up. The church hasn't just fallen apart physically. It's lost its purpose, and so has Carter.

He wonders if it all meant anything. After years of trying to help, trying to believe, all that's left is a building falling apart and a man who isn't sure he believes anymore.

II.

Reverend Carter steps outside the church and walks through the town he's called home for most of his life. But what he sees now isn't the town he remembers. It's broken, just like the church.

The Ramirez house used to be full of life. Cookouts, birthday parties, and music coming from the windows. Now it's boarded up, windows smashed in, and the front yard is filled with trash. Rosa, the mother, still works double shifts just to make ends meet. Her family? Torn apart. Her kids barely talk to her anymore.

A few blocks down, Maria sits on her porch, eyes tired and shoulders slumped. She's raising her grandkids alone. They're angry all the time, always yelling, sometimes disappearing for hours. She tries, but it's too much. She looks like someone carrying the weight of the world and losing.

Carter walks past the school next. It looks more like a prison than a place for learning. Tall fences, metal detectors, even armed guards. Just last week, a student got stabbed in the hallway. Drugs are everywhere. Kids are overdosing, and some don't make it. Carter has tried to help, offering to volunteer, to talk to the students, to pray with them. The school's staff no longer returns his calls. They've stopped believing anyone can fix this.

At City Hall, things aren't much better. Town meetings used to be boring, but now they end in yelling matches, sometimes with fists thrown. Half the council members have quit or been caught stealing. No one trusts anyone. The town is running on fumes and falling apart faster than anyone wants to admit.

As Carter walks through the streets, he feels something settle in his chest, not just watching a town fall apart. He's watching the end of a community that once cared.

III.

Back inside his office, Reverend Carter sits in the dark, watching an old video on a tiny screen. It's from the town's bicentennial celebration. The streets were full, people were smiling, and the church choir sang like they believed every word. Carter was younger then, full of energy and hope. He watches himself on the screen, laughing, shaking hands, and leading prayers, and it feels like watching a stranger.

Now? The laughter is gone. The choir is silent. The pews are empty. He pauses and stares at the frozen image of himself. "Where did it all go wrong?" he wonders. He thought faith would be enough to hold everything together. If he just kept preaching, praying, and showing up, the community would come back. But they didn't. They left, one by one, until he was the only one still holding on.

The words his father once told him echo in his mind: *"Faith isn't a feeling, it's a choice you make, even when everything feels lost."* Carter used to believe that. Now those words feel empty, like advice meant for someone stronger than he is.

He wants to believe. He really does. But each day, it gets harder. The silence in the church is louder than ever. The people he loved and served for decades are gone. And even when he prays, it feels like no one's listening.

Carter slumps in his chair, overwhelmed by sadness and doubt. The faith that once carried him through everything now feels like just another thing slipping through his fingers.

IV.

It starts with a soft knock.

Carter almost doesn't hear it. He's sitting alone, lost in thought, when the sound taps against the silence. He opens the heavy church door and sees a girl, maybe twelve or thirteen, standing there with a curious look and a nervous smile. Her name is Lily.

She says she's just looking around. She heard that this place used to be important. Carter raises an eyebrow. "Used to be," he says and steps aside to let her in.

Lily walks slowly down the aisle, eyes wide as she takes everything in. The dusty pews, the cracked windows, the faded altar, it's all new to her, even in its ruined state, she seems amazed. She runs her fingers along the wood and tilts her head at the broken stained glass. "It's kind of beautiful," she says, almost like she's surprised.

For the first time in what feels like forever, Carter smiles.

He watches her explore, asking questions about the church, the town, and why no one comes anymore. She's innocent but not clueless. There's sadness in her, too, but also something else. Curiosity. Maybe even hope.

Carter feels something stir inside him, a flicker, faint and fragile. He doesn't want to name it yet. But maybe, just maybe, Lily's presence is a sign that not everything is lost.

She looks at him before she leaves and says, "I think this place matters, even if people forgot."

After she's gone, the silence doesn't feel quite as heavy. Not yet anyway.

V.

For a little while, it felt like something was shifting.

Lily kept coming back to the church. She dusted off a few pews. Asked Carter if they could light a few candles "just because." Her quiet energy started to spread, and a few old faces trickled in, people Carter hadn't seen in years.

Andre came by one Sunday. He used to sing in the youth choir. Now he's taller, older, a man himself now, but with eyes that seem to carry a hundred disappointments. He sat in the back, arms crossed, face like stone. But he stayed the whole service. That alone gave Carter a sliver of hope.

Then there was Mrs. Darnell. She looked smaller than he remembered, like the years had folded her in. She walked in holding a Bible so worn it barely held together. She cried quietly through the hymns, her voice cracking on every note.

For one moment, Carter thought, *Maybe this could work.*

But it didn't last.

Andre showed up once more, then disappeared. "It's too late for all this," he muttered before walking out. "You don't fix something that's already dead."

Lily's classmates made fun of her for going to church. Called her weird. Said the place was cursed. She stopped talking about it at school, and eventually, she stopped smiling when she came.

Maria, already drowning in exhaustion, couldn't bring her grandkids. "They don't listen to me anymore," she said, eyes heavy. "I'm tired, Reverend. So tired."

Carter felt that weight in his bones. Every small spark fizzled out. No one stayed. No one believed enough. And just like that, the tiny flicker of hope faded back into the silence.

VI.

The storm hit fast.

Dark clouds rolled in like an army, thunder shaking the ground, lightning tearing through the sky. But what should've brought the town together only pushed it further apart.

Instead of helping each other, people panicked. They looted stores, fought over supplies, and screamed in the streets. Some even pulled guns. Carter, watching from the church steps, felt like he was witnessing the final unraveling.

He opened the doors wide, hoping people would come seeking shelter, peace, anything.

A few did. But they didn't come in calmly or gratefully; they came in angry, soaking wet, and blaming each other. Fights broke out in the aisles. Shouting filled the sanctuary. One man accused another of stealing food. A woman screamed that the church had done nothing for years and shouldn't be trusted now. Carter tried to speak, but his voice was drowned out by the chaos.

Then it happened.

Outside, Andre got into a fight. Carter saw it from the doorway. Fists flying, then a scream, then Andre on the ground, bloody, motionless, barely breathing. Carter ran to help, and the crowd fled. Andre's eyes fluttered open for just a second, full of pain and fear, and then glazed over as his breathing stopped.

Lily saw it all. She was standing near the church steps, shaking, crying. When Carter looked at her, she turned and ran. She didn't come back.

As the storm raged on, the church doors stayed open, but the sanctuary felt colder than ever. Carter sat down alone, drenched and defeated. Everything was already broken.

VII.

The storm passed, but nothing really changed. The sun came up the next morning, but the light didn't bring comfort, just more silence, more wreckage.

Reverend Carter sat at his desk, papers all around him, and picked up a pen. He had written to Bishop Langley before. He'd always tried to sound hopeful, even when things were falling apart. But this time was different.

This letter wasn't hopeful. It was honest.

He wrote about the empty church, about the people who had drifted away, and about how every single effort to bring them back had failed. He told the bishop that he hadn't just lost his faith in God. He had lost faith in people, in the community, and in himself.

He said he had tried, for decades, to hold it all together. To be the steady voice, the kind hand, the open door. But nothing worked. The world around him had crumbled, and now, he felt like just another broken piece.

"I don't believe I'm needed anymore," he wrote. "And I'm starting to think I never was."

This time, Carter didn't fold the letter and hide it in a drawer like he had in the past. He signed, sealed, and mailed it. His resignation.

It wasn't just a letter to his bishop. It was a final admission to himself and to the world that he was done. Not angry. Just tired. Empty. And maybe it was time to stop pretending anything could be saved.

VIII.

A year passed, but the town showed no improvement. It got worse.

St. Luke's Church was officially closed. The front windows were shattered. Graffiti covered the walls, some of it angry, some of it just nonsense. The doors were chained shut, and no one even tried to clean up.

The Ramirez house? Burned to the ground. No one knows for sure who did it, but everyone suspects it wasn't an accident. Rosa moved away without a word. Maria never made it out; she died quietly one night, stress and heartbreak finally taking their toll. There was no funeral.

The school shut down after too many fights, too many overdoses, and not enough teachers left willing to come back. The kids? They scattered. Some ended up on the streets. Others just vanished.

Downtown looked like a ghost town. Stores boarded up. Trash blowing through the streets. The town council fell apart completely, and nobody trusted anyone enough to lead. The state had to step in just to keep the lights on.

Carter still lived there. He walked the broken sidewalks like a shadow. The man who once believed in everything now believed in nothing. He passed people who used to wave and smile. Now they looked through him like he wasn't there.

And then one day, he saw her.

Lily.

She was older now, but not in a good way. The light in her eyes was gone, replaced by anger and something harder. She looked right at him but said nothing and just kept walking.

Carter turned and walked back to what was left of the church. The door hung crooked on its hinges. Inside, the altar was smashed, glass crunched underfoot, and everything smelled like mold and dust.

He sat alone, like always.

The church was gone. The town was gone. And Carter finally understood that maybe they were never whole to begin with. Maybe faith, unity, and hope were just stories people told themselves to feel safe.

Now, all that was left was in ruin.

Epilogue

The church stood silent for years, slowly falling apart one season at a time. Vines crept up the sides. Rain soaked through the roof until the inside was nothing but rot and shadows. Most people just avoided it. Some said it was cursed. Others didn't care enough to even wonder.

One spring morning, a truck pulled up. A man got out, middle-aged, wearing a dusty work jacket and holding a clipboard. He looked up at the old sign that used to say, "St. Luke's Church," now barely hanging by one screw.

Behind him, a small crew began pulling out boards and clearing trash. The man lit a cigarette, took a long drag, and said, "Tear it down."

That's how it ended.

No ceremony. No final service. No one came to say goodbye. Just silence… and then the sound of machines tearing through wood and stone, burying whatever was left of the past.

They built a parking lot there a few months later. People park their cars there now to get pizza from the shop next door.

Most don't even know a church used to be there, and those who don't care.

Lifeline

I.

It was one of those cold nights when the wind seemed to blow right through you. The kind of night where even the streetlights looked tired. Downtown Tampa wasn't the place you wanted to be after dark, especially not alone. Sirens echoed in the distance, growing louder, then fading again. Somewhere, someone was hurt. Again.

The streets were mostly empty, except for a few shadows moving from alley to alley like ghosts trying to stay hidden. A couple of old newspapers blew across the sidewalk. Broken glass glittered in the gutter. The whole city felt like it had been forgotten or ignored.

I pulled my coat tighter and kept walking. I didn't really have anywhere to go. Just walking to clear my head, I guess. I passed boarded-up shops, graffiti-covered walls, and the same old liquor store with the flickering "Open" sign.

People say Tampa isn't as bad as places like New York or L.A., but those people haven't been here lately. At least not at this hour on this side of town. It's not just the crime; it's something deeper, like the soul of the city is tired. It gave up a long time ago, and no one noticed.

I walked past a man sitting on a bench with a trash bag full of who knows what. He didn't ask for money. Didn't even look up. Just stared off into the dark like he was waiting for something. Or maybe someone. I've seen enough of these streets to know that not everyone out here is dangerous. Some of them are just lost.

I kept walking. The church bells rang in the distance, slowly and sadly, like they were counting down the end of something. Maybe they were.

II.

Tampa used to be a place people loved. Back in the day, downtown was filled with small shops, food stands, and people laughing on the sidewalks. You didn't have to worry about walking to your car at night. Now? Things are different.

It's like the city aged too fast, and no one knew how to take care of it. The buildings still stand, but they're they are old. Windows are broken, stores are empty, and everything feels like it's falling apart. Even in the daylight, it's not the same.

The truth is that people don't really talk about Tampa much. It's not as flashy as Miami or as famous as Chicago. But it's getting worse, and no one seems to notice. Or maybe they just don't care. These days, you can't go two blocks without seeing someone sleeping on the sidewalk, wrapped in whatever blankets they could find. And honestly, some of them don't even wake up.

Most folks avoid eye contact. They keep walking, acting like they don't see the man digging through the trash or the woman curled up by the bus stop. Some assume these people chose this life. That they're addicts or lazy or just don't want help. And sure, yeah, some of them might be. But not all.

I've met people out there who had real jobs, real lives. Some just caught a bad break and never recovered.

III.

I met a man once who said he had worked for NASA. It was close to three in the morning when I saw him.

I was walking past the shelter, one of those places that open late and fill up fast. Sometimes, people line up hours before the doors open. The shelter was full, and he was just sitting off to the side, leaning against the wall, seeing if someone was going to leave and open a spot. He wasn't sure if he wanted to go in at all.

He looked older, maybe in his mid-fifties. Gray in his beard, worn-out sneakers, layers of clothes that didn't quite fit. But there was something different about him, something in the way he held himself. Calm. Still. Like he was thinking hard about something big.

I nodded at him as I passed. He looked up and nodded back. "You're out late," he said, voice scratchy but kind.

"Could say the same about you," I replied.

He chuckled, just a little. "Fair enough."

I don't usually stop and talk to people this late at night, not because I'm scared, but because you never know who's in a good mood and who isn't. But something told me this man wasn't looking for trouble. He seemed to need someone to talk to.

So, I sat down on the nearby curb. We didn't say anything for a minute or two; we just listened to the wind and the buzz of an old streetlight overhead. Then he said, "You ever lose everything, kid?"

I shrugged. "I've lost a few things."

He gave me this look like he was trying to decide whether to trust me with his story.

"I worked for NASA once," he said finally. "A long time ago. Not that anyone would believe me now."

I raised an eyebrow but didn't say anything. I've heard enough stories out here to know the truth doesn't always look the way people expect it to.

"They laid me off after the Challenger exploded," he went on. "Told us they'd call us back when things started up again. Only... by the time they did, I didn't have a number. Or a place. Or anyone left to tell me they were looking."

His voice cracked a little, but he kept going. He told me about how fast things fell apart: divorce, missed bills, sleeping in his car, and then losing the car, too. And just like that, he was on the street.

He didn't ask me for anything. Not money, not food. He just wanted someone to hear him. And for whatever reason, that night, I was the one who did.

IV.

"I wasn't always like this," he said, eyes locked on the ground. "I used to have a life. A good one."

He told me he worked with computers and electronics, dealing with high-level technology. Said he was part of a team that helped monitor systems on one of the space shuttle missions. It's not the kind of job you just fall into. He went to school, worked hard, and climbed his way up.

"When the shuttle blew, they shut everything down," he said, voice low. "We were told it was temporary. Just a pause. They'd call us when things started moving again. It turns out NASA's shuttle program was shut down for almost three years."

Time passed, and bills stacked up. His wife couldn't take the stress, and one day she left. She took the house, the car, and everything but the clothes in his closet. He said he tried to hold on, picked up odd jobs, and worked security for a while, but nothing stuck.

"When you go from being somebody to being nobody, it messes with your head," he said. "You stop calling people because you're embarrassed. You stop answering the phone because you know it's just going to be bad news. And eventually… the phone stops ringing."

He said the worst part wasn't losing the job or the house. It was losing the feeling that he mattered.

"I remember the first night I slept outside," he said. "I thought it was just for one night. A weird little bump in the road. But one night turned into a week. A week turned into a year. And before I knew it, I wasn't even me anymore."

He paused and rubbed his hands together like he was trying to warm up something deeper than just his skin.

"Maybe NASA did try to call," he said. "Maybe they had a spot for me. But where were they supposed to find me? I didn't even know where I was half the time."

It hit me then how fast things can change. One bad break. One twist of fate. That was all it took to send someone crashing from orbit straight to the street.

And all he wanted at that moment was to be seen. To remind someone that he was still there.

V.

He leaned back against the wall and stared up at the sky. "It's funny," he said. "I used to track satellites and monitor the shuttle. Now I track where the cleanest bathroom is."

He meant it as a joke, but it didn't land that way. There was too much truth behind it.

After losing his job and home, he said it felt as though the world had erased him. He applied for help, went to shelters, looked for temp work, and sought government assistance, but everything needed paperwork. And to get the paperwork, you need an address. It was a loop with no exit.

"I used to carry my résumé in a folder," he said. "It got rained on one night. After that, I stopped trying."

He told me about sleeping under a bridge during a storm and waking up with water up to his ankles. About having a decent pair of shoes stolen while he was using the bathroom in a gas station. About going three days without food and finally breaking down and eating scraps from a dumpster behind a pizza place.

"I never touched drugs," he said. "People assume I must've. But no, I stayed clean. Doesn't mean much, though. You start to look like an addict even if you're not."

He said the shame was the worst part. Worse than the cold, worse than the hunger. "There's this moment," he said, "where you look in the mirror and don't recognize yourself. And then another moment, later, when you stop looking in mirrors altogether."

I didn't know what to say to that, so I didn't say anything.

He filled the silence with random memories scattered. A daughter he hadn't seen in years. A cat he used to have named Rocket. The sound of coffee brewing in the morning. It was like he was trying to hold on to pieces of who he used to be before they slipped away for good.

By now, the air had gotten colder. The sky was turning from black to dark blue, the morning wasn't far off.

VI.

The sky was starting to lighten just a little. That soft gray that shows up before the sun makes up its mind. The streetlamps flickered like they were getting ready to call it a night.

The man stood up slowly, stretching like someone who hadn't moved in hours. He rubbed his back and looked down the street toward the shelter entrance. A few people were coming out, bundled in hoodies and blankets.

"You going to go in?" I asked.

He shook his head. "Not tonight. Too crowded. Too loud. Too many rules."

I pulled a granola bar from my coat pocket and held it out. "You sure? You could at least take this."

He looked at it, then at me. "Thanks," he said, but didn't take it. "But I'm good."

I didn't argue. I just nodded and set it down on the bench between us.

He shoved his hands deep into his jacket and looked down the road like he had someplace to be, but we both knew he didn't. Maybe that's what hurt the most. Not being anywhere, not being expected anywhere.

He turned to me and said, "Thanks for listening. Most people don't." And then got up and walked away. No big goodbye. No dramatic moment. Just quiet steps fading down the block.

I sat there for a minute longer, watching the sun try to rise. I kept hoping he'd turn around or come back or something. But he didn't. I sat there, picked up my granola bar, and slipped it back into my pocket.

VII:

I went back to the shelter the next night, just in case he showed up. He didn't.

I checked again a few nights later. Still nothing. I even asked around, but no one knew who I was talking about. Some people just disappear like that. No name, no record, no one looking for them. They just fade.

I kept thinking about the things he told me about NASA, about losing everything, about not recognizing himself anymore. I wondered how much of it was true. Maybe all of it. Maybe none of it. He could've made the whole thing up for attention. Or he could've been exactly who he said he was. I guess I'll never know.

But here's the thing: I don't think it matters.

That night, he needed someone to talk to. Not to fix him. Not to save him. Just to listen. And for whatever reason, I happened to be that person. Maybe that's all some people ever really need. A voice in the dark. A small reminder that they're still human.

It stuck with me the way his story unraveled, like threads from a sweater, until there was nothing left but the man sitting on a cold sidewalk at 3 a.m.

You pass people like him every day. You don't always see them. But they're there. Carrying stories is too heavy for one person. Stories they'll probably never tell. Unless someone stops and listens.

I've thought a lot about that night. Sometimes, I wonder what would've happened if someone had just reached out to him sooner. If someone had answered the phone when he called for help, sent a letter, or knocked on his door before he lost everything. Maybe that would've been his lifeline. The thing that kept him from falling so far.

But life doesn't always work like that.

We like to think people end up where they are because of their choices. And sure, choices matter. But so does timing. So does luck. And sometimes, all it takes is one bad break for everything to come crashing down.

That's the part people forget. How fragile it all is. That night didn't change the world. It didn't fix his life. But it changed something in me. I saw the truth behind the eyes of someone who most people would've walked right past. And I started thinking differently, not just about the homeless, but about how easily someone's story can go untold.

I never saw him again. Maybe he moved on. Maybe he didn't. I'll never know.

But I do know this: everyone has a line, something they're holding on to. And sometimes, when the world stops listening, that line slips from their hands.

So now, when I see someone sitting alone on a bench or wandering with their whole life in a plastic bag, I don't look away. I remember that night. I remember the story. And I remember the man who fell from orbit.

Because everyone deserves a lifeline.

Author's Note

This story was inspired by something I overheard when I was sixteen, working alongside my dad at a cold-weather shelter in Florida. My dad ran the place, and one night, he spoke briefly with a homeless man who claimed to have worked for NASA. He told my dad that after the Challenger explosion, he lost his job, and things just fell apart.

It was only a two or three-minute conversation, but it stuck with me probably because I've always been fascinated by space. What happened after that? How does someone go from working at NASA to sleeping on the streets?

Years later, I decided to take that short exchange and build a story around it. I imagined what his journey might've looked like, told it from a first-person point of view, and filled in the blanks with pieces of other stories I heard while working those shelters.

Because that was one of the most important lessons I learned during that time, everyone out there has a story. Some are heartbreaking, some are unbelievable, and some just needed someone to care enough to listen. Helping at those shelters taught me a lot about people.

I wrote this story as a tribute to the man who once reached for the stars and to all the others I met who had lost something but still kept going. May we never forget that behind every face, there's a life worth knowing.

—Brett C. Persson

Room 7A

I.

The train platform buzzed with quiet movement. No one spoke. They never did. Talking wasn't forbidden, not exactly but it drew attention, and attention could get you flagged.

Lena stood in line like everyone else, facing forward, an emotion tracker flashing a steady blue glow on her wrist. Blue meant calm. Blue meant safety. She kept her breathing even, even though her heart had started to race. She wasn't sure why.

A screen above the platform blinked to life. The face of the Chancellor filled the screen with sharp eyes and a smooth voice, too perfect to be real.

"Harmony is strength. Obedience is peace. You are safe because you are loyal."

The crowd didn't react. The message repeated twice before fading into the weather forecast: gray skies again, with a slight chance of fog.

The train hissed into the station, doors sliding open with a practiced whoosh. Lena stepped inside, taking her assigned spot on the standing rail. Cameras scanned the car. Her wristband pulsed once still blue.

On the ride to Central District, Lena scanned through her government-issued planner. Today's tasks: review citizen behavior reports, file emotion variance forms, and monitor social feed patterns. Nothing unusual. Nothing dangerous.

As she closed the planner, something caught her eye on the floor near the exit: just a scrap of old paper. A cleaning bot rolled toward it, but before it could scoop it up, she leaned over and picked it up. Quick. Quiet.

It was a torn page from a book. Real paper, yellowed and worn. On it, written in shaky handwriting, was a single line:

"I dream of stars they say no longer shine."

Lena's breath hitched. Her wristband blinked yellow for a second warning. She quickly folded the page and slipped it into her coat pocket. The band returned to blue.

She looked up. The camera above the door had turned toward her. She held her face still. No expression. Just the blank mask she'd worn for years.

The train came to a stop. Central District. She stepped off with the others. The day was just beginning.

But something had already changed.

II.

Lena walked through the glass turnstiles at the Ministry of Public Order, her boots echoing on the polished floor. She nodded at the security bot. It didn't nod back, but it recorded her temperature, her heart rate, and the color of her emotion band. Still blue. Good.

She took the elevator to Level 6 and walked into her office, which had gray walls, gray chairs, and gray lights. The same "inspiration" poster hung over every desk:

"Silence is the sound of progress."

Lena sat, opened her terminal, and began reviewing reports. Citizen #82-394 had laughed too loudly at a food stand. #117-201 was reported for humming an unregistered tune. Lena filled in the forms, noting the emotion levels recorded at the time of the incidents. Mild curiosity. Slight amusement. Suspicious.

She clicked submit. Just another day. But her thoughts kept drifting to the note in her coat pocket. She hadn't looked at it again. She didn't need to. The words were burned into her mind:

"I dream of stars, they say no longer shine."

A few hours later, a message appeared on her screen. It was simple:

**WELLNESS REVIEW: REPORT TO ROOM 243 – 14:00
Subject: Emotion Irregularity Detected – ID #F-328-Lena**

Her stomach dropped. She swallowed hard and kept her face still, even though no one was watching. She had to be careful.

She stood and walked calmly to the lift. Her wristband blinked blue barely. It hovered on the edge of yellow.

Room 243 was small and cold, with no chairs. A screen on the wall blinked to life as she stepped inside.

"Citizen Lena," said a soft, genderless voice. "You showed an unregistered emotional spike at 08:42 this morning. Please explain."

Lena's mind raced. She couldn't say "I found a poem." That would be a confession. She couldn't say "I don't know," either. That would raise suspicion.

"I had a brief memory of my brother," she said quietly. "He died during the Freeze Out seven winters ago. The memory surprised me. I'm sorry."

A pause.

The voice replied, "Grief is permitted in limited form. But your pattern showed…curiosity. Was there a trigger?"

"No," Lena lied. "Just a passing thought."

"Very well. You will be assigned a recalibration video tonight. Please absorb it fully. We will check your emotion band tomorrow morning."

The screen went black, and she left the room, sweat gathering at the back of her neck. She knew they hadn't believed her. But they hadn't punished her either. That was worse. It meant they were watching. Waiting.

Back at her desk, she reached into her coat pocket, just to feel the edge of the paper.

It was still there. And for a second, so was something else.

Not fear. Not grief.

Something like…wonder.

III.

That evening, Lena took the transit home under the dim gray glow of the city's artificial sky. She sat in the back of the rail car, staring out the smudged window, the note pressing against her leg like it had weight. Like it was alive.

She passed the same billboards, the same cameras, the same empty faces. "*Unity Is Freedom.*" "*Feelings Lie—The State Knows Best.*" No one looked at each other. No one smiled.

As she neared her housing block, she saw a small crowd gathered at the edge of the plaza. It was not a protest; those never lasted, but something was happening.

She drifted closer.

A boy, maybe seven, had drawn on the pavement with a piece of yellow chalk. Just one image: a bird in flight.

It was beautiful.

Two security drones floated down like insects. One flashed red, the other deployed a voice command:

"Cease activity. Step away from the ground."

The boy froze. His mother reached out, but an officer pulled her back. The boy was taken by the arm and led away. The chalk was crushed beneath a boot.

The crowd dispersed in silence.

Lena stood there a moment longer, her jaw clenched. She could hear her heartbeat now. She hadn't remembered it ever being this loud.

Suddenly, it wasn't just the poem in her pocket. It was the boy. It was the bird. It was the way everyone turned their heads like nothing had happened.

She went home, bypassed the assigned recalibration video, and opened her desk drawer. Inside was her stack of state-issued feedback slips, the kind meant for writing praises to the Ministry.

She took one.

Her handwriting was slow, careful, almost shaking as she copied the line again: "I dream of stars they say no longer shine."

She folded the slip and sealed it with the standard "Voices of the People" sticker.

The next morning, on her way to work, she passed the Ministry Dropbox, just a narrow slot built into the concrete wall.

She paused.

There were cameras nearby, and her wristband hummed softly, glowing a cautious yellow. She slipped the note in. Then she walked away. For the first time in her life, she didn't look back.

IV.

Lena barely slept that night. Every creak in her apartment made her sit up straight. Every flicker of the streetlamp outside seemed like a searchlight.

She told herself they wouldn't care. It was one slip of paper. Anonymous. Untraceable.

But she also knew better.

By morning, her eyes were heavy, and her nerves felt stretched thin. She got dressed slowly, her hands stiff, her wristband already pulsing a soft yellow. She took the long way to the train station, avoiding the Ministry's eye-level facial scanners. It didn't matter. They always knew.

At her desk, everything looked the same. For an hour, nothing happened. Then the screen on her monitor blinked red.

REASSIGNMENT NOTICE: REPORT TO ROOM 7A.

Not a Wellness Review. Not a routine check-in.

Room 7A was something else.

Lena stood. She didn't speak to anyone. No one looked up. That was the rule: when someone was called, you pretended they were never there.

The hall to Room 7A was colder than the others, lined with mirrors instead of screens. She caught her reflection and barely recognized it. Pale. Eyes too wide. She was still holding her ID pass as it might protect her.

Inside the room was a single chair facing a blank wall. A tall man in a gray coat waited. No badge. No name.

"Sit," he said.

She obeyed.

"You submitted something yesterday," he said. "Handwritten. Unassigned. Unapproved."

She didn't speak.

"You could be removed for that."

Still, Lena said nothing. She wasn't sure if her silence was a sign of strength or surrender.

Then the man did something unexpected. He leaned forward and placed a folded slip of paper on the table. Her paper. He opened it.

"I dream of stars, they say no longer shine."

Then he said, quietly, "Do you believe that?"

Lena blinked. It wasn't the question she expected. She nodded, just once.

The man looked at her for a long time. Then he smiled, a real, tired smile and whispered, "You're not alone. Someone will contact you."

Her heart thundered. Was this real? A trick? A test? Before she could ask anything, he stood and left. She remained in the chair, staring at the folded paper, unsure if she had just been saved... or marked.

V.

The next morning, Lena woke before her alarm. The city outside was still asleep, but her mind wasn't. The memory of the gray-coated man's words spun circles in her head.

"You're not alone."

She didn't know what that meant. Was he part of something real? Or was it a deeper trick, one more test designed to catch those whose minds drifted toward rebellion?

There were no answers.

At work, everything was the same. The trains ran on time. The announcements blared the usual slogans. Her desk sat waiting for her, sterile and square. The same "inspiration" poster still hung on the wall.

Her coworkers didn't say a word. Neither did she.

She powered on her terminal, expecting to see her usual task queue. But instead, something new blinked on her screen: a message waiting.

There was no subject line. No name. Just one line of text:

"Even in the silence, something dares to breathe."

Lena stared at the screen for a long moment. Her wristband glowed steady blue.

For the first time in years, the color didn't feel like obedience.

It felt like control, *her* control.

She closed the message, opened a blank report, and began typing. The same reports, the same names, the same system. But now, buried deep in her chest, something had shifted.

She didn't know if the message meant someone would reach out. Or if she was now expected to be the one who would.

But either way, she was no longer dreaming of stars. She was becoming one.

Whispers of the Neon God

I.

The city never really slept. It buzzed and blinked day and night, always lit by giant screens and neon signs. People filled the sidewalks like rivers, moving fast but never really *seeing* anything. Most of them stared down at their phones, eyes glued to glowing screens, thumbs tapping like they were trying to stay alive.

Ethan blended in with them. Same steps. Same screens. Same silence.

Every morning, he rode the train to work. Nobody talked. No one smiled. The only sounds were the screech of metal on tracks and the soft ding of digital notifications. He used to notice the music people played in their earbuds or the books they carried. Now, everyone just stared into the glass phones, tablets, and digital ads. Even the train windows played ads on repeat.

Ethan worked as a graphic designer in a tall glass building with automatic doors and smart elevators. His whole job was designing ads that popped bright, flashy, and eye-catching. He used to love it, but now it all felt fake. As if he were just feeding the machine that kept people quiet.

At his desk, he stared at the screen for hours. Moved colors around. Picked fonts. Answered emails with short replies. Half the time, he wasn't even sure if the people he talked to were real or just automated messages pretending to be coworkers.

Lunch break? He sat alone, scrolling through news that didn't matter, watching videos that didn't make him laugh.

At home, things weren't much better. Anna, his girlfriend, still lived with him. But most nights, they sat on the couch staring at their own screens. Sometimes, they talked about groceries, work, and bills. But never about anything deep. Not like they used to.

Ethan didn't know when the world had changed. Maybe it hadn't. Maybe *he* had. But lately, something felt... off. Like the silence around him wasn't just quiet. It was heavy. Cold. Like the whole city was holding its breath.

And that night, the dream came again. Just like it had for the past few weeks.

Fog rolled through empty streets. Neon lights blinked like dying stars. And in the distance, tall, still, and glowing, stood the figure. The Neon God.

Watching.

II.

Ethan woke up with his heart racing. His room was dark except for the soft blue glow of the digital clock. 3:17 a.m. The dream had felt so real, like he'd been in those foggy streets, standing in front of that huge glowing figure. He could still feel the silence, thick in his chest.

He sat up and rubbed his face. "Just a dream," he whispered. But he didn't believe it.

The next day, things felt... off. The world looked the same: people buried in their devices, ads flashing on every surface, but Ethan noticed how nobody really *talked*. Sure, there were words. Office small talk. A few texts. But there was no feeling in them. Just noise that didn't mean anything.

Even Anna seemed distant. At breakfast, she asked how he slept, but she didn't wait for the answer. Her eyes were on her phone; thumb scrolling through news or work or who knows what. Ethan mumbled something, and she nodded, not really listening.

At work, it got worse. While designing a new ad for a phone company, Ethan saw the same colors from his dream, blinding pinks, eerie greens, and blinking blues. It made his skin crawl. The city in his dream had been covered in light like that.

He looked around the office. No one seemed bothered. People typed, clicked, and scrolled. Nobody looked up. It was like they weren't really there, just bodies going through the motions.

That afternoon, he stood by the office window, staring at the street below. Crowds of people flowed by, all glued to their screens. It hit him then: this wasn't just a bad dream. The silence was real. It had taken over the city.

And no one seemed to notice.

That night, Ethan told Anna about the dream. "There's this... figure," he said. "Tall, glowing. Like a god made of neon lights. And everything's covered in fog. Quiet. Too quiet."

Anna looked at him, then gave a small laugh. "You've been working too much," she said. "Maybe cut back on caffeine."

"I'm serious," he replied, voice sharper than he meant. "It's more than a dream. It's like... something's wrong with everything. Like people don't *feel* anything anymore."

She sighed and turned back to her phone. "Maybe you just need a break."

But Ethan knew it wasn't him. It was the world, and the silence was only getting louder.

III.

Ethan started to keep a notebook. Not for work, not for lists. Just... to write down what he saw. What he felt. What was *wrong*?

He didn't tell anyone. Especially not Anna.

He wrote about the silence, the dream fog, and the strange way neon signs seemed to *watch* him. He even sketched the Neon God's tall, faceless arms out, as if it wanted to be worshipped. Every night, the dream returned, and every morning, he remembered more. He remembered the streets. The chill. The way the light stung his eyes.

He thought about talking to someone, so he booked an appointment with a therapist. Dr. Harris.

The office was clean and quiet. Too quiet. The kind of quiet that hums behind your ears.

Ethan tried to explain everything. The dreams. The strange feeling that no one was *present* anymore. The way the world had gone hollow.

Dr. Harris nodded politely, taking notes. "You're under a lot of stress," he said. "The world moves fast. Maybe you're feeling disconnected."

"No," Ethan said. "It's not *me*. It's everyone else."

More nodding. More calm, careful words. But there was something in Dr. Harris's eyes like he was reading from a script. Like he wasn't really hearing Ethan at all.

On the way home, Ethan saw a man trip on the sidewalk. People walked around him. No one stopped. No one even looked. The man stood up slowly, brushing himself off, totally alone in a crowd of hundreds.

That night, the dream changed. This time, Ethan tried to *speak* to the Neon God. He shouted, begged, cursed. But no words came out. His mouth moved, but no sound escaped.

He woke up gasping. Sat on the edge of the bed, sweating, hands shaking.

In the bathroom mirror, he whispered, "I'm still here." But the reflection didn't look sure.

At work, Ethan barely spoke. His coworkers didn't notice. Anna didn't say much either, but when she did, her voice seemed... distant. Like it had been recorded ahead of time.

Ethan had stopped sleeping through the night. He started walking the city alone, looking for signs of something real. Something alive.

He watched a street performer one night, strumming a guitar no one could hear over the buzz of passing ads. The man looked right at Ethan and smiled like he *knew*.

Ethan wanted to ask him something. Anything. But the moment passed. The man disappeared into the fog.

The world wasn't just quiet anymore. It was cracked, glitching, and Ethan was the only one who noticed.

IV.

Ethan couldn't keep pretending. Something was broken in the world. Not just around him but *inside him,* too.

The silence had started to spread. It wasn't just people who were not talking. It was like they didn't *feel* anything anymore. No warmth. No kindness. Just robotic replies and blank stares. He watched couples sit together in cafés, both scrolling on their phones. Kids with virtual headsets at the park. A man crying on a bench, completely ignored.

It was like humanity had gone offline.

One night, while walking through an old alley lit by a flickering sign, Ethan saw something just a small sticker on a brick wall. It read: **"You are not alone. The God is not real."**

His heart jumped.

He came back the next night. And the next. Eventually, he found more signs. Hidden messages carved into concrete, painted on the backs of street signs. **"Don't bow." "Silence is control." "Remember how to feel."**

They led him to a dusty bookstore in a quiet part of the city. The windows were covered. Inside, a woman named Marla greeted him with a nod. No smile. Just a quiet look that said, *you're not crazy.*

There were others. Five or six people. All different ages. All carrying the same haunted look in their eyes.

They shared stories of strange dreams, of seeing the Neon God in reflections, of feeling like something was missing from the world.

One man, Marcus, shared how his wife had stopped calling him by his name. Just said, "Good morning," "Dinner's ready," "Good night." Over and over. Like a loop. One day, she didn't even blink.

Ethan didn't feel comforted. Not really. If anything, it made everything worse. It meant the silence was real, and it was spreading.

Marla showed him old news clips, studies, leaked documents, and articles about tech companies pushing new emotion-dampening features.

Quiet pills, calm filters, and AI tools that would answer texts *for you.* A world where people no longer needed to think or feel.

"It's all by design," she said softly. "The silence is the product."

Ethan's hands were shaking. All this time, he'd thought maybe he was just losing it. But now he wondered if that would've been easier.

Still, he wasn't sure if the group was helping or just feeding the fear. Every answer led to more questions. More uncertainty.

That night, the Neon God came again. But this time, Ethan didn't run. He walked straight into the light.

V.

The dream felt different this time.

It wasn't just fog and flashing lights. It felt *real*. Like Ethan had stepped out of his body and into a world made of smoke and static.

He walked through narrow streets, the buildings around him tall and cold, their windows blank like eyes that had forgotten how to see. Neon signs blinked in every color, ads, faces, and symbols. They buzzed louder than ever, but not a single voice could be heard.

Then he saw it. The Neon God.

It rose from the center of the city like a tower of light and shadow, glowing but empty. It had no mouth. No eyes. Just a giant shape, pulsing with power. Screens wrapped around its chest, flashing images of happy people, shiny gadgets, and perfect lives.

But none of it felt real. It was all fake. Plastic joy.

Ethan stood frozen as the god looked down without really *looking*. The silence hit him like a wave, pressing against his chest, pushing the breath out of his lungs. He opened his mouth to scream, but no sound came.

All around him, people knelt. Bowed. Their faces lit by glowing screens clutched in both hands like holy objects.

"Why?" Ethan tried to say. "Why did we let this happen?"

The god didn't answer. It never did. But in that silence, Ethan finally *understood*.

It wasn't a god at all. It was a mirror.

A reflection of everything humanity had given up: connection, emotion, meaning. All traded for convenience. For distraction. For silence.

Tears slid down Ethan's face, but no one noticed. No one looked up.

In the dream, he ran toward the god. Clawed at it. Punched the screens. Screamed with everything he had, even if the sound never came.

"I'm still here!" he shouted into the void.

The god cracked. Just a little. A flicker. A glitch.

And then Ethan woke up, gasping, drenched in sweat.

His alarm buzzed beside him. 6:00 a.m. Outside, the city hummed as always. But something had changed.

At least... inside him.

VI.

The next morning, Ethan walked through the city like always. Same blinking signs, same people, eyes locked on screens. The same mechanical voices coming from speakers and phones.

But Ethan was different now.

He didn't look at his phone. He watched *people* instead—their blank faces, their quiet mouths, their tired eyes. And it hurt. Really hurt. Because now he could *feel* it. The silence wasn't just around them. It was *in* them. It had taken root.

He tried to speak to a man at the coffee shop, just a simple "Hey, how's your morning?" The man blinked, nodded once, and went back to scrolling.

He tried again with someone else. "Do you ever feel like something's missing?"

The woman gave a polite smile. "Sorry, I'm in a meeting," she said, tapping her earbuds and walking away.

That night, Ethan sat on a bench in the city square, surrounded by people. Music played through speakers overhead. Screens flashed ads every few seconds.

But no one was talking.

He whispered to himself, "This isn't living. It's sleepwalking."

Just then, a small boy, maybe ten, walked past with his family. The boy looked up from his screen and noticed Ethan sitting alone. Their eyes met for one brief second. The boy's steps slowed.

And then... he *smiled*. Just a little. Ethan smiled back.

The boy's mother called his name, and he quickly looked down at his screen again, hurrying to catch up.

But for a second, a *second*, he had looked.

Ethan stayed on that bench long after the crowds moved on. The silence still pressed in all around him, thick and heavy.

But now, there was a crack in it.

Small. Quiet.

But real.

Author's Note

Whispers of the Neon God was born from a question that kept circling in my head: What happens when we trade connection for convenience?

I've spent more time than I care to admit walking through crowded places where nobody looks up, where conversations feel rehearsed, and where silence doesn't mean peace, it means something's missing. This story isn't just about a man haunted by dreams. It's about a world that feels too quiet in all the wrong ways. A world where empathy is getting drowned out by distraction.

The inspiration came from Simon & Garfunkel's *"The Sound of Silence,"* a song I've loved for years. Its haunting lines, *"People talking without speaking, people hearing without listening,"* felt more like a warning than lyrics. So I asked myself, *what if someone actually heard that silence growing? And what if it started to speak back?*

Ethan's story is about waking up. Not just from a dream but from the slow sleep of apathy. Maybe you've felt that strange emptiness, too, in a world full of noise.

Hopefully, something in this story made you pause and wonder if you, on some level, have been bowing to your own version of the Neon God.

Thanks for reading.

—Brett C. Persson

Not Even a Whisper in the Silence

Chapter 1

The church was quieter than it had ever been. No songs. No prayers. Just the sound of old wood creaking under Nathaniel's boots as he stepped up to the pulpit one last time.

The sun was low, casting long shadows through the stained-glass windows. Dust floated in the light like tiny spirits still hanging around, waiting for someone to notice them. The place smelled like old hymnals and memories, both of which hadn't been used in a while.

Nathaniel looked out at the empty pews. He could still picture where folks used to sit. Mrs. Smith, in the third row, was always knitting during the sermon. The Williams kids were in the back, whispering and laughing until their mom gave them that look. And Tom Harding, faithful as a sunrise, hadn't missed a Sunday in twenty years until the day Nathaniel stopped preaching.

He placed his hands on the pulpit. The wood felt worn and familiar. This had been his place. For years, this was where he stood, shouting about heaven, warning about hell, and trying to make sense of the world with nothing but a Bible and a fire in his heart, but that fire had gone cold.

"I guess this is it," he said out loud, though there was no one to hear him. His voice bounced around the empty room. "One last sermon."

He pulled out a small, folded piece of paper from his pocket. It wasn't a sermon, not really. Just some words he'd jotted down the night before. He unfolded it slowly, like it might fall apart in his hands.

"I used to believe," he read. "With everything I had. I believed in prayer. I believed in miracles. I believed there was a reason for everything." He paused. The silence felt heavy.

"But then the prayers stopped working. The miracles never came. And the reasons... well, they never made much sense."

Nathaniel looked up at the cross on the wall behind him. It was crooked; it had been that way for years. He used to think it added character. Now it just seemed tired, like it had been holding up too much for too long.

"I'm not angry," he said, folding the paper again. "Just... done."

He stepped down from the pulpit and walked down the center aisle slowly, like it was a funeral march for something he used to love. At the back of the church, he stopped and turned around one last time.

"This place gave me a voice," he said, almost whispering. "But it also took my questions and turned them into sins."

He pulled the door shut behind him, locking it with a heavy click. He dropped the key into the church's old mailbox. It landed with a metallic thunk that echoed across the porch.

And just like that, he walked away. Not from a building. Not from a job. From a life he used to believe in.

Chapter 2

Nathaniel was ten when he learned that not all prayers are answered.

His mom had been sick for a while, but nobody really said how bad it was. She still smiled, still tucked him in at night, still told him everything was going to be okay. But even then, he could see the truth in her eyes. They looked tired, like her soul was slowly being pulled out of her.

The church had held a special service for her one Sunday. Everyone gathered around, laid hands on her, and prayed. Nathaniel had never prayed so hard in his life. He squeezed his eyes shut so tight it hurt. He begged God to fix her, and he promised he'd be good forever if God just made her better.

The pastor had knelt down beside him afterward and said, "God heard you, son. He hears every word. If your faith is strong, He will answer." So, Nathaniel waited. Two weeks later, she was gone.

The house felt empty after that. Not just because she wasn't there, but because something else had left with her. Hope, maybe. Or trust. He wasn't sure.

At the funeral, he sat in the front row, holding a crumpled tissue in one hand and his mom's old cross necklace in the other. The pastor talked about heaven and how she was in a better place. People around him nodded and wiped their tears. Some even smiled, like that made it all okay.

Nathaniel just felt cold.

That night, he crawled into bed and prayed again. Not for healing. Not for miracles. Just for a sign. Anything. A warm breeze. A flicker of light. Her voice in a dream.

Nothing came.

He stared at the ceiling until his eyes burned. Then he whispered, "Did I not pray hard enough?"

No answer.

It was the first time Nathaniel felt completely alone.

Not just in his room, but in the universe.

Chapter 3

Nathaniel was twenty-three the first time someone called him *Pastor Cross*. He still remembered how weird that sounded. The name belonged to someone older, wiser, and probably with less student debt. But it was real. He'd finished Bible college, done his internship, and landed a job at a small church just outside Tallahassee.

He poured everything into that place.

Sunday sermons. Wednesday night Bible study. Youth group pizza nights. Hospital visits. Weddings. Funerals. He did it all because that's what a good pastor is supposed to do. And back then, Nathaniel wanted to be better than anything else.

His sermons were on fire. People say that all the time. "You're on fire for the Lord," they'd say. "God's really using you." And he believed it. He *felt* it. There was this deep, buzzing energy in his chest every time he preached. Like God Himself had lit something inside him, and the words just came pouring out.

He'd study scripture late into the night, highlighting verses, scribbling notes in the margins, and connecting dots that made his head spin and his heart race. The Bible was alive to him. A living, breathing message. And he was the messenger, but even in those early days, the questions never fully went away.

Sometimes, he'd read a passage that didn't make sense. Or one that felt... off. Like when God ordered entire cities wiped out, including children. Or when He hardened Pharaoh's heart just so He could show off. Nathaniel would circle those parts and write "Come back to this" in the margins.

He never really came back.

Until one day after the service, a man named Dr. Calvin approached him. He was a retired science teacher with silver hair and a soft voice that always made you lean a little closer.

"That was a good message today," Calvin said. "Mind if I ask you something?"

"Sure," Nathaniel said.

"What do you think about evolution?"

Nathaniel smiled politely. "I believe God created the world."

"Of course. But do you think He could've used evolution to do it?"

Nathaniel paused. "Maybe. I mean, it's not exactly what Genesis says, but... maybe."

Calvin nodded thoughtfully. "Just something to think about. The universe is big, Pastor. Really big. And sometimes, the more I learn, the more I think we've only scratched the surface of what's true."

That stuck with Nathaniel more than he expected. He found himself staring at the stars a little longer at night. Reading a few articles that Calvin left on his desk. Nothing crazy. Just... wondering.

He didn't share those thoughts with his congregation. Not yet. Not while the fire was still burning strong.

But in the quiet moments, when the church was empty and the lights were low, he started to feel something shift.

The fire in his bones was still there, but it had started to flicker.

Chapter 4

It was the summer Nathaniel turned thirty-eight when everything cracked wide open.

The church was doing well. Sunday attendance was strong, the youth group had grown, and the food pantry they ran every Friday had become a big part of the community. On the outside, things looked solid. But behind the scenes, something dark had started to surface.

It began with a whispered conversation after service. A teenage girl, Emily, had asked to speak with Nathaniel privately. She was quiet and nervous, eyes darting to the door even though it was closed.

"He touches me," she said, barely above a whisper.

Nathaniel blinked. "What?"

"Mr. Jenkins," she said. "The deacon."

At first, Nathaniel didn't want to believe it. Deacon Jenkins had been with the church for decades. He taught Sunday school. He prayed loudly. He always helped with the offering and gave the best hugs.

But Emily didn't flinch. Her voice cracked, but her words were steady. "I told my mom. She said I must be confused. She said not to stir up trouble."

Nathaniel asked all the right questions. He documented everything. He even went to the elders about it, expecting action. Expecting justice.

Instead, they told him to drop it.

"Deacon Jenkins has done so much for this church," one of them said. "We can't throw that away over a teenager's confusion."

"She's not confused," Nathaniel had snapped. "She's scared."

"Then let her pray about it. God will bring peace."

Nathaniel left that meeting feeling like he couldn't breathe. He sat alone in the sanctuary that night, staring up at the wooden cross hanging over the pulpit.

He prayed.

He begged.

He shouted in the empty room, "Where are You?"

No answer.

No sign.

Just silence.

A few weeks later, Emily took her own life. She left behind a short note and a Bible with the pages torn out of the Psalms.

The funeral was small. Her mother sat with stiff shoulders, face like stone. Jenkins didn't even attend.

Nathaniel wanted to scream. He wanted to tear the cross off the wall and set it on fire. Instead, he returned to the pulpit the next Sunday and delivered a sermon titled "The Silence of God."

He didn't name names. But everyone in that room could feel it. The weight. The fury. The grief.

Some nodded along.

Others whispered afterward that he'd "lost his fire."

He hadn't lost it.

He was finally seeing what had been hiding in the shadows all along.

And for the first time in his life, Nathaniel wondered if God had ever been there at all.

Chapter 5

They didn't call it a trial, but that's what it was.

A closed-door meeting with the elders. No congregation. No support. Just Nathaniel, a few men in suits, and a Bible sitting between them like a silent judge.

"We're concerned," Elder Brooks had started. His voice was calm, but his eyes were sharp. "Your recent sermons have caused division."

Nathaniel sat still. "Division, or discomfort?"

"There's a difference?"

He didn't answer. He didn't have to.

They went down the list. Questioning doctrine. Stirring doubt. Refusing to let go of the incident with Deacon Jenkins. Even after the girl's death, the elders insisted there was no "proof." No one else had come forward. The deacon had "stepped down quietly," and they called that closure.

Nathaniel called it cowardice.

"You're undermining the authority of the church," another elder said. "You're preaching confusion instead of truth."

"I'm preaching honesty," Nathaniel replied. "The truth is... we didn't protect her. We failed her. And instead of seeking justice, you buried it under prayer and politeness."

Brooks leaned forward, folding his hands. "You were once a great pastor, Nathaniel. But somewhere along the way, you started believing in yourself more than you believed in God."

They told him he could step down quietly, too. Save face. Move on. Maybe even find another church willing to overlook his "rough patch."

But Nathaniel didn't want another pulpit. He wanted the truth.

"I won't lie to people just to keep my job," he said. "If asking questions gets me excommunicated, then so be it."

And with that, it was over.

He turned in his office keys, packed up his books, and walked out the back door. No send-off. No prayer circle. Just a few awkward nods and someone muttering, "We'll pray for you."

He didn't want their prayers. What he wanted was for someone, anyone, to admit that faith should never cost a girl her life.

That night, Nathaniel sat on the hood of his car in the church parking lot. The building stood quiet behind him, lights off, doors locked. Just another shell of what it pretended to be.

He looked up at the sky. No thunder. No fire from heaven. Just stars.

And for the first time, he didn't feel like he'd been cast out of God's house.

He felt like he'd finally walked out of a cage.

Chapter 6

Nathaniel now went by "Nate." Just Nate. No title. No pulpit. No more polite smiles from church ladies or handshakes from deacons who couldn't meet his eyes.

He lived in a small apartment above a bookstore in Tampa. The ceiling leaked when it rained, and the AC groaned like it was on its last breath, but it was his. Quiet. Simple. Safe.

He taught night classes at the community college: Introduction to Philosophy and Critical Thinking 101. It wasn't glamorous, but he liked the questions his students asked. Real questions. Honest ones. Not the kind you already knew the answer to before you opened your mouth.

He kept a thick, beat-up notebook on his desk titled *Faithless Fire*. That was the book he was writing. Or maybe just living. It started as scattered thoughts, old sermon notes scribbled over with black ink, Bible verses crossed out and replaced with questions like:

What if morality is older than religion? If God is love, why do churches so often choose silence? Does purpose have to come from heaven, or can it come from us?

Some nights, he stayed up until 3 a.m. writing. Other nights, he just stared at the page and let the silence wash over him. Not the empty kind he used to fear. Not the silence that followed a prayer and made you wonder if you were talking to yourself.

This silence felt different. Peaceful. Real.

One afternoon, after class, a student named Mariah stuck around to talk. She was quiet in lectures but always took sharp notes and tilted her head when something didn't make sense.

"Can I ask you something kind of personal?" she said.

Nate nodded. "Sure."

"Were you always an atheist?"

He smiled. "Not even close."

She raised an eyebrow. "So... what happened?"

He thought about how to answer. About Emily. About the silence. About the stone faces around that elder's table. About the God who never showed up.

"I stopped pretending," he said finally. "And I started looking for answers that didn't require me to lie to myself."

She didn't say anything for a second. Then she nodded slowly. "That takes guts."

"I don't know about that," he chuckled. "Maybe just a tired soul."

After she left, Nate sat at his desk and opened the notebook again. He flipped to a blank page and wrote in big, messy letters:

Reason doesn't give all the answers. But at least it doesn't punish you for asking.

He underlined it twice, then leaned back in his chair.

The fire that once burned in his bones was still there, but it had changed. It didn't rage from a pulpit anymore. It didn't need smoke and thunder.

Now, it burned steadily and quietly. Like a lantern in the dark.

Chapter 7

The call came late on Wednesday afternoon.

"Reverend Wallace is in hospice," the voice said. "He's asking for you."

Nate hadn't heard that name in years. Reverend Thomas Wallace, his old mentor. The man who first told him he had "the fire of a prophet." The same man who'd sat across from him at the table the day he was excommunicated.

He almost didn't go. But something in him, curiosity, maybe, pulled him there anyway.

The hospice room was small and smelled like hand sanitizer and wilted flowers. Reverend Wallace looked thinner than Nate remembered, his skin pale, like paper left too long in the sun. Machines beeped softly beside the bed, keeping time like a metronome.

"Pastor Cross," Wallace said, a faint smile on his lips.

"I don't go by that anymore," Nate said, pulling a chair beside the bed. "Just Nate now."

Wallace chuckled, then he winced. "Old habits."

There was a long pause. The kind that's heavy, like the air itself knows something important is about to be said.

"I read about your upcoming book," Wallace finally said. "*Faithless Fire*, right?"

"Still writing it."

"You always were a writer," the old man said. "You made God sound like poetry."

Nate looked down. "Yeah. Back when I still believed He was listening."

Wallace shifted slightly in the bed. "You think He stopped listening?"

"I think," Nate said slowly, "He was never there to begin with. We were just talking to ourselves and calling it prayer."

The old man didn't argue. Not right away. He just stared at the ceiling, like maybe he was asking it something, too.

"I've been praying a lot lately," Wallace said. "Trying to make peace."

"Has He answered?"

Wallace gave a soft laugh. "You always did ask the hard questions."

Nate leaned forward. "Tell me something, Tom. Do you really believe... still?"

Wallace closed his eyes. "I believe in what I tried to do. I believe in kindness and in helping people. I don't know if there's a heaven for sure, but I believe there is, I truly do. It's called having faith."

Nate nodded. "I believe in helping people and kindness, too. Just not the part where you need a sky-father to make them matter."

For a while, neither of them spoke. The machine beeped. A nurse walked by in the hallway, humming off-key. The world kept turning.

Finally, Wallace turned his head toward Nate. "I'm glad you came."

"I didn't come to fight," Nate said. "Not this time."

"I know."

"I just... needed to know if you still thought I was lost."

Wallace smiled. "No, son. You were never lost. Just walking a different path."

He closed his eyes again, and Nate watched his chest rise and fall, slow and shallow.

"I hope you find peace," Wallace whispered.

"I already have," Nate said.

He stayed for a while longer, sitting in silence next to the man who had once given him everything, and then taken it away, but in the end, forgiveness didn't need words. Sometimes, the last debate isn't about who's right.

It's about letting go.

Chapter 8

The sun was just starting to rise as Nate reached the overlook.

It was quiet up there, nothing but wind through the tall grass and the distant sound of birds waking up. He parked the car, grabbed the small wooden box from the passenger seat, and made his way to the edge of the cliff.

The view stretched out for miles. Hills rolled like soft waves, and the sky was streaked with orange and gold. It looked like the world was exhaling.

He opened the box slowly. Inside were his mother's ashes. They'd been sitting in his closet for years, waiting for a moment like this, though he wasn't sure what made this morning the right one.

Maybe it was seeing Wallace. Maybe it was finally finishing the last chapter of *Faithless Fire*. Or maybe it was just time.

He held the box against his chest for a moment. "I hope you knew how much I loved you," he said softly.

Then he stepped to the edge and scattered the ashes into the wind.

They swirled and danced, carried off by a breeze that didn't need permission. And just like that, she was gone again, but this time, it felt different. It's not like a loss. Not like silence, but like a return.

He stood there a while longer, hands in his pockets, watching the sun break through the clouds.

"I used to think I'd see you again," he said. "In heaven. Somewhere bright and perfect. But now... I think this was it. This life. This moment. This love."

There was no voice from the clouds. No whisper in the wind. Just light, air, and the sound of his own breath.

And yet, somehow, it was enough.

He turned back toward the car, the empty box under his arm, the morning sun warming his back.

He didn't feel empty. He felt alive, and as he walked away from the edge, he whispered one last thought, not a prayer, not a plea.

Just the truth.

"Heaven was empty. And that made this life, this moment, everything."

"When I stopped searching for heaven, I found the sacred peace and serenity in sunrises, in silence, and in simply being."
— *Nathaniel Cross, Faithless Fire*

JUST ONE MORE DAY

BRETT C. PERSSON

Part I

The room was dark except for a single lamp in the corner, casting a soft yellow glow across the cluttered floor. Empty soda cans, a half-eaten bag of chips, and a few old takeout boxes sat in lazy piles around the bed. It smelled like old sweat, dust, and something sour, like life had just stopped trying here a long time ago.

Alex sat on the edge of the bed, elbows on his knees, staring at the nightstand. His eyes didn't blink much. They were locked on the cold, metal revolver lying beside his phone. He didn't cry. He didn't scream. He just sat there, empty.

He reached for the gun, picked it up slowly, and turned it over in his hand. The weight of the gun made his arm drop a little. It wasn't heavy because of the metal; it was heavy because of everything it meant.

His voice cracked as he whispered, "Does anyone even care?"

Outside, the world kept spinning. Cars drove by. A dog barked. Somewhere, someone was laughing. But not here.

Here, it was just silence… and the sound of a hammer clicking back into place.

Part II

That morning started like any other. Alex got up late, skipped breakfast, and barely made it to work on time. He didn't care much anymore, but he still showed up. That had to count for something, right?

The boss didn't even wait an hour before calling him into the office.

"We're letting you go, Alex," she said, without even looking him in the eyes. "It's not working out."

Just like that. No warning. No second chance. Just done.

He didn't say much. Just nodded, grabbed his jacket, and left. Outside, the sun was way too bright, and the world felt too loud. His heart pounded, but not from anger; it was numbness.

He walked for hours with nowhere to go. Texted his sister. No reply. Called his old sponsor. Straight to voicemail. Even the group chat from his recovery meetings was quiet.

By late afternoon, he was sitting on a bench, staring at nothing, wondering how everything had slipped away. He used to be clean. He used to have hope. He used to laugh.

Now? Just this deep, empty feeling like something inside him had rotted and died without anyone noticing.

"I got nothing left inside," he muttered. And for the first time in years, he believed it.

Part III

Alex wandered through the city like a ghost. He didn't have a plan; he just walked wherever his feet took him. He passed old places that used to mean something: the diner where he had coffee with his sponsor, the bus stop where he used to joke with his sister after work, and the corner where he used to sell pills before he got clean.

Now, they were just places filled with ghosts of who he used to be.

He stopped at a bridge and stared down at the water below. It was quiet there, except for the cars behind him and the wind brushing past his face. For a second, he thought about jumping.

Just doing it. Ending everything. But his body wouldn't move. He cursed under his breath and kept walking.

Later, he passed the homeless shelter where he used to volunteer. He saw a kid outside, maybe eighteen, shivering, arms wrapped tight around himself. Alex paused but didn't say anything. He just kept walking.

He stopped at a pawn shop and bought a small box of bullets with the last $20 in his wallet. The guy behind the counter didn't even blink. Just took the money and gave him a nod.

Back home, he poured himself a drink, sat on the edge of the bed, and stared at the gun again.

"Just give me the courage," he whispered, hands shaking.

Outside, the streetlight buzzed. Inside, he raised the gun and closed his eyes.

Part IV

Alex sat there for what felt like forever, the gun resting heavy in his hand. His finger hovered over the trigger, but it wouldn't move. His hand was shaking so badly it almost felt like the gun was shaking, too.

He closed his eyes and tried to picture what it would feel like, just silence. No more pain. No more pretending. No more anything.

But instead of peace, a memory came rushing in.

He returned to the shelter two years ago. A kid, barely a teenager, had overdosed in the bathroom. Alex had found him just in time and called 911. He stayed with him, talked to him, and kept him breathing until help came. That kid had cried into Alex's shirt, thanking him for saving his life.

Then came another memory: his mom, years ago. Wrapping him in a hug after one of his first clean months. Her voice was soft and shaky when she said, "You matter, Alex. Don't ever forget that."

His eyes snapped open. His chest ached like he couldn't breathe.

"But that was before," he said aloud. "That was when I still mattered."

Tears slid down his cheeks. He tried to hold them back, but they came anyway. His whole body trembled. The gun was still in his hand. His finger moved, just a little, toward the trigger.

But he slammed the gun down on the floor instead, hard. It didn't go off. It just clattered across the wood, spinning for a second before coming to a stop.

Alex curled up on the bed and cried like a kid. For everything. For nothing.

Part V

Alex lay there on the bed, eyes red and swollen, staring at the ceiling like maybe it had answers. The room was quiet, except for the hum of the refrigerator and the occasional sound of a car driving outside.

His head was spinning. One minute, he wanted it all to stop. Next, he was remembering things, good things he hadn't thought about in years.

He reached for his phone. His hands were still shaking. One new missed call. His sister.

He stared at the screen, heart racing. His thumb hovered over the call-back button, but he didn't press it. He couldn't. What would he even say?

Hey, I almost killed myself. What's up with you?

Still, he opened their old texts. The last message from her was just a few hours ago: **"Let me know if you want to grab dinner soon. Miss you."** He had never replied.

Alex called her and apologized to her for not getting back to her. They talked for several minutes. Alex had almost told her about his job and how he felt, and then decided against it. These were his problems, not hers.

Alex set the phone down next to the gun. He didn't want to hold either of them anymore. They both felt like choices, and he didn't trust himself to choose.

He stood up and looked at himself in the mirror. His face was pale, tired, older than he remembered. But he was still here, for now. He sat back down. He waited and just began to think about the choices he had to make. His hand would move from the phone to the gun as his internal struggle fought for a solution.

Part VI

His sister pulled into the driveway a little after midnight. She hadn't planned on coming over, but something about Alex's voice when they talked had scared her. It was too flat. Too quiet. Something was off, and she couldn't get the thought out of her mind.

She knocked on the door. No answer.

"Alex?" she called. Nothing.

The door was unlocked, which wasn't like him. Her heart started to race. She stepped inside slowly, the smell of dust and something sour hitting her nose. The house was dark, except for a faint light coming from the bedroom.

She called out again, a little louder. Still no reply.

When she walked into the room, she saw him. He was on the floor beside the bed, slouched over, the gun still in his hand. His eyes were closed. His chest didn't rise.

For a moment, she just stood there, frozen. Then she dropped to her knees beside him, grabbing his shoulders, shaking him.

"Alex! No, no, no, no, please."

But he was gone.

On the nightstand, next to the half-drunk glass of water, was a torn scrap of notebook paper. Just a few words in his handwriting:

"I fought it as long as I could. I just couldn't feel anything anymore. I'm sorry."

Her hands trembled as she read it. Tears poured down her cheeks. She didn't scream. She just held him and whispered, "I'm sorry I didn't come sooner. I hope you have your peace."

Outside, the world kept turning. Somewhere, someone was laughing. But in that room, the only sound of a sister crying while she held her dead brother.

Dead Cold Winter

Prologue

It was a deadly cold winter, the kind of cold that bit through the skin and clung to the bone. The sun had just begun to fall behind the prison walls, bleeding red and orange across the sky, as if trying to remind the world of the life it once gave. But John Winter hadn't seen a sunset like that in 27 years. Not without bars in the way.

The steel doors groaned as they slid open behind him. No ceremony. No justice. Just the end of a sentence that should never have started.

He took a step forward, his boots crunching the frost-covered ground. The air stung his lungs. The world was quieter than he remembered. Or maybe he was just quieter inside. Something had been left behind in that cell, something that once hoped. What was left now was colder. Sharper.

Hank Jackson leaned against the hood of his rust-dented Oldsmobile, a cigarette burning low between his fingers. He didn't speak right away. Just watched John with the uneasy reverence of someone who had touched a ghost.

"You're free," Hank finally said, flicking the ash into the wind.

John glanced at the sky, at the distant sun trying to push warmth into a place that had long since forgotten what warmth was.

"No," John said, his voice low and gravelly from disuse. "I'm finished being caged. But I'm not free. Not yet."

Hank opened the passenger door, but John didn't move. He was looking out over the barren hills, where the cold rolled in like fog and shadows stretched long and quiet.

"They think time fixes things," John said. "But time doesn't heal lies. It just buries them."

Hank gave a slow nod. "You got a second chance now. What you do with it..."

John cut him off. "I already know what I'm gonna do."

He turned toward the open door, one foot still in the winter dusk, the other stepping into a different kind of darkness, the kind you carry with you.

Behind him, the prison gates slammed shut with a mechanical finality.

Justice had frozen twenty-seven years ago. Now it was time for the thaw.

Chapter One

The door clicked shut behind him like the punctuation on a long, bitter sentence. John Winter adjusted the collar of the gray coat Hank had brought, the wool stiff with cold and years in a closet. It smelled like mothballs and stale air, but it was warm. Warmer than anything he'd worn since '68.

He paused outside the gate, letting the cold settle into his skin like it belonged there.

"Christ, you look like a ghost," Hank said, pushing himself off the car. "Or maybe a corpse they let out too soon."

John offered a thin smile, the kind that didn't touch the eyes. "Maybe they did."

They shook hands, but it wasn't warm. It was just something people did when they didn't know what to say.

Hank opened the passenger door, but John didn't get in right away. He stared at the prison, at its lifeless bricks, at the towers with their blind eyes, at the walls that had swallowed his twenties, thirties, and most of his forties.

"Twenty-seven years," John muttered.

"You said that already," Hank replied gently.

John nodded, more to himself than Hank. "Just making sure I believe it."

Inside the car, the heater whined as it struggled to warm the cold air. John sat stiffly, his body unfamiliar with space and silence. He held himself like he was waiting for the next command, the next meal bell, the next hour of the yard.

Hank drove slowly as if speeding might break the fragile illusion that John was truly free.

"I put a bag together," Hank said. "Clothes, cash, the basics. Even got you some music, thought maybe it'd help you catch up to the world."

John didn't respond. His eyes were on the landscape, flat fields, broken fence lines, the occasional tree stripped bare by winter's grip. It was all so still. Dead, almost. He knew how it felt.

"You ever think they'd let you out?" Hank asked.

John shook his head. "No. And then, somewhere along the way, I stopped caring."

Silence filled the car again. It wasn't awkward, just heavy.

Hank finally cleared his throat. "You got a place to go?"

John nodded slowly. "Got a few things to take care of first."

Hank didn't ask. He didn't have to. The cold in John's eyes told him everything.

"You should lay low," Hank said. "Enjoy your life. What's left of it."

John turned his head, just enough to meet Hank's gaze. "I didn't get life. My life got stolen."

They drove on, past shuttered gas stations and silent farmhouses. As they crossed into the edge of town, John noticed things he remembered: half the diners were gone, the old theater had been turned into a megachurch, and the corner store where he used to buy Rachel cherry sodas was now a vape shop.

"Lots changed," Hank said.

"Not enough," John replied.

They pulled into a small motel off the highway. Hank had paid in advance, under a different name. Privacy. Distance. The usual post-prison protocol for someone the system pretended to pity.

As John stepped out, Hank grabbed his arm.

"Whatever you're planning…" he said, eyes sharp now. "Don't."

John stared at him, that same quiet fury under the surface. "I'm not planning anything."

Hank let go, not because he believed him, but because he knew better than to argue with a man who'd lived two decades in a cell for a crime he didn't commit.

John stepped into the motel room without looking back. The door clicked shut behind him. Alone now, with nothing but his thoughts and a suitcase full of borrowed time.

He sat on the edge of the bed, opened the duffel bag, and pulled out an old leather-bound notebook.

Inside were names.

Three of them.

Raymond Holloway. Paul Carpenter. Martin Gaines.

He set the book on the table, opened a pack of cigarettes, and lit one with a shaky hand. The smoke curled into the ceiling like a prayer or a curse, depending on who was watching.

John Winter didn't believe in justice anymore. He believed in revenge, and revenge was coming.

Chapter Two

Paul Carpenter jolted upright in bed, sweat soaking through his undershirt, his breath ragged and loud in the silent room. His hand instinctively reached for the Beretta he kept in the nightstand. It was already cocked.

The room was dark. Still. Cold.

Beside him, Sue stirred. "Paul?" she mumbled. "What is it?"

Paul didn't answer. He stared at the bedroom door, cracked open just enough to see the hallway bathed in dim light. For a moment, he could have sworn he saw a shadow move, tall, lean, silent.

"It's him," Paul whispered. "John Winter. He's back."

He leaped from the bed and stumbled toward the door; gun raised with shaking hands.

"Paul!" Sue's voice was sharper now, alarmed. "What the hell are you talking about?"

He flung the door open, gun ready to fire. But there was nothing. Just air. Just silence. Just guilt.

Sue reached him and slowly touched his arm. "It was a dream," she said. "You're dreaming again."

Paul's breathing slowed, but the fear lingered. "No," he said, staring into the empty hall. "It was real. He's out."

Sue led him back to bed, and they sat on the edge together. Paul lit a cigarette with trembling fingers, the tip flaring orange in the darkness. He took a long drag before exhaling the memory of the nightmare.

"You remember that case from before we met?" he asked. "The murder trial. Three people. Small town panic."

Sue nodded. "Vaguely. That was twenty-seven years ago, right? Before we met."

"He got out," Paul said, voice flat. "John Winter. He got out yesterday."

Sue turned to him, suddenly alert. "I thought he was serving life."

"So did I," Paul muttered. "Turns out life doesn't mean what it used to."

"What does this have to do with you?"

Paul stared at the floor for a long moment. Then he stood, walked to the window, and opened it. The cold air rushed in like punishment. He smoked in silence before answering.

"They paid me," he said at last. "I threw the case."

Sue didn't speak. Her breath caught in her throat.

"I was young. Stupid. A fixer named Martin Gaines came to me, saying John was guilty and deserved the needle, not a lawyer. Offered me a twenty grand to take a dive, to tank the case, and I took it."

Sue stood slowly, as if something sacred had cracked inside her. "You never told me this."

"I buried it," Paul said. "And for a while, it stayed buried. Until about six months ago. Word got around that John's case was getting reopened. Evidence mishandled. Witnesses recanted. The DA's office didn't want to admit fault, but the court of appeals didn't care. And now he's out."

He turned to her. "He's coming for me."

Sue crossed her arms. "You don't know that."

"I do," he said. "I would. If it were me, I'd want blood."

A long silence passed between them, broken only by the wind rattling the windowpane.

"Did you call the police?" she asked.

"They said there's nothing they can do," Paul replied bitterly. "No threats, no contact. They won't babysit me because I've got a guilty conscience."

Sue sat back down on the edge of the bed, eyes heavy with disbelief. "You helped send an innocent man to prison. And now you're worried he's going to do to you what you did to him."

"I didn't kill anyone," Paul snapped.

"No," she said softly. "You just lied and let someone else fall."

Paul crushed his cigarette into the ashtray. His hands were shaking again.

"He's not the same man he was," Paul said. "You don't come out of a place like that whole. You come out cold. Hollow. Hungry."

Sue looked at him, really looked at him, and realized something terrible.

"You don't feel bad for what you did," she said. "You feel bad that he's coming for you."

Paul didn't answer.

Chapter Three

The driveway was lined with bare oaks, their skeletal limbs clawing at the gray sky. John Winter pulled the car over a block away and turned off the engine. He didn't need to get any closer. He already knew the house.

Raymond Holloway had once worn the black robe like a crown. Now he wore oxygen tubes in his nose and a wool blanket across his knees. The internet had done its job: a quick search revealed everything, his retirement speech, photos from charity events, and a recent piece in the *Gazette* about "a life of justice well served."

Justice.

John's jaw tightened as he stepped out of the car and walked the rest of the way.

No guards. No cameras. No alarms. Just the quiet, rich stillness of a man who had outlived accountability.

The front door was locked. But John was inside in just a few minutes.

John let himself in like a ghost returning to the scene of its murder. The house smelled of old books, fading cologne, and slow decay. A jazz record was playing low in the background, Miles Davis, if he wasn't mistaken.

"Hello?" a weak, rattling voice called. "Is someone there?"

John followed the sound. The judge sat in a large leather recliner near the fireplace, a thick book resting on his lap. His eyes were glassy, rimmed with yellow. His mouth twitched, unsure if he was looking at a memory or a man. An oxygen tank sat next to him with tubes that ran to the judge's nose.

"I know you," Holloway said, voice trembling. "I know that face…"

"You should," John said, stepping into the light. "You looked down on it from five feet up in your robe. That day in court. December second. Nineteen sixty-four."

The judge paled. The book fell from his lap.

"John Winter," he whispered.

John gave a small nod. "Took you longer than I thought."

"I... I hadn't heard they let you out."

"They didn't let me out," John said. "They admitted they were wrong. But not you."

The old man leaned back in the chair, wheezing. "I was just doing my job."

"You weren't doing your job. You were following orders."

"I had no choice," Holloway said. "People were scared. Three brutal murders. The town wanted blood. They were going to come after my family. After me."

"They came after me instead," John said. "And you let them."

The judge looked away. "What do you want from me?"

"I want you to tell me the truth," John said. "Before it's too late."

Holloway was silent.

John pulled out a small voice recorder and placed it on the table beside the judge. He hit the red button. "Start with the bribe."

The judge closed his eyes, the old facade crumbling. "It was Martin Gaines. Said the DA's office needed it to go a certain way. Said the people needed a conviction, or there'd be riots. He always brought money. Told me the defense attorney had been handled, and I needed to keep my mouth shut. And I did."

"Why?"

"Because I thought you were guilty, still do in fact," the judge said, opening his eyes. "Because it was easier. Because it paid my mortgage and got my daughter into Yale."

John leaned closely. "You stole my life for a fucking tuition check."

"I'm sorry, but I was helping send a guilty man to prison for what he did. It didn't seem wrong at the time." Holloway whispered.

John stared at him, his expression unreadable. Then he stood. From his coat, he pulled a vial. Colorless liquid. Fast. Quiet.

The judge looked at it and then up at John. "Please…"

"You gave me a life sentence," John said. "I'm giving you mercy."

He pressed the vial to the judge's oxygen intake, letting the poison seep into his system like the truth had seeped into his soul. Slow. Unforgiving.

Within minutes, Judge Holloway was still.

John picked up the recorder, rewound the tape, and listened to the confession once. Then he turned off the jazz, stepped back into the snow, and closed the door behind him.

One down.

Chapter Four

Martin Gaines lived in a glass fortress on the edge of the city. Floor-to-ceiling windows, marble floors, a private elevator, and a wine cellar bigger than John's entire childhood home. Men like Gaines always built high walls, as if money could keep out consequences.

John didn't bother with the front entrance. He waited until the sun went down, watched the doorman leave, and slipped in through the loading dock beneath the building. The keycard he'd cloned earlier that afternoon worked like a charm. A gift from a sympathetic janitor with a gambling problem.

Elevator. 21st floor. Private residence.

The penthouse was all steel and silent, the kind of place where echoes sounded expensive.

John found Gaines in the kitchen, swirling a glass of red wine like he was trying to hypnotize it. His back was turned, his voice low and amused.

"I was wondering when you'd show."

John didn't speak.

Gaines turned around slowly, eyes settling on the silenced pistol in John's hand. He didn't flinch. Just smirked. "They told me you were smart. Patient. I figured you'd come eventually."

"Then why haven't you run?" John asked.

"Because men like me don't run. We negotiate."

John stepped forward, the muzzle of the gun now inches from Gaines' chest. "You orchestrated it. You paid Paul. You leaned on the judge. You ruined my life."

"And you're still alive," Gaines said. "Which is more than I can say for a lot of the people in that courtroom back then."

John's grip tightened.

"But look," Gaines continued, stepping carefully to the sideboard. "I've got something better than apologies. Proof."

He opened a drawer and pulled out a slim leather file. Tossed it on the counter.

John kept the gun on him but opened the file with his free hand. Inside: photographs, wire transfer slips, a handwritten ledger with names, Paul Carpenter, Judge Holloway, and even the original district attorney. And one more: **Ethan Ray**.

The real killer.

"You want justice?" Gaines said. "That's your golden ticket. Ethan Ray paid to have you buried. Paid me to sweep up the mess."

"Why are you giving this to me?" John asked.

"Because I'm old, and I'm tired," Gaines said. "And because maybe, just maybe, I'm not the devil you think I am."

John flipped through the pages, heart steady. The proof was here. He could feel it. Everything he'd suspected lay bare rotting beneath the polished tiles.

"I'm not going to kill you," John said finally.

Gaines exhaled, relieved, smug.

"I'm going to make you useful," John added, lowering the gun.

That was the last thing Gaines heard before John swung the butt of the pistol into his temple.

When Martin woke up, he was tied to a chair, barely conscious, head pounding, mouth taped shut. John sat across from him, calm as a priest at confession.

The camera was already rolling.

John ripped off the tape. "Talk. On record. The truth. Everything."

"I already gave you the file—"

"The file is for the world," John said. "The tape is for me."

Gaines swallowed hard. "Fine."

He confessed. Name by name. Date by date. How Ethan Ray had killed those people and pinned it on the closest nobody. How the system was paid off, one man at a time. How Gaines had tied the bow.

When the confession was over, John turned off the camera. "Thank you," he said, almost kindly.

Gaines looked at him, blood crusting on his lip. "So... what now?"

John leaned forward. "Now you answer for it."

The corkscrew was small. Stainless steel. John bore and twisted into his carotid artery. It took less than two minutes for Gaines to bleed out.

John left the wine cellar, the metallic smell of blood in the air.

The camera. The files. The tape.

Two down.

Chapter Five

Paul Carpenter hadn't slept in three days.

The house felt colder now, even with the heat turned up. The shadows stretched longer. The creaks in the floorboards were louder. His wife, Sue, had gone to stay with her sister. He told her it was for her safety, but really, he couldn't stand the way she looked at him now, with pity, with shame, with disgust.

He stayed locked in the study. Curtains drawn. Gun in his lap. Cigarette butts overflowed in the ashtray. A class of bourbon sweated on the desk, untouched.

Every noise made him flinch. Every silence made him worse.

He had started seeing things. A face in the window. A shadow in the hallway. A voice behind the door was whispering his name.

Paul didn't know when he finally passed out, head and gun on the desk, but when he opened his eyes, the bourbon glass was gone.

And John Winter was standing across the room.

No words. No grand entrance. Just a man standing in the study like he'd always belonged there.

Paul didn't reach for the gun. He knew better.

He stood slowly, hands shaking. "It was Gaines," he said. "He made the offer. I was just a pawn. You must believe me…"

"I don't have to believe anything," John said.

"I didn't know the truth," Paul pleaded. "Not back then. I thought you were guilty. The whole town did. I… I convinced myself I was doing the right thing. That you deserved it."

"And now?" John asked, a voice like winter wind. "What do you believe now?"

Paul swallowed hard. "Now I believe I was a coward."

John nodded slowly. "That's the first honest thing you've said in thirty years."

He stepped forward, placing a flash drive on the desk.

"What's that?" Paul asked.

"Your confession," John said. "I've already sent a copy to Detective Dana Ruiz. She's putting the pieces together. But this one... this is for you. So, you can hear yourself say what you did."

Paul sat back down. His hands trembled as he touched the drive, like it might burn him.

"I'm sorry," he whispered.

"I'm not here for apologies," John said.

Paul finally looked up, eyes glassy. "Then why are you here?"

John reached into his coat. The gun was silent. A soft click. A bright flash.

Paul's body collapsed against the desk with a dull thud. The confession drive clattered to the floor, landing beside a tape labeled **"Redemption."**

John stood for a long moment, watching the smoke curl toward the ceiling. Then he turned off the light and walked out the back door into the night.

The next morning, Detective Dana Ruiz arrived at the Carpenter residence. She'd already been investigating the death of Judge Holloway and the disappearance of Martin Gaines. Now, Paul Carpenter was dead too, with a bullet in his chest and a folder of taped confessions sitting in plain sight.

No fingerprints. No trace.

But she knew.

She stood at the doorway, looking out toward the street.

Somewhere, John Winter was watching. Waiting.

She said nothing.

Chapter Six

Detective Dana Ruiz had seen plenty of dead men before. But never like this.

Three bodies in three weeks, each more high-profile than the last. A disgraced judge was found dead in his recliner. A corporate fixer bled out like livestock in his own wine cellar. A former defense attorney was shot execution-style in his study. All connected. All with one thing in common.

John Winter.

She'd read the transcripts from his trial. Studied every line of cross-examination. Watched the interviews with blank-faced jurors. Even sat down with the prison guards who'd seen him off that morning three weeks ago. They all said the same thing:

"He wasn't angry. He was *focused*."

Now she stood in her office, holding a plain manila envelope that had arrived by courier. No return address. No fingerprints. Just her name was written in tight, clean lettering across the front.

Inside, there were answers.

A flash drive with a neatly typed label: **"Ethan Ray."**

A series of signed statements from Judge Holloway, Paul Carpenter, and Martin Gaines, each detailing their role in the conspiracy.

And finally, a photo.

Ethan Ray, smiling beside a politician at a charity gala. The same man who, according to these statements, had orchestrated the original murders, then pinned them on a scared 21-year-old kid named John Winter.

Dana slid the flash drive into her laptop. The screen lit up with a video.

Gaines, eyes swollen and lips cracked, sat slumped in a chair. He spoke slowly, clearly, as if reading from memory.

"Ethan Ray killed those people. He didn't just frame John Winter, he *used* him. John was just some poor bastard in the wrong place. I paid off the judge, leaned on the DA, and delivered the money to Carpenter. It was all about control. Ethan didn't want a trial. He wanted closure."

Dana paused the video. She sat back, staring at the wall. The pieces clicked into place one by one. She didn't need more proof.

She needed a warrant.

Two Days Later

Ethan Ray was arrested at his office, a high-rise, corner suite, wearing an expensive suit. He didn't resist; he just laughed, as if it were a misunderstanding, a bad headline.

But the evidence was airtight.

The confessions. The ledgers. The wire transfers. Even his own men flipped to avoid going down with him.

Within 24 hours, Dana had secured enough to bury him. But there was one thing she couldn't find.

John Winter.

The Night After the Arrest

Dana sat alone at her desk, the clock creeping past midnight. She pulled out a folder labeled "WINTER, JOHN," then slid it into a locked drawer.

She'd done her job. Justice had finally been served. But something about it still haunted her.

She looked out the window at the snow falling in soft silence over the city. Somewhere out there, he was watching. Not just her, but the whole damn world.

A man who had every right to burn it all down but chose precision instead of chaos.

A man who did what the system wouldn't. She whispered it to the empty room, just once.

"Thank you."

Chapter Seven

The cemetery was quiet beneath the snow, a cold stillness that seemed to hush even the wind.

John Winter stood at the top of the hill, a single red rose in his hand, the collar of his coat pulled high against the wind. The tombstones stretched out around him like frozen teeth, each one whispering the name the world had forgotten. But not this one. Not her.

Rachel Anne Maddox

August 12, 1946 – April 3, 1989

"You are loved beyond time."

The words etched in stone struck harder than the bullet he'd left in Paul Carpenter. He didn't cry, hadn't in years, but something inside him cracked like thin ice.

Rachel.

The only person who had ever believed in him when no one else did.

She used to sit across from him behind thick prison glass, her fingers curled around the phone receiver, smiling like time hadn't swallowed them both whole. Even when the appeals were denied. Even when hope turned bitter. She stayed. Until the visits stopped.

He never blamed her. Not when she stopped writing. Not when the news came that her heart had finally given out.

John knelt slowly in front of the headstone, brushing snow from the granite with his glove.

He reached into his coat pocket and pulled out an old photograph, faded from time, the edges curling. It was the two of them, summer of '64, sitting on the hood of her dad's truck, drinking cherry sodas and laughing like nothing bad could ever happen.

He placed the photo gently against the base of the stone, then set the rose beside it.

"I made them pay," he said, voice low and rough. "All of them."

The wind carried his words away, as if even it wasn't allowed to hold onto them.

"I found out who really did it. I gave it to someone who would do what the courts never could." He paused. "You always said I should try to forgive. I tried, Rach. I really did."

He closed his eyes.

"But I'm not that man anymore. The one you used to love. He didn't survive that place."

John stood, brushing snow from his knees. He lingered for a moment longer, looking down at the grave like he might sink into it.

"I wish you could've seen it. The sky tonight it's the same color it was the day we first kissed."

A faint smile flickered on his face, vanishing just as quickly.

He turned, walking slowly through the snow back toward the road, his footprints the only sign he'd been there at all.

As he disappeared into the falling dusk, the wind shifted.

Soft.

Still.

And somewhere between the trees, a whisper that was quite sound:

"You are loved beyond time."

I Learned to Drink My Coffee Black in Rehab

Chapter 1

John Franks woke up with a sock stuck to his cheek and a stale slice of pizza balanced on his chest like it belonged there. For a moment, he thought he was in a pizza commercial gone terribly wrong.

Then reality hit.

The couch cushions were on the floor; his phone was blinking with fourteen missed calls, and something he hoped was ketchup was crusted to his forehead.

He groaned, sat up, and checked the time. 11:47 a.m.

"Perfect," he muttered. "Only four hours late for work. Again."

His phone buzzed. A voicemail from his boss.

"Hey John, it's Carl. Listen… we're gonna have to let you go. It's not just the late shifts or the time you accidentally emailed that weird meme to corporate. It's… everything. I hope you get the help you need. And please stop replying to all staff emails with gifs."

John sighed and tossed the phone into an empty cereal bowl. It bounced out, of course, because even gravity seemed to be against him.

He stood up slowly, like an old man or a sad giraffe, and shuffled to the bathroom. He opened the cabinet, grabbed what he thought was toothpaste, and smeared it on his toothbrush. One second later, he was spitting out minty shaving cream into the sink.

"Okay," he said to the mirror. "That's it. I'm done. I need help. Or at least instructions for basic survival."

The mirror, like most people in John's life lately, offered no response.

John didn't have a big, dramatic breakdown. No screaming. No tears. Just this quiet moment where he realized… he was tired. Tired of pretending he was fine. Tired of acting like he didn't need help. Tired of shaving cream breath.

He needed to change something. Fast.

Later that day, after a long call to his insurance (and one argument with a robotic voice named "Megan"), John signed himself into rehab.

He packed exactly three pairs of socks, two T-shirts, one wrinkled hoodie, and a travel mug he hadn't used since 2016.

That night, while lying on a strange bed that smelled like lemons and nervous sweat, John whispered to the ceiling, "Please don't let this be the worst mistake of my life."

It wasn't, but it would include some very bad coffee.

Chapter 2

Sunny Hills Rehab looked nothing like the brochure.

The building was a faded beige, with a broken porch swing that squeaked in the wind, as if haunted by ghosts of bad decisions. The sign-out front had a sun on it, but someone had drawn sunglasses on the sun and a cigarette dangling from its mouth. John wasn't sure if it was vandalism or marketing.

He stepped through the front door and immediately ran into a life-sized cutout of a smiling nurse holding a clipboard.

"Welcome to Sunny Hills!" the cutout read.

John flinched. "Thanks for the heart attack, Cardboard Cathy."

At the front desk sat a woman in her fifties with a beehive hairstyle so tall it probably needed its own ZIP code. She glanced up and said, "You must be John. Sign in. No gum, no outside snacks, and definitely no sarcasm."

John paused. "So... just my personality is banned then?"

She didn't laugh. Instead, she handed him a name tag and pointed toward a hallway that smelled like burnt toast and old hope.

"Orientations in Room 3, then after that is time for group. You're in Group B. Good luck."

John walked down the hallway and into a room with mismatched chairs and a giant poster that read *FEELINGS ARE NOT OPTIONAL.*

Sitting on one of the chairs, cross-legged and barefoot, was Doug. He wore cargo shorts and a tank top that said, *"Spiritual Warrior,"* though he looked more like a guy who had once tried to punch a vending machine for stealing his Doritos.

"New guy!" Doug shouted, grinning. "I'm Doug. I got kicked out of three rehabs before this one. This place? Total upgrade. The pillows are fluffier, and nobody judges you for screaming into a laundry basket."

"Cool," John said. "That's totally on my checklist."

"Also, the coffee's free!" Doug added, holding up a mug. "But it's black. No sugar. No cream. Builds character."

John glanced into the mug. The coffee looked like something drained from an engine.

He sat down and scanned the room. Across was Sally, who wore twelve bracelets and a smile that didn't seem entirely legal. She gave John a big wave.

"I'm Sally," she chirped. "I've been here for three weeks and cried in every room, including the broom closet. But it's okay. Feeling your feelings is part of healing!"

John gave a polite nod. He wasn't sure if he should be comforted or concerned.

Then, in the corner, sat Stan. Stan was tall and wiry, wearing a T-shirt that said, "Caffeine Is My Religion." He was staring at the ceiling, as if trying to read messages from space.

Stan spoke without looking down. "They say aliens invented coffee. That's why it makes us feel more alive than water ever could."

Doug leaned over to John and whispered, "Stan's been here forever. Nobody knows why. Some say he just wandered in one day and never left."

John wasn't sure what to say. These were his people now.

A staff member named Marty walked in and clapped his hands. "Group B! Let's get started. Today's topic is: Accepting Help. But first… anyone want to share something good from their day?"

Doug raised his hand. "I found a Cheerio in my pocket. I think it was from 2019, but I ate it anyway. That's called living in the moment, right?"

Sally applauded. Stan muttered something about "cereal gods."

John just blinked.

Welcome to Sunny Hills.

The coffee was awful. The people were weird, but maybe… just maybe… this was exactly what he needed.

Chapter 3

John had faced many scary things in his life, including awkward first dates, surprise dental bills, and the time he tried to fix his own toilet. However, nothing quite prepared him for group therapy.

He sat in a circle of folding chairs with Doug, Sally, Stan, and three other people who looked like they'd rather be anywhere else, including a dentist's waiting room playing country music.

Marty, the counselor, stood in the middle of the circle with a clipboard and the kind of overly chipper voice that only people who truly believed in "emotional breakthroughs" could pull off.

"Alright, Group B," Marty said, clapping his hands like a preschool teacher, "let's talk about our feelings!"

John shifted in his seat.

Doug leaned over and whispered, "Don't worry. Just say something about your inner child and you'll fit right in."

"I barely like my *outer* adult," John whispered back.

Marty looked at John. "You're new, right? Why don't you start us off?"

Of course.

John cleared his throat. "Uh… hi. I'm John. I've been here for, like, twelve hours. I think I accidentally drank part of a scented candle in the dining hall. I'm still alive, though, so that's something."

Marty smiled. "Thanks for sharing, John. What brought you here?"

John paused. The honest answer was complicated. It involved loneliness, a lot of poor choices, and one truly terrible night, which included karaoke and a taco truck. But instead, he said, "I guess I just got tired of being tired. Also, my toothpaste turned out to be shaving cream."

Sally gasped. "That happened to me, too! Mercury is totally in retrograde."

Stan nodded, as if this was an obvious cosmic truth.

Doug raised his hand. "Speaking of cosmic, I'd like to share. Last night, I had a dream I was riding a dolphin made of Cheetos. I think it means I need to face my fear of swimming *and* artificial cheese flavoring."

Marty scribbled something down. Hopefully not, "Doug is a lost cause."

Then it was Sally's turn. She held a purple crystal in one hand and a tissue in the other.

"I just want to say," she sniffled, "that today I didn't cry when I dropped my breakfast muffin. I just picked it up, whispered 'thank you for your journey,' and ate it anyway."

Everyone clapped like she'd won a Nobel Prize.

John looked around, unsure if he was on a reality show or in an actual therapy session. But weirdly... it didn't feel bad. These people were strange, sure. But they were trying. They were showing up. And for the first time in a long time, so was he.

When it was Stan's turn, he stood and pointed dramatically to the ceiling.

"I believe we're all on this planet for a reason," he said. "Mine is to decode the truth inside every cup of coffee."

Doug raised his mug. "Preach, brother."

Stan sat back down like he'd just dropped the mic.

By the end of the session, John felt something weird. Not joy. Not peace. Something smaller, but real.

Hope.

And heartburn, but that was from the candle coffee.

Chapter 4

The next morning, John shuffled into the dining room like a zombie in search of brains, or in his case, caffeine.

The smell of something burned and slightly acidic filled the air. A large metal coffee urn sat in the corner, next to a stack of mismatched mugs that looked like they had been stolen from various garage sales.

He grabbed a cup with a cartoon duck on it that read, *"Waddle I Do Without Coffee?"* and poured himself a drink.

It looked like motor oil. It smelled like disappointment.

Doug strolled up beside him, holding a mug that said, *"Bean Me Up, Scotty."*

"No sugar. No cream," Doug said proudly. "It's the rehab way."

"Yeah, well, I like my coffee to taste like hope," John muttered, staring into the black swamp in his cup.

Doug clapped him on the back. "Hope is a trap. Bitter builds character."

Sally floated behind them, holding a thermos covered in unicorn stickers. "Black coffee is sacred," she said. "It cleanses the soul. Like sage, but in your stomach."

John raised the mug to his lips. He braced himself.

He sipped.

He gagged.

He coughed into his elbow like he'd just inhaled a small fire.

"Good, right?" Doug said, totally serious.

"It tastes like regret," John said, wiping his eyes. "Regret and possibly old shoe leather."

Stan appeared out of nowhere like a caffeine ninja. "That's because it's *real*. No sugar to lie to your face. No cream to smooth the edges. Just the truth."

"I didn't come here to be attacked by my beverage," John replied. But the weird thing? He kept drinking it.

He took another sip. Still terrible. Another. Slightly less terrible. He sat down at the table with the others, and the coffee warmed his hands. Then, strangely, his chest.

It wasn't the flavor that grew on him. It was the ritual. The quiet. The sitting-down-with-other-broken-people part.

No phones. No distractions. Just people with shaky pasts, weird dreams, and awful coffee.

Doug told a story about the time he tried to build a go-kart out of office chairs and bungee cords. Sally showed off a new tattoo of a flamingo riding a bicycle. Stan explained how coffee was probably how aliens first contacted Earth.

And John? He listened. He sipped. Eventually, he stopped grimacing after each gulp.

Maybe drinking your coffee black wasn't about becoming tough. Maybe it was just about learning to face things as they are, bitter, bold, and unfiltered.

Like life.

Or like Doug, who just spilled coffee down his shirt and didn't even notice.

Chapter 5

By his second week in rehab, John had learned three important things:

1. Group therapy wasn't as scary as it sounded.

2. Sally owned more crystals than most museums.

3. Doug should never, ever be left alone with laundry baskets.

It happened on a Thursday, right after the morning mindfulness session (which was basically everyone trying not to fall asleep while listening to whale sounds).

John walked into the hallway and found Doug wedged into a plastic laundry basket like a turtle wearing a bad idea.

"I was trying to make a personal cocoon," Doug explained, his knees poking out on both sides. "For emotional rebirth."

John blinked. "You're stuck."

Doug nodded. "Very."

Sally ran in, gasped, and immediately pulled out her phone. "Wait, don't move! I need a picture for my healing blog."

Marty eventually arrived with a crowbar and a deeply exhausted expression. "I'm not even surprised anymore," he said, prying Doug free.

Despite the chaos and the mild injury to Doug's pride, John couldn't help but laugh. A real laugh. The kind that caught him off guard and echoed through his ribs.

It felt good. Like maybe something inside him was finally unclenching.

Later that day, during group, Marty asked everyone to talk about what they were ready to let go of.

John hesitated. He'd been holding onto a lot: guilt, shame, bad habits, that one voicemail from his ex he kept pretending he hadn't listened to fifty times.

When it was his turn, he stared at his hands for a moment.

"I think I'm ready to let go of pretending I'm fine all the time," he said. "I used to wear this mask, like I was always in control, even when I was falling apart. I was miserable, but I made it look like a joke so people wouldn't ask questions."

The room was quiet.

Then Sally leaned over and patted his shoulder. "That was brave," she whispered.

Stan added, "Masks block brain waves. You made the right choice."

Doug gave him a thumbs-up. "Also, I think the basket thing was symbolic. You know, being trapped… by your own emotional laundry or baggage."

Marty just nodded like this was the most normal conversation ever.

John felt lighter. Not fixed. Not perfect. Just… a little more honest with himself.

That night, he drank his coffee black without flinching.

And when Doug sat down beside him with a new bruise and a grin, John said, "So, what's the moral of today's story?"

Doug sipped his coffee, winced, and said, "Don't trust baskets. Or your feelings. Or baskets full of feelings."

John laughed again.

Yeah, maybe letting go was messy, but so was life.

And somehow, it was starting to feel manageable, with just a splash of bitter coffee and a whole lot of weird friends.

Chapter 6

John stood by the front doors of Sunny Hills Rehab with his tiny duffel bag, a coffee-stained hoodie, and a knot in his stomach the size of a grapefruit. Today was his last day.

He had survived three weeks of group therapy, cafeteria mystery meat, daily affirmations, black coffee, Doug's constant barefoot adventures, and at least two of Sally's moon ceremonies.

And now he was leaving.

"Well," said Doug, slapping him on the back, "you didn't explode. That's progress."

"Thanks," John said. "You've been… weirdly helpful."

"That's my whole thing," Doug replied proudly. "Weird. Helpful. Occasionally flammable."

Sally ran up, carrying a goodbye gift wrapped in what looked like a bath towel.

"I made you a 'hope bundle,'" she said, handing it over. "It's got a healing stone, a feather I found near the dumpster, and a small note of encouragement I wrote during my 'emotional fog bath' yesterday."

John blinked. "I… thank you?"

Sally smiled. "Hold it against your chest during thunderstorms. Or traffic."

Then Stan stepped forward, holding something wrapped in tinfoil.

John stared at it. "Is that… a hat?"

Stan nodded solemnly. "A tinfoil helmet. To protect your brain from toxic thoughts and microwave waves. Especially in grocery stores."

John grinned. "I'll treasure it forever. Probably in a drawer. Far away."

Stan whispered, "That's what they expect. Stay unpredictable."

Marty appeared next, clipboard in hand. "John, before you go, do you want to say anything to the group?"

John looked around the room at the stained couch, the buzzing light above the coffee station, the people who had somehow become his oddball little tribe.

"Yeah," he said, clearing his throat. "I just want to say thank you. I came here feeling like a broken mess. And I still feel like a mess... but not a broken one."

"And I learned that it's okay to ask for help. That our feelings won't kill us. And most importantly... I learned to drink my coffee black."

Doug stood and clapped. "He's one of us now!"

Sally wiped a tear. "He's bitter and awake, just like the rest of us!"

Stan saluted.

John walked out the doors with the sun on his face and a strange sense of peace in his chest. The world outside remained the same: loud, messy, and unpredictable. But John wasn't.

He was a little braver. A little clearer. A little more real, and as he stepped into his new beginning, he took one final sip of his black coffee and whispered to himself,

"Still terrible. But somehow... kind of perfect."

Chapter 7

It's been six months since John walked out of Sunny Hills Rehab with a duffel bag, a rock that "channels moonlight," and a tinfoil hat he swears is still in a drawer somewhere.

His life isn't perfect. He still has weird dreams. He still avoids karaoke bars. And some days, feelings come rushing in like a flash flood during monsoon season.

But he's sober.

He has a job at a local bookstore now, where he alphabetizes self-help books and secretly leaves encouraging sticky notes inside the ones he thinks people need most.

He calls his sister again. He even joined a support group in town, where nobody's tried to build a cocoon out of laundry baskets... yet.

And every morning, he pours himself a mug of hot, black coffee.

No cream. No sugar. Just bitter, bold, and honest.

The first sip still makes his face twitch.

But the second sip? That one tastes like something else.

Not perfection. Not peace, but progress, and for John Franks, that's enough.

Well, that, and maybe a good donut on Fridays.

Known Destiny

Chapter 1

Brandon's earliest memories weren't filled with toys, cartoons, or playgrounds. They were filled with silence, the kind of silence that made your heartbeat louder. He was five years old, lying face down on the old brown carpet in the living room, staring at the frayed threads near the couch. He didn't know why, but something about that day felt worse than usual.

Maybe it was the way the hallway was too quiet. Maybe it was the dog, how it had stopped barking, like it knew something was about to happen.

Then the front door creaked open.

Brandon froze. He could hear the slow, dragging steps of boots crossing the tile floor. Then the sound changed, thump, thump, thump, as the heavy footsteps hit the hallway's wooden floor. Each step grew louder, closer.

His father was home.

Brandon's small Matchbox car sat forgotten on the table. The one rule: never leave anything out. He had forgotten. His stomach twisted.

A loud, slurred voice cut through the air. "Who left this piece of junk on my table?!"

A second later, the door flew open. The knob slammed against the wall. His father's hand reached out, rough and shaking, and grabbed Brandon's shirt, lifting him off the ground like he weighed nothing.

Brandon couldn't look away. His father's face was just inches from his. His breath hit him like a storm, hot, sour, and sharp. The smell of whiskey. The stink of cigarettes. But there was something worse hiding underneath it all. Something rotting.

Brandon didn't know what a soul was, not back then, but whatever his father had inside him, it smelled wrong. Broken. Evil.

"Do you think I work all day so you can leave your trash everywhere?" his father shouted, his spit spraying across Brandon's cheek. His eyes were red and wild. His voice was full of hate.

Brandon didn't answer. He couldn't cry. He couldn't even breathe. He just stared, wondering if monsters had fathers, too.

Then came the shove.

It wasn't a punch, not this time, but it knocked Brandon down hard. His knees burned against the carpet. His chest hit the floor. He didn't make a sound.

His father's voice moved on, yelling at his mom in the kitchen. Something about the TV being too loud. Something about dinner tasting like soap.

Brandon stayed where he was. Not because he was too hurt to move, but because the floor felt like the only safe place left. He curled up against the couch, small fingers gripping the edge as he tucked himself into a tight ball, like a leaf falling from a tree, already half-dead.

The smell of his father's breath lingered in the room long after the yelling stopped. It was the kind of smell Brandon would never forget.

Even now, all these years later, a whiff of whiskey and cigarettes in a crowd could stop him cold. His heart would race, and his body would stiffen. It was like his brain couldn't tell the difference between past and present.

That smell wasn't just about alcohol or bad habits. It was something deeper. Something twisted and cruel, leaking out from the inside of a man who should have protected him, but never did.

Even as a little kid, Brandon had felt it. He didn't have the words for it back then, but he knew. His father's soul was rotten. And God, in some quiet way, had been warning him all along.

Chapter 2

Brandon was nine the day everything changed forever.

It was one of those rare, peaceful afternoons. The sunlight poured through the living room window, making the dust in the air sparkle. Brandon sat cross-legged on the carpet, building a tower of blocks with his little sister, Kaylee.

She was two, with chubby cheeks and bright eyes that lit up when she laughed. Her giggles were soft and full of life, the only real happiness in that house.

Kaylee had her toy farm spread across the floor. She carefully placed a tiny plastic pig in a pen made of metal fence pieces. One of the pieces wouldn't snap into place, so she tossed it away with an exaggerated, "Uh-oh!"

Brandon chuckled. "It's okay," he said gently. "I'll fix it."

She toddled off, dragging her favorite doll behind her. Neither of them noticed where the broken fence piece had landed, right in the middle of the floor, just a few steps from their father's recliner.

A loud bang shook the house. The front door had slammed open. Brandon's body tensed. His heart started racing.

Their father was home too early.

The sound of boots stormed through the doorway. Then a moment of angry silence as his father removed his boots in the foyer, wet from the puddles left by the rain earlier.

Suddenly, a scream, low and filled with rage, followed by the sharp crash of breaking glass.

"WHAT THE HELL IS THIS?!"

Brandon turned and saw him, his father, hopping on one foot, blood trailing from the other. A thin metal rod stuck out from the bottom of his foot. The piece from the toy fence.

Brandon's heart dropped.

His father yanked it out and threw it across the room. His eyes scanned the space like a wild animal. And then he saw her.

Kaylee.

She stood frozen near the couch, holding her doll. Her big brown eyes were wide with confusion, too young to understand fear.

He stomped toward her.

Brandon's mouth opened, but nothing came out. His voice was stuck somewhere deep inside his chest.

Their father grabbed Kaylee by the arms. She shrieked and kicked as he shook her. "Stupid little… You think you can leave your crap all over MY house?!"

"Dad, STOP!" Brandon shouted, finding his voice at last. "It was an accident!"

Their mom rushed in from the kitchen, screaming, "Put her down! PUT HER DOWN!"

But he didn't listen. His grip got tighter. His shaking turned violent.

Brandon's heart pounded so hard it hurt. Kaylee's cries turned into gasps. Her feet kicked in the air.

Then came another scream, this one from their mom, as their father lashed out and kicked her in the stomach. She crumpled to the floor, groaning in pain.

Brandon went back into the corner of the room. He couldn't move. His legs felt like they were filled with cement. All he could do was cry.

Then everything froze.

The front door burst open splinters flying. A deep voice shouted.

Mr. Jenkins.

Their neighbor had kicked the door down.

For a split second, no one moved. The only sound was the angry, ragged breathing of Brandon's father.

Then, he spun.

Once. Twice.

On the second turn, he let go of Kaylee.

She flew.

Time seemed to stop.

Brandon locked eyes with her. Her arms reached out. Her mouth was open in a silent cry. Her small body twisted in the air like a dropped toy.

She hit the fireplace.

Headfirst.

THUD.

CRACK.

Then came the sound of metal tools falling from their hooks. One of them, a sharp poker, landed with a clatter… and stuck where it shouldn't have.

Right through her head.

For a moment, there was no sound.

Then came the scream.

His mother's.

Brandon didn't remember if he screamed, too. But the neighbors said they heard him. Said it sounded more like howling than a cry.

Mr. Jenkins didn't hesitate. He charged their father and tackled him to the ground. Fists flew. Yells filled the air. Blood hit the walls. It took the police to pull Mr. Jenkins off.

Brandon's father didn't wake up for four days. Kaylee never woke up again.

They never let Brandon see her after that. He didn't want to. That image, her flying, the sound of her head hitting stone, the sight of that metal rod, it haunted him. Still did.

His father spent a month in jail, waiting for trial. But he never made it to court.

Someone stabbed him in the shower.

No one found out who did it. No one really tried to.

And Brandon?

He just tried to survive the silence that came after the storm.

Chapter 3

After the ambulance and the squad cars were gone, after the yellow tape had been removed and the whispers in the neighborhood started to fade. People saw Mr. Jenkins as a hero, but he felt he was just a little too late, he didn't get to save Kaylee.

They all saw what Mr. Jenkins saw, a monster who had it coming.

Back then, Brandon didn't feel confused or guilty. He felt relief. For the first time in his life, he felt safe. He was glad. And if he was honest with himself, he was happy the man who hurt his family was gone.

That happiness didn't last.

As Brandon got older, his feelings began to shift. At first, it was just a question that whispered through his mind at night, *Was it right to feel good about someone dying?*

He found the answer slowly, with time and faith.

Becoming a Christian didn't erase Brandon's past, but it gave him a new way to see it. He began reading the Bible that his mom had given him. Not just reading it but really trying to understand it. And what he learned was that being a Christian wasn't about pretending to be perfect. It was about facing your pain, your past, and still choosing something better.

Forgiveness wasn't a one-time thing. It was a battle. There were nights Brandon lay awake, screaming into his pillow so no one would hear. Nights when he prayed, even though he didn't know if he believed in anything. Nights when he begged God to help him let go of the anger that burned like fire in his chest.

But slowly, painfully, he forgave his father. Not because his father deserved it, but because Brandon couldn't move forward without it.

Anger had chained him to the worst moments of his life. Forgiveness was the only key that could set him free.

He didn't know where his father's soul went after death. That wasn't his place to say. But deep down, Brandon believed that when a man meets God, something changes. No one walks away from that kind of truth untouched.

It gave him hope but also served as a warning.

He thought about Mr. Jenkins sometimes. To Brandon, the man had been a hero that day. He did what no one else could. He stepped into a nightmare and fought back.

But even heroes pay a price.

Brandon saw it in his eyes afterward, how Jenkins looked older, heavier somehow, like he'd been carrying something invisible on his back. They never talked about it. But Brandon knew. Violence, even when it feels right, leaves a scar.

Mr. Jenkins tried to help afterward. He brought groceries, fixed their broken fence, and even read books to Brandon while his mom rested. For a while, he was the kind of man Brandon wished had been his dad. But eventually, Jenkins stopped coming around.

Brandon didn't blame him. That house was full of ghosts. Maybe the man just needed to breathe somewhere without screams echoing in the walls.

Some people rescue you and disappear. That doesn't mean they weren't sent by God.

Brandon stayed. He had no choice. Every day, he walked past the fireplace. The stains had been scrubbed, the tools replaced, the furniture rearranged, but the memory never left.

Still, the hardest part of healing wasn't about forgiving his father. It was about forgiving himself.

Brandon had been nine. Just a kid. He knew he couldn't stop what happened. But sometimes, knowing something in your mind doesn't stop your heart from hurting.

He wondered, what if he'd grabbed Kaylee first? What if he'd hidden the toy? What if he'd stood between her and their father?

It was a heavy question to carry. Sometimes, it still weighed him down. But if he could speak to another survivor, someone else carrying the same guilt, he knew what he'd say.

"You didn't deserve what happened. You didn't cause it. And you don't have to carry it forever."

That was why he told his story. Because pain didn't get the final word. Not when grace was still on the table.

Chapter 4

The house was too quiet.

After the trial, after the funeral, after the police cars stopped coming and the neighbors stopped dropping off casseroles, silence took over. It spread like mold, filling every room, clinging to the air and the furniture. Everything slowed down. Everything stopped.

Brandon was ten when he started cooking his own dinners. Nothing fancy, just soup from a can, frozen waffles, or scrambled eggs if the stove decided to work that night. He'd push a chair over to the sink when he was done, to reach the faucet and rinse the dishes. He always did the dishes. It gave him something to do, something to control.

His mother didn't come out of her room much anymore. Some days, she didn't speak at all.

Brandon would knock gently on her door, whisper, "Dinner's ready," and set a plate on the floor. Most mornings, he'd find it untouched, cold, the food starting to dry and curl at the edges.

After a while, he stopped asking if she was okay. He stopped hoping she'd sit at the table again.

Sometimes, he would place two plates on the kitchen table and sit across from the empty chair. He'd talk like she was there. "School was okay," he'd say. "I made a friend named Cody, or you should come outside tomorrow. The tulips are blooming again."

She never answered. But the tulips bloomed anyway.

The living room still carried a strange, heavy scent, iron and ashes. The fireplace hadn't been used since the day Kaylee died, but the smell never left. It lived in the bricks and the carpet, and in Brandon's memories.

At school, Brandon wore the same jeans for days. No one said anything, but he noticed how some kids avoided him. Teachers gave him that quiet, sad look, like they already knew too much but didn't know what to say. He always left class last, dragging his steps, hoping to stay invisible just a little longer.

There was one place where he felt a bit of peace.

Across the street from the school stood a small church with a white bench tucked under a willow tree. Brandon would sit there in the afternoons, watching sunlight filter through the branches. The leaves whispered in the wind, and sometimes, when everything else felt heavy, he'd sit there and whisper, "Are you still here, God?"

And when the wind rustled the leaves just right, he liked to imagine the answer was yes.

On his eleventh birthday, no one remembered. Not his mother. Not his teachers. Not even the kids at school.

He walked home in the rain, his socks soaked, shoes squishing with each step. That night, he made himself a peanut butter sandwich and turned on cartoons. He tried to laugh at the silly voices and wild characters, but everything blurred until he couldn't tell if it was the screen or his tears.

Later, curled up in the corner of his bed, he spoke out loud. "God, if you're listening… please just tell me what I'm supposed to do."

No voice answered him. But the next morning, something had changed. When Brandon walked into the kitchen, his mother was sitting at the table.

Her hair was messy, her skin pale, her eyes dull. She didn't say a word. But she looked at him, really looked at him, for the first time in a long time.

That look didn't fix anything. It didn't bring back the laughter or erase the weight they were both carrying. But it said: *I'm still here. Barely. But I'm here.*

And for Brandon, that was enough.

Chapter 5

Brandon had never liked the stillness of the house.

It wasn't just quiet; it felt heavy, as if something invisible was pressing down on his shoulders. He was twelve now, used to silence. But that day was different. The quiet didn't feel empty. It felt wrong.

He dropped his backpack near the door. "Mom?" he called out.

No answer.

That wasn't unusual, but the uneasy feeling wouldn't leave. His arms tingled. Something wasn't right. He checked the bedroom. Empty. The bed was still made from the morning.

The bathroom, nothing there. The living room looked the same as always, dim, dusty, forgotten. The kitchen smelled faintly of burnt toast from breakfast. Dishes were still in the sink, untouched.

Brandon stood in the hallway, unsure of what to do next. That's when he smelled it.

It wasn't a strong odor, not enough to make him gag. But it was there, a strange, acrid smell. It reminded him of gasoline and blood. Something that didn't belong. His eyes landed on the door to the garage.

He didn't want to go in.

But something pushed him, something deeper than fear, something heavier than curiosity. His hand hovered over the doorknob. He paused, then turned it and stepped inside.

The air was thick. Foggy. Hard to breathe. He coughed and blinked against the haze. The car was parked backwards.

That's when he saw the hose. It ran from the exhaust pipe into the back window of the car, sealed tightly with strips of gray duct tape. The engine wasn't running anymore. Everything was still. But the fumes hadn't cleared. They hovered in the air, silent and deadly.

"No..."

He hit the garage door button, and sunlight exploded into the space, cutting through the haze. He rushed forward, his legs weak beneath him, his heart slamming in his chest.

And that's when he saw her. She was in the driver's seat.

Still.

Pale.

Her eyes were open, but empty.

Brandon couldn't breathe. Brandon stumbled backward, then fell hard onto the floor. He didn't feel the pain. He didn't feel anything.

He curled into himself, shaking, his cheek pressed to the cold garage floor. The world stopped. All that remained was his breath, fast, shallow, and the crushing silence of a house that no longer had anyone left in it.

He didn't know how long he had stayed there. It could've been ten minutes or it could've been hours.

It was Mr. Jenkins who found him. The old man had been driving by, and something had caught his eye, the open garage door maybe. But as he drove by, he noticed Brandon lying on the floor like a forgotten doll.

Mr. Jenkins called the police. He wrapped a blanket around Brandon. He held him and whispered, "It's going to be okay," even though they both knew it wasn't.

Brandon didn't cry. Not at first.

First, his sister.

Now his mom.

It felt like the world had erased his family, one by one, like they were never meant to stay. He felt hollow. Alone. But even then, deep in that darkness, something inside Brandon refused to give up completely.

He still believed in God. Because if he didn't, then none of it meant anything.

Kaylee's death... his mother's pain... his survival, it would all be pointless. And Brandon couldn't live with that. He couldn't live in a world where all that suffering had no meaning.

So, he chose to believe. Not in a God who caused the pain, but in a God who walked through it with him. A God who wept when Brandon wept. A God who didn't erase suffering but stood beside the broken and held them up.

That belief didn't fix everything. But it gave Brandon something to hold on to. It didn't start his mission. But it stopped him from running from it.

Chapter 6

The room had gone quiet.

Brandon sat at the table, gripping the edge like he might fall if he let go. His eyes were low, staring at something far beyond the floor. His Bible was clutched tightly against his chest, not like a book, but like a shield.

He hadn't spoken in a while.

The silence wrapped around them like a heavy blanket. No one dared break it. Finally, Brandon spoke, his voice low but steady.

"Every day," he said. "I wonder if it broke something in me." His gaze lifted, and there was no sorrow in his eyes this time. There was fire.

"People love calling me crazy," he continued. "Fanatic. Unstable. I've heard it all." He leaned forward, and his voice sharpened.

"But how else does a kid survive what I did unless he *knows* there's something bigger than the pain?"

He paused. Then let out a small, bitter laugh. "Of course, my faith is a coping mechanism," he said. "So is breathing."

The edge in his voice rose.

"You think I made it through that house, through that blood, that silence, those nights with no one, by accident?"

He pushed back his chair and stood. The legs scraped loudly against the floor. "I wasn't lucky," he said. "I was *carried*. I was *chosen*."

He stepped away from the table, pacing now, the words pouring out of him like steam.

"God spoke to me. Not in thunder. Not in fire. But in whispers. In the quiet moments between sobs. When the world went black and I was still breathing, somehow, I heard Him."

Brandon's hands shook at his sides.

"You want to talk about madness?" he snapped. "Madness is pretending this world makes sense without God. Madness is watching someone like my father destroy everything and thinking it's just bad luck. Madness is standing over your mother's body and saying, Well, that's just life."

His whole body trembled. But his voice held firm. "I'm not mad," he said. "I'm *awake*."

He turned and walked toward the window. Outside, birds were chirping. A breeze danced across the surface of the pond. It was a peaceful scene that didn't match the weight in his voice.

For almost a full minute, he said nothing. Just staring out the glass, his hands pressed gently against the windowsill.

Then, softer than before, he spoke again. "I don't want to be angry," he said. "But people, they give up on God because He doesn't give them what they want."

He shook his head. "They say, 'If God were real, He would've stopped it.'"

A long pause.

"But they forget… free will is the price of love. God didn't make us puppets. He let us choose. And sometimes, people choose evil."

Brandon turned around. The fire in his eyes had dimmed—but not gone out. Now, there was something else. Something deeper. "Grace," he said, "is what comes after."

He wiped sweat from his brow, his breathing slowing as he crossed the room and returned to his chair. This time, he sat carefully. Slowly. His hands rested on the Bible again, steady now. Calm.

"I'm sorry I lost it a little," he said. "I didn't mean to explode."

He paused, searching for the right words.

"It's just… I carry it all. Still. Every day. But carrying it doesn't mean I'm broken."

He looked up, his voice quiet but sure. "It means I haven't given up."

Brandon sat straighter. The fire hadn't burned out. It had settled into something stronger. "You asked if I thought it broke something in me," he said. "And yeah... it did."

He tapped the cover of his Bible once. "But God doesn't use the unbroken. He uses the ones who've been shattered and still choose light."

There was silence again, but this time it felt peaceful, not heavy.

Brandon smiled.

It wasn't big. But it was real.

"I'm not doing this for the people who think I'm insane," he said. "I'm not doing this for the critics or the doubters."

His eyes shone, calm and full of purpose.

"I'm doing it for the ones still stuck in the dark... the ones who think there's no way out." He leaned forward, almost whispering. "I want them to know, they're wrong."

Chapter 7

Brandon sat quietly, his hand resting gently on the cover of his Bible. This time, he wasn't clutching it. His fingers relaxed against the leather, and his eyes drifted to the window, watching the trees bend with the wind.

He had talked about his faith, about his mission. But there was something deeper that still lingered in the room. Something he hadn't said out loud yet.

"I forgave my father," Brandon said quietly. "And I forgave my mother."

He paused, his voice steady—but softer now.

"But the one I still struggle with… is me."

He was thirteen when he entered his third foster home.

The hallway smelled like mildew and burnt eggs. He stood there, holding a black trash bag that sagged under the weight of his few belongings: a couple of shirts, a half-used spiral notebook, and a toothbrush wrapped in tissue. That was all he had left of his old life.

The social worker patted him on the back, her voice kind but tired. "It'll get better now," she said.

Brandon didn't reply. She didn't know who she was talking to.

That night, lying on a top bunk that smelled like someone else's sweat, Brandon stared at the ceiling and whispered the same question he had whispered for over a year.

"Why didn't I do something?" Why didn't I grab Kaylee and run? Why didn't I scream louder? Why didn't I check the garage sooner? Why didn't I stop it?

He knew the answers.

He was a kid.

But knowing something in your head doesn't always reach your heart.

Even years later, the guilt still crept when things got too quiet. Brandon would sit with it, like an old friend he didn't ask to visit but couldn't turn away.

"I knew I was just a child," he said. "I *knew*. But I still couldn't feel it." He rubbed his thumb across the edge of the Bible, thinking.

"Guilt doesn't always come from what we do. Sometimes it comes from what we didn't do, what we *couldn't* do."

So, how did he start to forgive himself? He started by talking to God. Not in a church. Not with polished words.

But in broken whispers.

"I talked to God like He was the only one who wouldn't hang up on me," Brandon said. He told God he was sorry. He asked why he was the one still breathing.

At first, there was nothing. No signs. No sudden peace.

But slowly, overtime, something came to him. A quiet thought that returned again, and again: *You were meant to speak for the ones who no longer can.*

Brandon placed a hand over his chest.

"Forgiving myself didn't happen in one moment," he said. "It happened in layers. Like peeling back old wallpaper. Every time you tear a piece off, something uglier is underneath. Until finally, you reach the raw wood."

That's where healing began.

He still carried the guilt. But it no longer controlled him.

"People think forgiveness means forgetting," he said. "It doesn't. It means remembering—without letting it destroy you."

Brandon was seventeen the night something shifted. The church was empty. Everyone had gone home. The candles had burned low. The air smelled like wax and old wood.

He knelt near the front pew, tears streaking down his cheeks.

"I forgive you, Dad," he whispered. Then, softer still: "And I forgive me, too."

It wasn't the beginning of his ministry. But it was the end of his hiding. That was the night he stopped praying to be rescued.

And started praying to be *used.*

If you asked Brandon now what he'd say to someone who still feels unforgivable, Brandon wouldn't hesitate. He'd look them in the eye and say:

"Your scars aren't proof you're cursed. They're proof you survived." Then he'd lean forward and tell them the hardest truth of all: "Forgiveness isn't a one-time moment. It's a choice. One you make every single day, even when the pain whispers that you don't deserve it."

And then, finally, "You do. You always have."

Chapter 8

The air in the room had changed. Not lighter, exactly, but still.

Brandon sat upright, no longer trembling, no longer holding himself together with sheer will. There was something different in him now, something anchored. Something steady.

The kind of strength that only comes after you've walked through fire and decided not to stop. He had told his story. All of it, or at least, all that needed to be said.

And now, at the end of it, there was peace. Not the kind that comes from forgetting. The kind that comes from surviving.

Brandon's fingers rested lightly on the old Bible in front of him, the leather worn smooth from years of use. He didn't hold it like a weapon or a shield anymore.

He held it like a promise.

"I still believe I was chosen," he said without hesitation.

A small smile formed on his face, not forced, not for show, but real.

"When you survive what I've survived... when you've seen what I've seen... you stop caring about what people think."

He glanced at the Bible and ran his fingers along the edges. "God doesn't choose the strong," he said softly. "He strengthens the broken."

The room was quiet again, but not empty. It felt full, full of everything Brandon had lived through, and everything he still believed.

"Do I think all of it had to happen?" he continued, voice low, steady. "No. I don't think God *wanted* the pain. But I know He *used* it."

Brandon leaned back and looked toward the ceiling, like he was searching for a word just out of reach.

"I think sometimes," he said slowly, "the road to your purpose isn't paved at all. It's shattered. And every step cuts you open until you learn to bleed grace instead of bitterness."

His gaze returned to the present.

"And if someone out there is still waiting to hear their own calling?"

He paused, then answered without blinking.

"They've already heard it," he said. "If you're still breathing, there's still a reason. God doesn't waste breath. You have to listen to what is said."

Brandon sat in the quiet, letting the truth settle in the space between his words.

"You're here for something, even if it's just to hold a hand, or offer a kind word, or make it through one more day."

There was nothing dramatic about his tone. Nothing polished.

Just the truth. Honest. Raw. Real.

Brandon exhaled deeply and looked down for a moment.

Then he looked back up and spoke with calm conviction.

"I didn't survive all of this just to stay quiet," he said. "My story isn't clean. But it's mine. And maybe… maybe that's enough."

He reached down and opened his Bible, flipping through the pages gently. His hand stopped. His eyes found a verse.

He read it aloud.

"The light shines in the darkness, and the darkness has not overcome it." —John 1:5

He closed the book.

"That's how I live," he said. "That's how I survived."

He placed a hand over his heart.

"And that's how I know… this was always my destiny."

Brandon's words lingered, even after he stood to leave. The room didn't feel heavy anymore. It felt holy. His life wasn't a clean line. It was a scarred one. But he never pretended it wasn't.

And sometimes, the truth, just as it is, is the holiest thing of all.

Brandon stood quietly by the door, hands at his sides, Bible tucked beneath one arm. The fluorescent light above him flickered softly, humming like a tired voice that had nothing left to say. The walls were white, too clean, too blank, like they were trying to erase something no one could forget.

The lock clicked.

A guard in pale blue scrubs opened the door, nodding silently. Brandon gave a small nod in return and stepped out into the hallway. His bare feet padded gently along the cold tile, and the Bible thumped lightly against his ribs as he walked.

Inside the observation room, two doctors remained seated behind the tinted glass.

Dr. Keller leaned back, took off his glasses, and pinched the bridge of his nose. "Well," he muttered. "That was… something."

Dr. Morales crossed her arms, still staring at the door. "Every word of it. The detail. The pacing. It wasn't just a story."

"No," Keller agreed. "It was a testimony."

Down the hall, Brandon stopped outside his room. He turned to the guard and smiled, a soft, warm smile that had no edge to it. Just calm.

Then he stepped inside. The door closed behind him with a quiet click.

And the world outside moved on.

Laid to Ashes

They say the world ended in a blink, but that's not true.

It didn't happen all at once, like flipping a switch. No, it died slowly, burning, choking, falling apart piece by piece. First came the bombs. Then the sickness. Then the silence.

That was almost a hundred years ago.

I wasn't there, of course. I was born into the after. Born into a land where the air still tastes like smoke if the wind blows wrong, and where cities are nothing but rusted bones. People don't talk much about the time before. What's the point? There's no power, no satellites, no truth. Just stories, passed down like broken tools that don't quite fit anymore.

I live in a place called Dryridge. We've got a few wells, a fence made from scrap metal, and a patch of land dry enough to keep the worst things out. We're not fancy, but we survive. That's more than most can say.

But lately, things have been changing. A group came riding into town. Called themselves the Sanctifiers of the Flame. Said they could save us, give us food, order, purpose. Said they were sent by something holy.

Thing is, I've seen what fire leaves behind.

And I've learned that just because something burns bright… doesn't mean it's good.

— Jude Carver

Chapter 1

The sun had just started to rise, stretching long orange lines across the dirt, when Jude Carver stepped out of his shack. His boots crunched on the dry ground, and the morning air tasted like dust and rusted metal. Another day in Dryridge.

"Windmill's slow again," Emmett said, not even bothering with a "good morning." He was leaning against the fence, arms crossed, squinting into the wind like he was daring it to blow harder.

Jude rubbed the sleep from his eyes. "It's always slow when we need it the most."

He glanced toward the center of town. The old windmill, patched together from scrap car parts and steel beams, creaked in the breeze. It powered the well just enough to pull water twice a day if they were lucky.

Dryridge wasn't much to look at. A dozen or so buildings made from old trailers, shipping containers, and bits of a forgotten world. A fence ran around it, half-welded, half-wired together. Not pretty, but it kept out the worst of the wild.

Ruth waved to him from across the square, already setting up a small line of clay jugs by the well. Their daughter Anna skipped beside her, humming a song whose words no one remembered. Caleb, their twelve-year-old, was nearby, checking the water filter like he'd seen his dad do a hundred times before.

Jude felt a mix of quiet pride and fear. This place, they'd built it from nothing. And he'd do anything to protect it.

"I don't like the clouds," Emmett muttered.

Jude looked up. There weren't any clouds, just a faint haze on the horizon.

"Not clouds," Emmett said. "Dust. And riders."

Jude followed his gaze. Far off, just past the broken ridgeline, he could see movement, just small dots on the horizon.

"Scouts?" Jude asked.

Emmett shrugged. "Maybe. But they're coming straight for us."

Jude didn't like surprises. Not out here. Not after everything. He nodded once, firmly. "Let's get folks ready. Quietly."

They didn't panic in Dryridge. That was the rule. Panic got you dead.

Jude stepped onto the platform near the well and rang the old bicycle bell they used for meetings. One clang. Calm. Just a gathering.

People shuffled over, Ruth, Levi, and Sarah Beck, Elder Tobias with his cane tapping against the ground. Even Mira, the quiet girl who'd arrived a few months back and kept mostly to herself, showed up near the back, eyes sharp.

"We've got visitors," Jude said. "Not sure who yet. It could be travelers. Could be worse."

"What do we do?" Sarah asked, arms folded tightly.

"We don't show weakness," Emmett answered before Jude could. "We stand tall, like always."

Jude gave a small nod. "But we're polite. We let them speak first."

They waited.

An hour passed before the riders arrived. There were nine of them, all in white robes, faces clean, boots polished. That alone set off alarms in Jude's head. No one looked that put-together out here. Not unless they were pretending.

At the front rode a tall man with long white hair and a thick silver chain around his neck. His smile was gentle. His eyes were not.

He raised a hand in greeting. "Peace to you all," he called out, voice calm and smooth like he was preaching from a stage. "We come with blessings, not bullets."

Jude stepped forward. "Name's Jude Carver. This is Dryridge. Who are you?"

"I am Brother Malachai," the man said, bowing slightly. "We are the Sanctifiers of the Flame. We bring hope. And fire. In just the right balance."

Jude didn't smile. "That right?"

Malachai smiled wider. "We've helped many towns, given water, medicine, and purpose. All we ask in return is a bit of faith."

Emmett's hand hovered near the pistol at his side.

Jude kept his face still, but inside, something shifted. Faith, he thought, always comes with a cost.

And fire... fire always leaves something burned behind.

Chapter 2

They came in like ghosts from another world.

While most wanderers dragged behind tired horses and broken wagons, the Sanctifiers of the Flame rode in with purpose. Their white robes fluttered in the breeze, not even dirty from the road. Their saddlebags were full, their faces were clean, and not even one looked hungry.

That alone made folks uneasy, but still... Jude didn't turn them away.

He stood at the town's center, next to the well, as Brother Malachai dismounted. The rest of the riders stayed silent, waiting for their leader to speak first, like soldiers or true believers. Maybe both.

"Dryridge is a fine name," Malachai said as he looked around. "There's strength in it. It says, 'We endure.' I admire that."

Jude nodded slowly. "We didn't pick it for how it sounds. We picked it cause it's true."

Malachai smiled again, warm but careful. "We're not here to take over. We're here to serve. You'll find that our presence brings peace. Order. Resources you can't get on your own."

Ruth stepped up beside Jude, wiping her hands on a dusty cloth. "What's the catch?"

"No catch," Malachai said smoothly. "Just community. We believe in building something stronger together. And we ask for only a little faith in return."

Behind them, Emmett scoffed loud enough to be heard.

Malachai turned, not angry, but sharp-eyed. "Is there something on your mind, friend?"

Emmett didn't flinch. "I've seen plenty of people use 'faith' to get others to kneel."

Jude raised a hand before the tension could grow.

"We don't kneel in Dryridge," Jude said. "But we'll listen. If you really want to help, we'll accept your assistance. For now."

Malachai's eyes lit up. "You'll see. We bring more than just help. We bring rebirth."

By sundown, the Sanctifiers had set up their camp just outside the northern gate. They offered to sleep inside, but Jude politely declined. It was said that it was tradition to let guests rest outside the fence until trust was earned. Malachai had agreed, no offense taken, or at least none shown.

The town buzzed with quiet talk that night.

Some folks were excited. The Sanctifiers had brought crates of canned food, spools of clean wiring, even spare tools, things Dryridge hadn't seen in years. They offered medicine for the sick and clean water for the well.

"They've got to be connected to something bigger," Levi said during a small gathering by the fire. "There's no way they just travel around handing out supplies."

"Exactly," Emmett growled. "Which means they're not just passing through. They're recruiting."

Elder Tobias Vane leaned on his cane, staring into the flames. "Maybe we need recruiting. I'm tired of burying good people who die from things we used to cure with a single pill."

"Better to live free and sick," Emmett muttered, "than healed and owned."

Jude sat back, arms crossed. He didn't speak for a while. He was watching Mira.

She hadn't said much, but she was watching the Sanctifiers too. Not like the others. Not with wonder or hope. Her eyes were narrowed. Nervous.

Finally, Jude turned to her. "You know them?"

She jumped slightly at the question, then nodded slowly. "I've seen their kind before. Not these exact ones, but close enough."

"And?"

She looked down. "They talk nicely. Smile a lot. But fire doesn't smile. It burns."

Jude didn't press further. Not yet.

Instead, he stood and looked north, toward the white tents glowing in the moonlight just beyond the wall.

He didn't trust Malachai. Not completely. But he also couldn't ignore the way his people looked when they saw that food. That medicine.

He felt like a man standing at the edge of a cliff, wind at his back, wondering if the bridge in front of him would hold—or snap the moment he stepped forward.

Chapter 3

The next morning, Dryridge woke to the smell of baking bread.

That alone was enough to put people on edge.

Real bread, warm, yeasty, soft, wasn't something folks around here had tasted in years. Not unless you count the flat, sun-dried ration cakes Ruth made from old flour and wild seeds. But the Sanctifiers? They had ovens. Portable ones. And flour that hadn't gone gray.

Children gathered near their camp, sniffing the air and whispering. A few of the white-robed followers handed out small loaves like blessings, smiling as they touched each child's head and spoke words no one really listened to.

Emmett stood nearby, arms crossed. "They're softening us up."

Jude walked beside him, watching as Brother Malachai handed a small bundle to Elder Tobias. "They're smart," Jude said. "Too smart."

Malachai turned, as if hearing them, and gave a short nod.

Later that day, they assisted in repairing the town's broken water tower. Their people worked fast, organized, and efficiently. No complaints. No charge.

Ruth watched from the porch, her arms folded.

"Are you thinking what I'm thinking?" she asked Jude as he passed by.

"I think a lot of things," Jude said. "Lately, none of them are good."

Ruth didn't smile. "People are starting to like them. You need to be careful."

"I am."

"You're also tired. And you've got two kids depending on you not to screw this up."

Jude stopped. Turned. "You think I don't know that?"

She stepped closer, softer now. "I think you do. But I also think you want to believe they're what they say they are."

Jude didn't answer.

Because she was right.

That night, the Sanctifiers held a gathering outside their tents. They set up torches in a perfect circle and invited everyone from Dryridge to come to hear "The Word of the Flame." Most of the town showed up, drawn by the food and the strange peace that seemed to come with these people.

Jude sat in the back, beside Emmett and Mira. Ruth stayed home with the kids.

Brother Malachai stood in the firelight, arms outstretched, voice smooth like polished stone.

"We live in a world of ash," he said, "because the old world refused to be cleansed. It held on to its greed, its chaos, its broken systems. But the Flame does not lie. It purifies. It strips away weakness until only truth remains."

People nodded. Some whispered amen. A few closed their eyes like they were in some church from a time long gone.

Malachai continued. "We do not come to rule. We come to heal. We come to burn away the sickness of this land. And when the fire is done... all that remains will be clean."

Jude leaned toward Mira. "He's not talking about fire like an idea, is he?"

Mira's voice was low. "No. He means actual fire."

Later that night, as most folks headed home full of bread and belief, Mira stayed behind near the gate.

Jude found her staring at the white tents like they were graves.

"You've seen this before," Jude said, stepping up beside her.

Mira didn't answer right away. Then: "When I was twelve, my village welcomed a group like them. Different name, same robes. Same talk about purity. They helped us rebuild our church. Then one night, they said it was 'unclean' and burned it down with people inside."

Jude went quiet.

"My cousin tried to leave. Said it didn't feel right. They called her a traitor. Said she carried darkness. She was gone the next day."

"You think they'll do that here?"

Mira looked at him, eyes sharp. "I think they already have a list."

When Jude got home, Ruth was sitting on the porch with a lantern.

"How was the sermon?"

"Fire and forgiveness," Jude said, sitting beside her. "Mostly fire."

"You believe him?"

Jude stared out into the dark. "I believe people don't come bearing gifts unless they want something back."

Ruth reached over and took his hand. "Just don't wait too long to figure out what."

Jude nodded. Because something was off. And deep down, he knew...

If you play with fire too long... You don't just get burned. You turn to ash.

Chapter 4

It happened just after midnight.

Jude was walking the fence, as he did every few nights when sleep wouldn't come. The stars were bright, the wind was still, and Dryridge was quiet, but his gut wouldn't settle. Something about the way Malachai smiled. Something about the way the Sanctifiers never argued, never stumbled, never hesitated.

Too perfect. Too polished.

He was near the north gate when he heard the whisper.

"Jude."

He turned fast, hand on his knife.

Mira stepped out from behind the old supply shed, her eyes wide, voice urgent.

"We need to talk. Now."

They sat in the shadows by the fence, out of earshot from both the town and the Sanctifier camp.

Mira pulled something from her coat—a small, folded piece of worn cloth. Inside, it was a map, hand-drawn and marked with red circles. Names. Places. All crossed out.

"This is a record," she said. "Sanctifier settlements. Towns they've 'helped.' Every one of them... gone."

Jude studied the map. Some of the names he recognized. Old settlements. Places people used to trade with. Now they were ghost stories.

"What happened to them?" he asked.

"They don't leave survivors," Mira said. "At least, not the ones who don't obey."

"Why?"

"Because obedience is everything to them. It's not about faith. It's about control. Malachai preaches fire, and when people stop listening, he lights the match."

Jude's jaw clenched. "You've seen it?"

"My cousin was burned alive for questioning him. And when I ran... they called me a defector. A danger. If they find out I told you anything—"

"They won't," Jude said quickly. "I won't let that happen."

Mira looked at him, her face tired. "It's not just about me. It's your town now. Your family. You need to get them out, or be ready to fight."

Jude folded the map and slipped it into his coat.

"I need more proof."

"You don't," Mira said. "But I get it. You want to believe there's still good out there. So did I."

The next morning, Malachai stood at the center of town beside Elder Tobias.

He smiled, calmly as ever. "This morning, we ask for a small offering of trust," he said. "We've discovered one among you who has... strayed. An older man. He's confessed to hoarding water and refusing to share it with the sick."

A murmur spread through the crowd.

Jude's stomach dropped.

"We don't punish out of anger," Malachai continued. "We cleanse out of mercy. Tonight, we will hold a purification ceremony. He will be released from his sins by flame."

"What the hell is he talking about?" Emmett said from beside Jude.

"They're going to burn someone," Mira whispered, voice cracking. "Right here. In front of everyone."

"Who?" Jude asked, already dreading the answer.

An older man was dragged forward by two Sanctifiers—thin, dazed, barely able to stand.

Jude recognized him immediately. Henry Lowell. One of the town's oldest settlers. Half-blind, harmless. He barely had enough water for himself, let alone to hoard.

"Jude," Ruth said, arriving breathless. "He's innocent."

Jude didn't move. Not yet.

Malachai raised his hands. "We invite you all to witness this sacred moment at sundown. Let the Flame show you the path."

Back at Jude's home, the leaders of Dryridge gathered: Emmett, Ruth, Tobias, Levi, and Sarah, even a few of the younger farmers. They packed into the main room, voices tense.

"This is insane," Sarah said. "We can't let them do it."

"If we stop them, they'll turn on us," Tobias said, his cane tapping nervously. "We're outnumbered."

"They won't stop with Henry," Mira said. "They never do."

Levi looked at Jude. "You've got to make a call."

Jude stared at the floor, silent.

Emmett broke the silence. "You know what we have to do. You've known since the minute they rode in."

Jude nodded slowly.

"Then we stop the ceremony," he said. "And if they draw weapons, we draw faster."

Outside, the sun was beginning to fall. Torches were already being lit.

And in the center of town, the Sanctifiers were building something tall, made of wood, wrapped in rope—

A pyre.

Jude's hand gripped the hilt of his knife. It was time to stop the fire before it spread.

Chapter 5

The sky burned orange as the sun dropped behind the ridge, and the Sanctifiers' torches flared to life one by one.

In the center of Dryridge, they had built a towering pyre, just as Mira said they would. Rough wood, thick rope, and a single post rising from the middle. Henry Lowell stood tied to it, his head slumped to one side, too weak to speak.

The crowd gathered slowly out of fear, others out of curiosity. Most didn't believe it would really happen. Not here. Not in their town.

But Jude knew better.

He stood at the edge of the square, Emmett beside him, his hand resting on his rifle. Ruth was just behind them, holding Anna close. Caleb watched from the shadows, fists clenched.

Brother Malachai stepped forward, arms open like a preacher before a packed church.

"Tonight," he said, "we free a soul from corruption. We show our faith not in words... but in flame."

Jude took a breath, then stepped into the torchlight.

"That's enough."

The crowd turned. Gasps echoed through the square.

Malachai's smile didn't falter. "Ah, Jude. Have you come to witness the cleansing?"

"I've come to stop it."

Murmurs broke out around the square. Emmett raised his rifle just a little, not quite aiming—yet.

Malachai tilted his head. "You speak boldly for someone who accepted our help. Who ate our bread? Who drank our water?"

"And I thank you for that," Jude said. "But Dryridge doesn't burn its people."

Malachai's eyes narrowed. "Then perhaps you don't understand the Flame."

Jude took another step forward. "I understand you're using fear to control people. I understand you tied an old man to a pole with no trial, no voice, and no proof."

Malachai's smile broke. "Proof? His sin is clear. He hoarded water during a drought. He confessed it."

"Under what pressure?" Jude shot back. "You scare people into obedience and call it purity. That's not faith. That's tyranny."

The torches crackled in the silence.

Then Malachai raised one hand, and his robed followers moved in unison, forming a circle around the pyre.

One of them stepped forward, holding a torch toward the base.

That was the moment Jude's voice rang out, hard as stone. "Drop it. Or we drop you."

Guns were raised. Shouts broke out. Townsfolk scattered. Some drew knives. Others just ran.

The Sanctifier with the torch hesitated, then dropped it. Not onto the pyre, but to the ground.

Malachai hissed something low under his breath and turned to run, pushing through the line.

"Emmett!" Jude shouted.

"I see him!" Emmett sprinted after Malachai, gun raised.

The scene turned chaotic. A Sanctifier lunged at Jude, and they wrestled in the dirt. Jude slammed the man's head into the ground and stood, breathing hard.

Ruth was already untying Henry, tears in her eyes. "You're okay now," she whispered. "You're okay."

Mira darted into the crowd, helping a few stunned townsfolk to safety, her eyes scanning for more threats.

A single gunshot echoed from the northern end of town.

Jude froze.

He ran.

He found Emmett down by the edge of the chapel that the Sanctifiers had been building. A bullet wound bled from his side, but he was still standing, still alive.

Malachai was gone.

"He ran," Emmett said through gritted teeth. "Took two with him. The rest... scattered."

Jude helped him sit against the chapel wall. "We'll find him."

"No," Emmett said, gripping Jude's arm. "We wait. He'll come back. People like that always do."

Jude looked toward the smoke still curling from the torches. Henry was safe. The town had stood its ground, but something inside him knew this wasn't over.

Not yet.

That night, as the fires were put out and the wounded tended to, Jude sat alone outside his home.

Ruth brought him a cup of water. "You did the right thing," she said.

He nodded but didn't answer.

Across town, the half-finished chapel loomed in the dark, silent, cold, and waiting.

Chapter 6

Morning came heavily, dragging sunlight across the dusty ground like a worn-out blanket. Dryridge wasn't celebrating. It wasn't cheering. It was just... quiet.

The kind of quiet that happens after a storm when you're still counting the damage.

Henry Lowell was alive, but barely. Ruth and Sarah were tending to him in the old trading post, now turned into a makeshift clinic. A few townsfolk were helping Emmett, who'd been patched up with thread and liquor, but he stayed pale and stiff, a reminder that peace came with a price.

Jude stood near the chapel the Sanctifiers had been building, hands on his hips. The white structure was almost finished, with strong walls, clean corners, and a tall wooden spire that cast a long, sharp shadow across the ground.

"You should tear it down," Mira said behind him.

He didn't turn. "Part of me wants to burn it to the ground."

"Then do it."

"But another part wants to leave it up. As a warning. A reminder of how close we came."

Mira was quiet for a moment. "They'll come back, you know."

"I'm counting on it."

By mid-afternoon, word had spread. Some of the Sanctifiers had slipped out during the chaos. Others dropped their robes and blended in with the town. A few were still loyal to Malachai and hiding in the wild.

Levi brought news from the southern trail.

"There's movement down by the riverbed," he told Jude. "Three riders, maybe four. Moving fast. Could be Malachai heading east."

Jude looked toward the horizon. "He's running."

"For now."

That night, Dryridge held a meeting, not by choice, but because people needed answers.

"We can't go back to normal," Tobias said. "Not after this."

"No," Jude agreed. "But we can go forward. Stronger."

"Stronger, how?" someone asked from the back.

"By remembering who we are," Jude said. "We don't kneel for bread. We don't burn our neighbors. And we sure as hell don't let anyone use fear to run this place."

The crowd went still.

Then someone clapped. Then another.

They didn't cheer, but they stood taller. Straighter.

Dryridge didn't need a sermon. It needed a backbone.

Later that night, Mira sat on the chapel steps, turning her Sanctifier sash over in her hands.

"You ever think about leaving?" she asked Jude when he walked up.

"All the time."

"So why don't you?"

"Because running never fixed anything. I've got kids. A wife. A town that nearly got swallowed up because I wanted to believe someone else had the answers."

Mira tossed the white sash into the fire pit.

"I used to think fire was sacred," she said. "But all it ever did was take things from me."

Jude looked out over the town, where families were checking wells, sharing food, and patching the holes in the fence.

"No," he said softly. "It gave us something, too."

"What?"

"A reason to fight."

Across the plains, under a sky filled with stars and silence, Malachai rode with two followers beside him.

He didn't speak. He didn't rest.

And in his hand, clutched tight, was a small iron cross covered in ash.

Chapter 7

Malachai came back three nights later.

He didn't ride in with banners or speeches this time. No torches. No songs. Just fire.

It started at the edge of the fence. A loud crack, then a flash, and one of the outer buildings went up in flames fast, shooting into the dark sky like a signal. The chapel lit next, flames licking up the spire Jude hadn't torn down.

By the time Jude threw on his boots and grabbed his rifle, half the town was already awake and shouting.

"They're here!" someone yelled. "The Sanctifiers are back!"

Jude met Emmett limping out from behind his house, a bandage still wrapped around his side, pistol already in hand.

"How many?" Jude asked.

"Can't tell. It could be five, maybe ten. Maybe more hiding in the dark." Emmett winced. "They're lighting the outside and trying to scare us out."

Mira appeared beside them, breathless but steady. "They're not trying to scare us. They're trying to trap us."

"What?" Jude turned to her.

"They'll circle the fire. Wait for people to run. Pick them off as they flee."

Jude didn't waste time. "Get everyone to the center. From a ring around the well. Ruth and the kids go underground, into the storage cellar under the trading post. Guard them."

Emmett nodded and limped off to spread the word.

Jude stared into the fire as it spread up the chapel, now nothing but a symbol of foolish trust.

Malachai had made his choice. Now Jude would make his.

They held the line just past the well.

Families huddled behind stacked crates and overturned wagons. A few older kids held knives. Some of the townsfolk carried hunting rifles or old shotguns. Emmett was already taking shots from a low wall, and Mira stood beside him, her eyes locked on the tree line.

Then, through the smoke, they saw him, Malachai.

He walked into the clearing like he owned it, robes scorched and tattered, but his eyes still burning with purpose.

He raised his hands.

"You turned from the flame," he called out. "And so, the flame has come to judge you."

Jude stepped forward.

"I've seen your judgment," he said. "It looks a lot like murder."

"Purification," Malachai said calmly. "Your town could have been part of something greater. But you chose rebellion."

"We chose freedom."

Malachai nodded, as if he were disappointed in a stubborn child. "Then burn with it."

He raised his hand.

Gunfire cracked the air.

A bullet hit the dirt at Jude's feet.

Another hit the crate behind him.

Then the night exploded into chaos.

Jude fired back, ducking low and moving fast. He weaved between flames and falling debris, his rifle kicking back into his shoulder. All around him, Dryridge fought like hell.

Mira dragged a wounded townsman to cover. Emmett barked orders while firing shot after shot, blood darkening the side of his shirt. Ruth had taken charge of the children, keeping them underground and quiet.

The chapel collapsed in the distance, sending sparks into the sky.

Jude saw Malachai slipping through the smoke toward the chapel ruins.

He followed.

They met in the heart of the blaze.

Malachai stood with a small torch in hand, his white robes glowing orange in the firelight. His face was streaked with ash, his eyes wild now, desperate.

"It always ends like this," he said softly. "The old burned down so something new can rise."

Jude raised his rifle. "Nothing's rising from this but bones."

Malachai laughed. "You can kill me. But I am not the flame. I am only its voice."

"You've said enough."

Jude pulled the trigger.

Click.

Empty.

Malachai rushed him, screaming, swinging the torch like a blade. Jude ducked, slammed his shoulder into him, and they both crashed to the ground.

They fought hard, fists, elbows, and knees, old men clashing like it was the end of the world all over again.

Finally, Jude grabbed a splintered beam from the collapsed chapel and drove it into Malachai's chest.

The man gasped, eyes wide, fingers twitching, then went still.

Smoke rose around them as Jude stood, breathing heavily, face cut, knuckles raw.

By dawn, the fires had been extinguished.

Dryridge stood scarred, battered, but breathing.

Jude walked through the remains of the chapel, now blackened beams and ash. He found Malachai's iron cross in the rubble and held it in his hand for a long time.

Then he dropped it.

Let it fall into the ashes like everything else that man had brought.

Epilogue

A week later, the smoke was gone, but the smell still clung to everything, like the town itself didn't want to forget.

The chapel was now just a memory. Nothing left but a black circle in the dirt and a few nails Jude found half-buried when he walked through the ruins. He kept one in his pocket—not as a trophy, but as a reminder.

Dryridge had buried its dead and tended its wounded. Emmett was still healing, albeit slowly and steadily. Henry Lowell, surprisingly, recovered well. Kids played again, but quieter than before. Everyone seemed a little more grown-up.

Jude stood at the edge of the town with a shovel in his hand and his boots half-buried in dust. Caleb was beside him, holding a burlap sack of seeds.

"You sure that'll grow here?" Caleb asked.

"Nope," Jude said. "But we're gonna try anyway."

They dug small holes and dropped in the seeds—beans, mostly, and a few they couldn't identify but figured were worth a shot. The earth was dry, but not dead. And that was enough.

Ruth came over with a tin cup of water and helped sprinkle it across the rows. Anna skipped nearby, pretending not to be interested, but keeping close all the same.

From across the square, Mira approached hands in her pockets. She looked different, now lighter. Not happy, exactly, but no longer hiding behind quiet stares and hesitation.

"I've been thinking about staying," she said.

Jude didn't stop digging. "Good. We need more people who know how to spot trouble before it sets up camp."

She smiled. "Might even build a little place of my own, off the west fence. Something small."

"Make it bigger," Ruth called. "You'll want a porch."

Mira smiled wider.

That night, Jude sat on the porch, Ruth beside him, both of them watching the stars in silence.

"You think they'll come back?" she asked.

"The Sanctifiers?"

"Or others like them."

Jude took a deep breath. "Probably. Fire always finds something new to burn."

Ruth leaned her head against his shoulder. "And what do we do then?"

"We stand," Jude said. "Same as we did this time."

He looked out across the town, scarred, tired, patched together but still here. Still alive because sometimes survival isn't about being stronger or smarter.

THE END

Eldkula II

Prologue

My head's pounding like it's been slammed into a bulkhead. Everything hurts: my ribs, my leg, my back. My skin's raw where the harness burned me. Every breath feels like I'm pulling fire into my lungs. It's hard to tell how bad it is, but I know it's not good.

I'm lying here on the floor of the *Icarus*, probably somewhere near the bridge. I think. I can't see much. My eyes won't open all the way. The lights above flicker in that annoying, busted way, and I can't lift my head enough to get a good look around. My left leg's twisted underneath me like it doesn't belong to me anymore. And the taste in my mouth? Blood. Warm, metallic, and all too familiar.

Something happened. No, *a lot* happened. It's all scrambled in my brain like a busted transmission. One second, we were cruising near Eldkula II, the next, chaos. I remember alarms, shouting, the sharp pitch of shields failing, and the deep rumble of something hitting the hull hard enough to knock us sideways.

I try to piece it together, but my mind's thick with fog. Not just tired and foggy. Like all my thoughts are underwater. I hear a noise, something distant, almost like someone calling out my name over the ship's comms. Or maybe that's just the blood in my ears.

The air smells of burnt ionized metal and scorched circuits. I know that smell too well. Something overloaded. Probably the forward cannons or one of the plasma drives. The last time I smelled that, we lost a third of the crew.

I know I'm not going to make it. That part is clear.

I can feel the blood pooling under me. I'm cold, even though the emergency systems are probably still holding the internal temperature steady at 22 degrees Celsius. Funny how fast the body starts giving up when it knows it's dying. My fingers twitch like they're trying to do something useful. Maybe press a button. Maybe calling for help. But the truth is, I don't think anyone's coming.

Still, I don't feel scared. Just... tired. I keep thinking about yesterday. Or maybe it was two days ago. Back when everything still made sense.

We were heading for Eldkula II, this rocky little planet orbiting a K-type star. Orange sunlight, cooler than Earth's sun but still bright. The planet's got a thick crust and weird magnetic fields that scramble long-range comms. That's why we were out here to investigate those signals. They didn't match anything we knew. Not pirate chatter. Not local miners. Not even rogue AI drones. Something... new.

Now I'm lying here, bleeding out, trying to make sense of it all.

Whatever attacked us wasn't human. And whatever it was, it knew how to fight in space. Smart. Precise. Fast. We weren't ready, not really. But we fought. And I think, I *hope*, we won.

I'm fading fast now. My vision's gone gray at the edges. My heart's thumping slower like it's winding down for good. I want to believe it mattered. That what we did out here in the black meant something.

So, I focus on that last thought. The one I want to hold onto as everything slips away:

We were the first to see them. The first to fight back, and maybe, just maybe... the first to win.

Chapter 1

43 Hours Earlier
Reliant Base Alpha – Eldkula IV
August 28, 2122 – Earth Standard Date

The sun over Eldkula IV wasn't like Earth's. It had that soft orange glow you'd expect from a K-type main-sequence star—cooler, dimmer, but somehow steadier. The kind of light that made everything look a little more dramatic, especially through the thick plexiglass windows of Reliant Base Alpha.

I sat at the comms desk, sipping a lukewarm bulb of synth-caf, staring at the scrambled signal feed looping across the monitor. It looked like noise. At first. But I'd been doing this job long enough to know that random static doesn't pulse every six seconds with perfect precision.

"You're seeing it too, right?" Lieutenant Harris asked from across the control pit, her voice low and steady.

I nodded. "Yeah. Not a glitch. Not a flare. Something's *broadcasting* that."

She pulled up the signal overlay. "Origin?"

"Triangulated to somewhere just above Eldkula II's upper atmosphere," I said, tapping the console. "And it's not a normal orbit, either. Whatever it is, it's moving too fast and too tight. Like it's... watching."

The room got quiet.

Eldkula II was a weird planet. Dry, rocky, and cold as hell, surface temps hovered around -40 Celsius even on a good day. It didn't have much of an atmosphere, just a thin layer of mostly carbon dioxide. Not enough for life. At least, it's not life like *we* understood. The planet had no known colonies, no mining posts, no satellites, nothing but rocks, wind, and ancient craters.

But someone, or something, was out there.

"Commander Vance wants a crew up there within 12 hours," Harris finally said. "He's prepping the *Icarus* for launch. You're on the manifest."

I looked over at her. "You sure? I just got back from the Yeltran Run four days ago."

She smirked. "Congrats. You're rested."

I sighed and stood up, brushing crumbs off my jumpsuit. "Fine. I'll run diagnostics on my gear."

Before I left the control room, I glanced back at the screen. The signal was still pulsing.

Once every six seconds.

Relentless.

Later That Day – Launch Bay 3

The *Icarus* looked sharp as ever, with a sleek, black hull lined with sensor panels and solar deflectors. She wasn't the biggest in the fleet, but she was fast and smart. An S-class combat and recon cruiser built for deep-space missions just like this. Thirty-seven crew, dual fusion cores, a forward plasma cannon array, and state-of-the-art AI support.

She'd seen her share of action in the Yeltran skirmishes and came back in one piece every time. Most of us had come back too. Not all.

"Suit up," Vance barked as I entered. He was already in his command gear, helmet clipped to his belt, eyes sharp like he hadn't blinked in hours.

"What do we know?" I asked, pulling my suit from the rack.

"Not much. Signal origin is confirmed low orbit over Eldkula II. Could be alien. Could be an old probe reactivated. Could be something else."

Something else. He didn't say the word we were all thinking.

Hostile.

Six Hours Later – En Route to Eldkula II

The *Icarus* hummed softly as we glided past the edge of Eldkula IV's atmosphere. Ahead of us, Eldkula II spun slowly in the dark. It looked like a rusted coin in the sky, reddish brown with jagged mountains and impact scars covering most of its surface.

Sensors still couldn't get a clean read. Some kind of interference, probably electromagnetic, kept bouncing our scans back. We could see the signal now, though. Right there on the radar. A small, fast-moving object, about the size of a gunship, orbiting just above the terminator line where night met day.

No calls were answered. No transponder codes. Just silence and that same pulsing frequency.

I sat in the lower flight deck with a few others, running through pre-battle checks.

"Think it's them?" Ortiz asked. She was our weapons specialist. Sharp mind, sharper aim.

"If it is," I said, "we'll be the first humans to make contact with a new race in over twenty years."

She grinned. "Let's hope they're friendly."

I didn't answer. Because deep down, I didn't think they were.

Chapter 2

Eldkula II Orbit
August 29, 2122 – 0300 Hours

We dropped out of lightburn just shy of Eldkula II's orbit, and the entire bridge went quiet.

There it was.

Hanging out above the planet's edge like a shadow. Not a ship, exactly not like anything we'd seen before. It wasn't broadcasting, wasn't moving like a normal vessel. It was just... there. Sleek. Black. No lights. No markings. It's the kind of thing that gives you a chill even though the space is already cold enough.

Vance leaned over the pilot's chair and narrowed his eyes at the viewscreen. "Tell me that's a rock."

"No, sir," said Toni from sensor ops. "Metallic. Too symmetrical. Hull material unknown. It's reflecting sensor pings oddly like it's... absorbing them."

"Could be some kind of stealth coating," I added. "Or a defense matrix."

Ortiz let out a low whistle from her seat behind the cannon array. "It's just sitting there. Like it's *waiting* for something."

"Or *watching*," I muttered.

We'd already adjusted our orbit to match. Close enough to scan, far enough to back off if things went sideways.

"Send a standard hail," Vance ordered. "Keep it on loop. Full spectrum."

Toni nodded and tapped the commands in. "Hailing on all frequencies."

We waited.

Nothing.

No reply. No static. No reaction at all.

Vance crossed his arms. "Alright. Let's send in a drone. Keep us back, give it space."

0314 Hours – Drone Launch

The recon drone launched clean from bay three, its small thrusters giving off a faint blue trail as it closed the distance. Its onboard cams gave us a better look.

Up close, the object looked even weirder. It was oblong, almost organic-looking. Smooth curves, no seams, no clear engines or weapon mounts. Just a black surface with a shifting shimmer like heat waves on the pavement. Every few seconds, the drone's signal hiccupped like it was being jammed, but just barely.

"Telemetry's acting up," Toni said. "Still stable, but whatever that thing is it's not passively sitting there."

Then, the screen glitched.

For just half a second.

Then again.

"Drone feed is—" she started, and then it was gone.

Just... gone.

No explosion. No debris. No warning. In one frame, the drone was there, and in the next, it wasn't.

Ortiz stood up, eyes wide. "What the hell just happened?"

"Something *took it*," I said. "That wasn't a malfunction. That was intentional."

"Red alert," Vance said, voice flat. "Shields up. Weapons charged."

The hum in the ship changed. Shields snapped into place with a faint shimmer around the hull. You could *feel* the power draw in the air. We were ready to fight.

Even if we didn't know what we were fighting.

0340 Hours – First Strike

It happened fast. One moment, the object was still. The next, it moved with no warning, no visible thrusters, just *bam*, it jumped. Not a warp. Not a burn. Just… a spatial blink. One second, it was out there, a few thousand kilometers away. The next, it was right in front of us.

"Incoming!" shouted Toni.

Before we could react, a beam of pure white light fired across our bow. Not a laser, something else. It bent around space like it was rewriting physics as it moved. The shields flared, overloading, and the ship rocked hard.

"We're hit!" someone yelled from engineering. "Front shields down to 23%!"

"Return fire!" Vance barked.

Ortiz let loose with everything. Plasma bursts. Rail slugs. Shock torpedoes. Our best tech. It all hit, but none of it seemed to matter. The thing absorbed it. Like it was built to *drink* energy.

"Nothing's getting through," Ortiz growled.

"No, it's learning," I said. "It's adapting."

Vance looked at me. "Then we need to be smarter."

The ship rolled hard to starboard. We pulled a tight arc around the object, trying to confuse it with heat flares and burst signals. It followed.

It was *toying* with us.

That's when I knew we weren't just looking at new tech. We were looking at a new species, and they weren't interested in peace.

0355 Hours – Retreat and Plan

We finally pulled back into a higher orbit, behind one of Eldkula II's magnetic ridges. It gave us a few minutes of cover to regroup. The alien ship didn't follow, but it didn't disappear either. It just floated there, pulsing, like a heart made of metal.

Everyone looked shaken. Even Vance.

"Alright," he said. "We're not dealing with pirates. Or rogue AI. This thing is smarter than us. Faster than us. We need to come at it sideways."

"Suggestions?" I asked.

"We use the planet," Vance said. "Set up a decoy beacon on the surface. Lure it in. Then hit it with a pulse bomb strong enough to fry its systems before it can react."

"That'll blow our entire stockpile," Ortiz said.

"It's that or watch this thing tear us apart."

No one argued. We got to work.

And all the while, that dark shape kept watching us.

Waiting.

Chapter 3

Eldkula II – Surface Deployment Zone
August 29, 2122 – 0630 Hours

We hit the atmosphere rough. Eldkula II didn't roll out a welcome mat.

The drop shuttle bucked hard as we cut through the thin, dusty air. Red rock blurred below us like rust-colored sandpaper. Outside, the wind howled at over 300 kilometers per hour, loaded with fine particles that scraped the hull like angry bees.

"Landing gear locked," Ortiz called out. "Touching down in five."

I braced myself and gritted my teeth. The shuttle slammed into the surface with a bone-rattling *thud*, kicking up a storm of grit. Through the viewport, I saw jagged cliffs and cracked ground stretching for miles. It was like someone had dropped a continent-sized piece of burnt toast.

"Welcome to Eldkula II," I muttered. "Population: us."

We stepped out into the chill. Even with thermal suits, the cold bit right through to the bone. -78 Celsius, the last scan said. It's not a place you'd want to vacation. The sky was a burnt orange, and Eldkula IV, our staging planet, hung like a dim coin in the distance.

The team moved fast. We had to. The idea was simple: drop a beacon broadcasting a false signal and make it look like a distress call. We loaded it with heat signatures and EM pulses to mimic a damaged ship's core. Hopefully, the alien would take the bait.

Then we'd blow it sky high with a pulse bomb built into the bait.

"Decoy beacon placed," said Toni. "Activating in thirty seconds."

I watched as she flipped the final switch. A soft whine built up in the air, barely audible over the wind.

"Signal's broadcasting," she confirmed. "Looks messy. Just like a crippled ship might sound."

Ortiz checked the detonator. "Pulse bombs armed. If that thing gets within a hundred meters, boom. No time to adapt to that."

Vance nodded, looking out toward the horizon. "Now we wait."

0715 Hours – The Approach

We were camped in a ridge about half a klick from the beacon, hiding under a metal overhang that gave us a line of sight and a bit of shelter from the cutting wind. The ship had eyes in orbit. *Icarus* was floating just above the magnetic interference field, ready to jump back in if needed.

And then... we saw it.

The dark shape slipped through the sky like it was swimming. No engine trail. No thrust. Just motion, smooth and silent. It was headed straight for the beacon.

"Contact confirmed," Vance said. "It's coming in fast."

It hovered for a moment above the beacon like it was trying to understand it.

"Hold," Ortiz whispered, thumb over the trigger. "Just a few more seconds..."

The ship lowered closer.

Fifty meters.

"Come on, just a little more..."

Twenty.

Then—

"NOW!"

Ortiz slammed the trigger.

0720 Hours – The Blast

The pulse bomb detonated with a flash brighter than the sun. No sound, just pressure and energy rippling through the valley. The dust shot skyward like a volcanic burst. My visor dimmed automatically, but even then, I could barely see.

We held our breath.

The blast should've fried everything with a central nervous system or at least anything running on an AI core.

But as the smoke cleared, we saw it. Still floating.

Damaged, but still there.

One side of the alien ship was glowing, like it had been partially melted. The smooth black hull had split open, revealing something beneath—something almost... alive. Pulsing, like veins made of light.

"What... is that?" Toni whispered.

"I don't know," Vance said, "but it's still moving."

0725 Hours – Retaliation

Suddenly, a blast of white light shot from the exposed side of the alien ship. It hit the ridge above us. The rock exploded, showering us with shards.

I hit the ground hard, my ears ringing. Ortiz shouted something, but it was swallowed by the chaos.

Another blast hit just meters from our position.

"They're angry now!" I yelled.

"Fall back!" Vance ordered. "Shuttle's inbound!"

We ran. The alien ship was slower now, wounded, but it was still dangerous. Every few seconds, it pulsed again, releasing short bursts of whatever weapon it used. It wasn't trying to kill us all at once; it was *sweeping* the area. Precise. Controlled. Like it wanted to study us as much as destroy us.

We barely made it back to the shuttle. The ramp closed just as another blast lit up the landing site behind us. If we had waited three more seconds, we would've been ash.

0800 Hours – Back Aboard the Icarus

Once we docked with the *Icarus*, medbots started patching everyone up. My shoulder was burned by a flying piece of heated rock. Ortiz had a cracked rib. Toni's helmet had a hairline fracture.

Vance paced the bridge, furious.

"That thing should've been vaporized," he snapped. "How did it survive that?"

No one answered.

I sat in my chair, pulling off my gloves. My hands were shaking. "It bled," I said quietly.

They looked at me.

"That thing out there. It's not just a machine. It's not just metal. It bled."

Chapter 4

Icarus – Command Deck
August 29, 2122 – 0930 Hours

I was still shaking when the alarms started again.

"Multiple contacts!" Toni yelled from the ops station. "They just *appeared* out of nowhere!"

The entire bridge went tense. Vance leaned forward over the command rail. "How many?"

"Three… no, four ships. It has the same shape and the same energy signature. They're smaller than the first but moving fast."

Vance didn't flinch. "Sound general quarters. All hands to battle stations."

The red alert lights kicked in immediately, painting everything in a deep pulse of danger. The *Icarus* groaned as the defense grid fired up shields, plasma arrays, railguns, torpedo tubes, and the whole loadout.

We'd planned for one unknown ship.

Now we had four more on the field, and the first one, the *wounded one*, was still hanging below us like a ghost.

0945 Hours – Second Contact

"They're flanking," Ortiz said, locking in firing solutions. "No standard attack pattern. It's like they're learning *as* they move."

"Because they *are*," I said.

The new alien ships were quick, almost insect-like, in the way they zipped around our defensive perimeter. They didn't talk, didn't warn us, didn't even *hesitate*.

They struck.

And we answered.

Plasma rounds lit up the dark like blue lightning. Our railguns punched out superheated tungsten slugs at hypersonic speeds. The *Icarus* spun and rolled, dodging two shots that sliced through empty space like white-hot spears.

We got one of them. Ortiz landed a direct hit that shattered the lead ship's hull. It didn't explode; it just crumpled like it was made of brittle glass and then *evaporated*. No debris, no pilot, and no power core. Just... gone.

"Did we even kill it?" she asked.

"Don't care," Vance growled. "Keep firing."

1000 Hours – Hull Breach

One of the alien ships got too close—real close. It rotated mid-flight, fired a burst of that warped light energy, and punched straight through our aft shields.

"We've got a hull breach on Deck 3!" shouted Engineering.

That's where the backup reactor and medbay were. I took off running.

Smoke filled the hallway. Lights flickered. I grabbed a rebreather from the wall and slid it on, heart pounding as I leaped over fallen support beams and debris. There was a deep hum in the metal—like the ship itself was groaning under pressure.

Then I saw it.

A crewman. Crushed beneath a collapsed bulkhead. I reached for him, but one look told me it was too late.

I kept going.

1010 Hours – Fighting Smarter

By the time I made it back to the command deck, we'd taken out another ship, but not without cost. The alien vessels were fast, but we were starting to figure them out. They turned poorly after sharp acceleration. They didn't use shields. And they seemed to pull power from that same pulsing core like the first one did.

"They're drawing from the wounded one," Toni said suddenly, pointing to the scans. "It's like the big one is a power node and the others are feeding off of it."

That was it.

"Cut off the node," I said, breathless. "We take out the damaged ship below. The others might drop."

Vance looked at me. "Are you sure?"

"Nope," I said, "but it's the best shot we've got."

1020 Hours – Between the Storms

The lights on the bridge had dimmed, flickering slightly as power rerouted to the plasma cannon. Everyone was in motion, running checks, prepping systems, watching the alien core ship drift below us like a wounded predator. But for a second, just one second, time stretched.

Toni stepped up beside me, her helmet tucked under one arm. Her cheeks were flushed, eyes tired but sharp.

"You look like hell," she said quietly.

I forced a half-smile. "You should see the other guy."

Her grin flickered, then faded. "This is going to be close."

"Yeah," I said. "Closer than I'd like."

She hesitated. Her fingers brushed mine, barely a touch, almost like she was checking to see if I was still real.

"When we get back," she said, voice lower now, "I owe you a drink. The real kind. No synth, no ration limits. Just you and me, wherever the hell we want to be."

I looked at her. Really looked at her.

"You mean that?" I asked.

She nodded.

"Then I'll hold you to it," I said.

And for a moment, the war, the ship, the cold edge of death waiting outside the hull, it all disappeared.

All that mattered was that promise.

I turned back to my console, hands steady again.

"Let's finish this," I said.

1025 Hours – The Push

We dove.

The Icarus banked hard, thrusters screaming as we cut through Eldkula II's upper atmosphere, pulling tighter than the ship was built to handle. The air outside burned red across the shielding—static flaring, hull groaning. The wounded alien ship loomed below, drifting like a half-dead leviathan, still leaking light from the breach we'd carved earlier.

"Target locked," Ortiz said, voice tight. "Plasma cannon at 98%. Railguns fully charged. This is our shot."

"Fire," Vance ordered.

The deck shook.

The plasma cannon discharged in a blinding white arc, thick and radiant, slicing through the black. Simultaneously, the railguns unleashed six tungsten rounds in tight formation, each one aimed at the exposed wound. It was a coordinated strike, a textbook kill shot—if the textbook had ever accounted for enemies like this.

The alien ship reacted too late.

The first plasma burst punched straight through the crack in its hull. The second hit a moment later followed by the slugs, which ripped deeper, past the shimmering skin and into the core. The impact didn't explode.

It *folded*.

The ship let out a ripple across the sky, like space itself was being crumpled. Time seemed to bend around it. The pulsing veins of light flickered, spasmed... then died. For one breathless second, everything froze.

Then the alien vessel collapsed inward like a dying star collapsing into itself, folding and twisting until it vanished with no sound, no debris, just absence.

Gone.

1030 Hours – Aftershock

Silence.

The battlefield went still, broken only by the faint hum of the Icarus stabilizing from the recoil.

Toni gasped. "Look!"

The three remaining alien ships stuttered in the sky, erratic, confused. One spun wildly out of formation, its trajectory breaking into an uncontrolled descent. It struck the atmosphere and burned, a dying star trailing fire behind it.

Another simply stopped. Like a puppet whose strings had been cut, it hung there, motionless.

"They're falling apart," Ortiz breathed. "They were feeding off the core. Like drones."

The third ship turned and fled, disappearing behind Eldkula II's curvature. Whether it escaped or died out of sight, we couldn't tell. But it didn't come back.

We'd done it.

We survived.

Vance didn't speak. He just stared at the empty space where the alien ship had been, jaw clenched, eyes glassy with disbelief.

But I couldn't stand anymore.

My vision blurred. My side throbbed like someone had jammed a hot blade between my ribs. I looked down. Blood soaked through my flight suit, warm and heavy, and suddenly I understood why the world was dimming.

Deck 3. The hull breach. I hadn't gotten clear in time.

My knees buckled. I fell.

And even as the Icarus steadied and the cheers rose from the crew, I lay there on the cold floor of the command deck, slipping into the dark.

We had made first contact.

And we lived to tell the tale.

Well… most of us.

Chapter 5

Icarus – Medbay
August 29, 2122 – 1100 Hours

I woke up to the low hum of medbots.

Everything was blurry at first, just soft lights, the smell of disinfectant, and the rhythmic hiss of oxygen cycling. I was lying on a padded med-table, strapped in by an auto-splint system. My chest felt like it had been stomped on. My leg didn't feel like anything at all, which was somehow worse.

A nurse-bot hovered nearby, its little mechanical arms adjusting IV lines and scanning my vitals. I turned my head slightly and saw Toni through the glass window of the medbay. She was talking to Vance. Her face was serious, eyes locked on a datapad.

They didn't notice I was awake.

I coughed, which made my ribs scream in protest. A warning icon blinked on the console beside me: *"Internal bleeding detected. Stabilization required."*

Yeah. No kidding.

1106 Hours – Briefing Debrief

Toni finally came in. She looked relieved to see me awake, but only just.

"You scared the hell out of us," she said, trying to smile. "Thought we lost you."

"Close enough," I muttered. "Did we... win?"

She nodded slowly. "We did. The alien core ship's gone. The rest scattered or powered down. Whatever they were, they were not talking. But the signal yours, the one you picked up on Eldkula IV, that stopped too. Just... silence."

I closed my eyes and let that sit.

Silence had never sounded so loud.

1125 Hours – Personal Log Entry 318B

They gave me a portable console, mostly to keep me awake. I wasn't doing great. The medbots were trying, but the damage inside me was worse than they expected. They didn't say it, but I knew the truth.

There wasn't enough time. So, I recorded my last log.

Log Entry 318B – Crew ID: Lieutenant Daren Holt
Status: Critical – Non-recoverable internal trauma

"Hey. If this message makes it to Command… or Earth… or anyone who cares, I just want you to know something: we made first contact. It wasn't pretty. It wasn't peaceful. But we held the line."

"The enemy was faster, smarter… and alien in every way that word means. Not just new tech, but also new biology. New logic. They weren't here to talk."

"We lost good people. But we stopped them."

"I don't know if more are coming. I hope not. But if they do… tell whoever's left to be ready."

I paused, the pain in my side making it hard to speak.

"Also… tell my sister I kept the photo of Mom. It's in my locker. She'll want it back."

I looked at the blinking light on the console. Still recording.

"Oh, and whoever's reading this… don't trust silence in space. If something's out there… it's probably listening."

I hit send.

1145 Hours – Countdown

The pain meds dulled the rest.

I could hear the muffled sound of voices and the soft vibration of the engines as *Icarus* corrected its orbit. Outside the medbay window, Eldkula II spun slowly below. Quiet. Still. Cold.

Toni came back once more. She didn't say anything; she just sat by the bed and held my hand.

"Hey," I said, my voice almost gone.

She leaned in.

"Promise me something."

"Anything."

"If they ever come back… hit 'em harder."

She smiled through her tears. "Deal."

1158 Hours – Final Systems Check

I watched the stars through the port. So bright. So far.

There's a moment when everything slows down. Not because of adrenaline but because your body *knows* it's shutting down. My breathing got shallow. My vision dimmed at the edges. My fingers went numb.

But I wasn't afraid.

Not anymore.

I'd done my part.

We all had.

Log Entry 318C – Final Status: Deceased in Action
Confirmed Time of Death: August 29, 2122 – 1159 Hours, EST

Epilogue

Earth Command Archives – Luna Station
September 16, 2122 – 1437 Hours, EST

The room was quiet, except for the soft clicking of keyboards and the low hum of data cores running at 40% capacity. Commander Elira Brand stood in the observation deck above Operations, hands clasped behind her back, staring at the screen in front of her.

A new message had just come in.

It had taken nineteen days to cross from the Eldkula system to Earth through encrypted deep-relay channels. The signal was flagged as a high priority, marked with a red icon: *Casualty Report Attached.*

She tapped the screen. A voice began to play.

"Hey. If this message makes it to Command… or Earth… or anyone who cares, I just want you to know something…"

It was a young voice. Steady. Calm. Not the voice of someone who knew he was dying, but someone who wanted his words to matter.

By the time the message ended, Brand hadn't moved.

The room behind her was silent. Dozens of officers had stopped what they were doing to listen.

One of the junior techs finally spoke. "Should we begin a formal debrief on the Eldkula Incident?"

Brand turned, her expression unreadable.

"Not yet," she said. "Let it sit for a minute."

She looked back at the dark screen. It now displayed a still image: a rocky planet with a thin atmosphere, one small black ship barely visible in the lower orbit, the *Icarus* floating above.

They didn't know what race had attacked.

They didn't know if it was truly over.

But they knew this:

Humanity had stepped into another corner of the galaxy. And it wasn't empty.

Final Entry – Earth Command Log

Eldkula II Incident: Confirmed hostile first contact. Five alien vessels engaged. Four destroyed. One is presumed to have recovered or escaped.
Status: Debrief ongoing. Surveillance initiated across nearby systems.
Personnel lost: 9 confirmed. Including Lt. Daren Holt.
Recommendation: Upgrade Frontier Protocols. Initiate Contact Contingency Code 7.

We are not alone, and we are not always welcome.

Relapse

Prologue

Fifteen years sober. That's what the chip in Neil's pocket said, just a little circle of bronze, worn at the edges from years of being rubbed between his fingers. A lot of people in the rooms looked at Neil like he was some kind of miracle. He had the job, the apartment, the clean record, and a calm, steady way of talking that made newcomers sit up and listen.

To the outside world, Neil had done what so many couldn't. He'd beat it.

He wasn't flashy about his recovery. He didn't preach. He just showed up at work, at meetings, at coffee shops with guys trying to stay clean one more day. His life wasn't perfect, but it was solid. Predictable. Safe.

But quiet doesn't always mean peaceful.

There were things Neil didn't talk about. Not even to his sponsor. Not even to himself.

The dreams. The shame. The way his hands still trembled sometimes when he walked by the liquor aisle at the store. The ghost of his old life still followed him around, not loud, but close enough to feel. A whisper in the back of his mind, always saying the same thing: *What if you slipped? Just once.*

Some nights, when the apartment was too quiet and the clock ticked too loudly, Neil would sit on the edge of his bed, rubbing that coin between his fingers like a prayer. Not because he wanted to drink, but because he was afraid he still might.

And that fear… that quiet, private fear… was the one part of his story no one ever asked about.

And maybe that's why it grew.

Chapter 1

It didn't happen all at once.

Neil didn't wake up one morning and decide to stop going to meetings. He didn't slam the door on his support system or toss his sobriety chip in the trash. No, it started slow, like a leak behind the walls. Barely noticeable at first.

He had a rough week at the center. A new kid arrived, angry and loud, flinching at every noise. Neil saw pieces of himself in the boy, but nothing he said seemed to help. Then the power went out during lunch, one of the pipes burst in the bathroom, and to top it off, the director reminded Neil that funding was hanging by a thread again. He went home that Friday with a headache pounding in his temples and an exhaustion that sleep couldn't fix.

Then Jack died.

Jack had been more than Neil's first sponsor. He was his friend. His anchor in the early days. The guy who took Neil to meetings called him out when he lied and once drove across town just to stop him from picking up a bottle. Liver cancer took him fast. Too fast. Neil stood in the back of the church, staring at the closed casket, trying to swallow the lump in his throat. Everyone else cried. Neil couldn't.

After that, things shifted. Neil started skipping meetings. At first, it was just once he told himself he was too tired. Then twice. Then he lost count. The guys he used to call every week got used to not hearing from him. One even texted to ask if he was okay. Neil replied with a thumbs-up emoji and didn't respond again.

He still went to work. Still paid his rent. Still made his bed. But the spark was gone. He moved through the days like he was underwater, everything muffled, slow, and far away.

He stopped praying. Stopped writing in his journal. Stopped picking up his phone when his mom called.

And the scary thing was... no one seemed to notice.

He started walking a different route to avoid the corner store where he used to buy whiskey. But he thought about it. Every time. Every day. Not because he wanted to, at least that's what he told himself, but because something inside him missed it. Missed the weight of the bottle. The quiet after the burn.

The armor he'd built for over fifteen years was beginning to crack, and Neil wasn't sure he had the strength to fix it.

Chapter 2

The bar didn't have a name worth remembering.

It sat on the edge of town like a secret people were too ashamed to tell. A dull red neon sign flickered in the front window, missing a few letters. Inside, the air was thick with the smell of old cigarette smoke, and the scent of stale beer permeated the walls. It was the kind of place where people didn't come to celebrate; they came to disappear.

Neil stood just outside for a while. Just watching. His hands were stuffed in the pockets of his jacket. He could feel the cold metal of his fifteen-year chip pressing against his leg. He didn't take it out. He didn't need to see it.

He already knew what it said.

He told himself he was just going in to get warm. Just to sit down. Just remember what it *used* to feel like when the noise in his head went quiet after the second or third drink.

He walked in.

No one looked at him. The bartender gave a nod like he'd seen a thousand Neils before. Maybe he had.

Neil found a seat at the bar. The stool wobbled under him. He didn't take off his jacket.

He ordered a soda first. Just to settle his nerves. He sipped it, stared straight ahead, and told himself he could leave at any time.

But he didn't.

Instead, he watched the bartender pour drinks for other people amber liquid in short glasses. The sound of the bottle hitting the wood. The clink of ice. It was like muscle memory every sound hitting somewhere deep in his brain.

Then the thought came. Simple. Familiar.

Just one.

It won't fix anything, but maybe it'll take the edge off.

He tried to shake it. Thought about Jack. About his mom. About the kids at the center who called him "Mr. Neil" like he was someone worth looking up to.

And then he thought about his dad.

He pictured his face—quiet, proud, the way he smiled at Neil the day he picked up his first-year chip. That smile had meant everything.

Neil closed his eyes.

"Whiskey," he said. "Neat."

The bartender nodded and poured.

The glass sat in front of him. Small. Simple. Deadly.

Neil stared at it for a long time. Twenty minutes, maybe more. He picked it up, then set it down. He picked it up again. His hand shook a little.

He thought about the people who still believed in him. His sponsor. His mom. His ex-wife.

He thought about the man he had been.

And then, like a crack snapping open in the middle of a frozen lake, something inside him broke.

"Fuck it," he whispered. "He's dead."

And just like that, Neil lifted the glass and slammed the shot back.

The burn hit his throat and dropped into his stomach like fire. His eyes watered. His heart raced. But somewhere in all of that chaos, something went still.

He didn't feel better.

He just felt… gone.

He slid the glass forward and tapped the bar once.

"Another."

Chapter 3

The second shot led to a third.

By the time Neil stumbled out of the bar that night, the sky had turned to ink, and his phone had a dozen missed calls from his mom. He didn't answer. He shoved the phone deep in his pocket and told himself he'd call her tomorrow. Maybe.

But tomorrow came with a hangover and the kind of guilt that wrapped itself around his chest like a belt. Still, even with the pounding headache and dry mouth, part of him felt... relief.

He had finally done it. The thing he feared the most.

And the world hadn't ended.

So when the night came again, and the memories started clawing their way out, Neil went back.

This time, he didn't order a soda first.

Within a week, the bar stool felt like home again. The bartender knew his name. The faces at the bar didn't ask questions. Neil liked that. He didn't want to explain. He didn't want to hear about chips and meetings and "one day at a time."

He wanted silence. He wanted to stop feeling everything. But alcohol wasn't enough.

The booze numbed the edges, but the hole inside him was still there, wide and deep and hungry.

One night, outside the bar, a guy offered him a few pills. "Just to level things out," the man said, like he was doing Neil a favor.

Neil didn't hesitate.

The pills took the sting out of everything. Made the nights smoother. Helped him sleep without dreaming. At first, it was just a couple here and there, Xanax, maybe a little Oxy. But the more he used, the more he needed. And when the pills ran out, someone offered him something stronger.

He told himself he'd just try it once. He lied. Within a month, Neil wasn't just drinking. He was using. Full-on.

His savings started disappearing. First, it was small things, like extra cash from his wallet and a skipped bill here and there. Then he stopped paying rent. Then he stopped showing up to work.

The director at the center left three voicemails. The third one wasn't kind. Neil never called back.

He sold his guitar. Then his TV. Then he pawned the watch his dad gave him on his ten-year sober anniversary.

Each time he traded something away, he promised himself it would be the last, it never was.

His reflection started to change. His eyes lost their light. His clothes hung off his body in a way they didn't before. He stopped shaving. He stopped caring.

Old habits returned as if they'd never left. He lied to people who still trusted him. Borrowed money with no intention of paying it back. He made excuses for the excuses, and worst of all, he stopped believing he could come back.

One night, he pulled that fifteen-year chip out of his jacket pocket. It had been riding there for weeks. He stared at it under the flickering streetlamp outside the pawn shop and thought about how proud he used to be. Then he dropped it in the gutter and walked away.

Chapter 4

For a while, Neil tried to pretend nothing was wrong. He cleaned himself up just enough to pass. He'd splash cold water on his face, brush his teeth to hide the whiskey on his breath, and throw on clean clothes, even if he hadn't showered in days. If you didn't look too closely, you might think he was doing okay.

And most people didn't look too close.

He made an appearance at a meeting one night, just to remind himself he could. He walked in, nodded to a few familiar faces, and sat in the back. He didn't share. He didn't even listen. His mind was a storm of static, replaying the last few weeks on a loop.

When the meeting ended, someone clapped him on the back and said, "Good to see you, man. Still going strong?"

Neil smiled. "Yeah. One day at a time, right?"

He left before anyone could ask more.

The truth was, Neil was no longer living one day at a time. He was living from hour to hour. Hit to hit. Lie to lie.

Every day, he woke up in a panic, trying to figure out where he was, what he had left to sell, or who he could call to get his next fix. But then he'd slip into a clean shirt, plaster a smile on his face, and lie to whoever needed him to be okay.

When he ran into his old coworker from the community center at the grocery store, he pretended he was just on vacation. "Needed some time off," he said, laughing. "Burnout's real, man."

The guy smiled and nodded. "Well, you look great."

Neil almost laughed at that. He had dark circles under his eyes, had lost ten pounds, and hadn't eaten a real meal in days.

But people see what they want to see.

At night, he told himself he still had control. He wasn't like *them*, the ones who ended up dead in alleys or twitching in gas station bathrooms.

He still had his apartment. Still had some money. Still had a line he wouldn't cross, until he crossed it. That line constantly moved.

He started stealing. Nothing big at first. A few bucks from his mom's wallet when she let him crash on the couch for a night. A ring she kept in the kitchen drawer. She never said anything, but he knew she noticed. Her eyes looked different now, less hopeful, more afraid.

She stopped asking how he was. He stopped visiting. Neil didn't want to see the disappointment on her face.

But no matter how deep he sank, he couldn't shake the shame. It clung to him like sweat. Every time he looked in the mirror, he saw both versions of himself: the man who had been sober for fifteen years... and the man who was breaking every promise he'd ever made.

He missed the old version. But he didn't believe he could get him back.

So, he kept pretending. Because pretending was easier than asking for help.

Chapter 5

Neil didn't mean to end up outside the meeting hall. He had just been walking. Wandering, really. His phone was dead. He hadn't slept. He couldn't remember the last time he ate something that wasn't from a gas station.

And then there it was, that church basement. The one with rusty folding chairs and the stale coffee. The one where he first told a room full of strangers that he wanted to live.

He stood across the street, hands buried deep in the pockets of his hoodie, staring at the door like it might burn him if he got too close.

Part of him wanted to go inside. Just sit down and listen, but another part, the louder part, told him he didn't belong there anymore.

Not after everything.

Not after the lies. The pills. The drinks. The stealing. The time he left his mom's house without saying goodbye, just because he didn't want her to ask him how he was doing.

Still, something pulled him forward. He crossed the street and stepped inside.

The smell hit him first: dust, old carpet, and coffee strong enough to chew. It was familiar, comforting in a weird way. A few people looked up as he entered. One of them, a guy named Marcus, did a double take. Neil hadn't seen him in years.

"Neil?" Marcus blinked, like he wasn't sure it was really him.

Neil gave a tight nod. "Hey."

There was a pause. Then Marcus smiled. Not the fake kind, either, "I'm glad you're here, man."

Neil sat down in the back. The chair creaked under him. His hands wouldn't stop shaking.

The meeting started. People shared stories about bad days, near relapses, real pain. Neil listened. He heard words he'd once said to other people. Heard pieces of himself in every voice.

And the weight in his chest got heavier.

When the basket came around, he passed it along. When the meeting ended, he stood up and left without saying another word.

He made it two blocks before he ducked into an alley and pulled out a flask. The whiskey hit harder than usual. Not because of the burn but because of the shame.

He wanted to stop. He didn't know how.

That night, he tried to write in the old notebook he used to carry when he was clean. The pages were dusty, but still there. He flipped through them, old quotes, bits of prayers, letters to his future self.

He stared at the last page, where he had once written:

"I'm worth saving."

He didn't believe it anymore, but he wanted to and for a brief second, that want lit something in him, like the tiniest ember in a pile of wet ash.

Then it flickered out, and he took another drink.

He had walked into that meeting hoping for something, a spark, a hand, maybe a reason to keep going. But the truth hit harder than any drink ever had:

Wanting to come back wasn't the same as being able to.

Chapter 6

Winter came early that year, and Neil wasn't ready for it.

He woke up under a freeway overpass, tucked inside a tattered sleeping bag someone had given him outside the shelter. His coat was gone, traded for pills the week before. His shoes were soaked. His body ached in places he didn't even know could hurt.

He hadn't showered in weeks. The stubble on his face was patchy. His fingernails were black. His teeth hurt. He didn't know if it was from the drugs or just the months of not caring.

There was no more pretending now. No more clean shirts. No more showing up. No more stories to tell people about how he was "just tired" or "taking time for himself."

This was the bottom. And it was cold.

Neil shuffled toward the gas station bathroom he sometimes used to clean up. But this time, the clerk stopped him at the door.

"Bathrooms for customers only."

Neil didn't argue. He just nodded and walked away.

He passed his old sponsor's house on the way back to his usual spot behind the liquor store. He didn't stop. What would he even say? *Hey, remember me? I used to be somebody.*

He had a dream that night. He was back at the center, teaching a writing class to the kids. One of them asked him how to spell the word "hope," and Neil couldn't remember. He woke up gasping, heart pounding, clutching his chest like it might fall apart.

Some nights, he thought about calling someone. Anyone, but the weight of shame was too much. It wrapped around him like a chain. And even if someone answered, what would he say? *I screwed it all up again? I lost everything? I need help?*

He no longer believed help was an option.

So, he wandered through his days like a shadow. Panhandled for change. Dug through trash cans behind fast food joints. Sleeping wherever he could find shelter.

The world felt far away. Like he was watching his life from the outside, screaming at himself to wake up, to do something, to crawl back to the people who still cared.

But he couldn't.

He couldn't even cry anymore. He was past tears. Past anger. Past anything that made him feel like a human being.

And then, one night, when the cold slipped all the way into his bones and the silence screamed louder than ever, Neil sat alone behind the bar where it all started. He looked up at the sky, stars faint behind the city glow, and whispered:

"I don't want to do this anymore."

He wasn't talking about the drugs. He wasn't talking about the cold. He was talking about living.

Chapter 7

Neil didn't plan it out. There was no note. No long goodbye. Just a tired kind of silence that had settled into his bones, the kind of silence that made even breathing feel like too much work.

It was raining, cold, and steady. He sat huddled behind a boarded-up convenience store, knees pulled to his chest, a dirty blanket wrapped around him like it could still protect him from anything.

In his pocket was a bag.

A mix of pills, powder, and something stronger than usual. He didn't even know what all of it was. A guy downtown handed it to him and said, "This'll shut it all off."

Neil didn't ask questions. He just nodded.

He thought about his mom.

She hadn't called in weeks. Maybe she finally gave up. Or maybe she just couldn't keep calling a phone that never picked up.

He thought about the center, the chalk drawings on the sidewalk out front, the smell of cheap markers, the sound of kids laughing when they forgot they were supposed to be angry.

He thought about Jack. He thought about the bar. That first drink. The shot glass that tipped everything over and he thought about himself, the man he used to be. The one who once stood up in a room full of broken people and said, "I want to live."

Neil pulled the blanket tighter and leaned his head against the wall. His body ached. His chest hurt. His stomach was empty.

The worst part was the nothing. He didn't feel scared. He didn't feel sad. He just felt done.

He took the mix out of his pocket and lined it up. His hands were shaking, but he managed. He always did. His last thought before he took it all in was strange.

Not about death. Not even about life.

He remembered a joke Jack used to tell during meetings, something dumb about coffee and donuts and how AA didn't promise you heaven, just freedom from hell if you showed up.

Neil smiled, just a little, and then the world blurred. His vision flickered. The wall behind him felt as though it was drifting away, as if he were floating or falling; it was hard to tell.

Sounds got distant. Then too quiet.

And then…

Nothing.

Epilogue

Marcus didn't hear about Neil's death until three days after it happened. He was at the Wednesday night meeting, refilling the coffee pot, when someone mentioned a body had been found behind the old convenience store. A man in his late forties. Overdose. No ID.

Marcus didn't want to believe it. He stepped out to make a few calls, checked with the shelter, and asked around.

Finally, someone Marcus knew at the county morgue confirmed it; it was Neil.

The words didn't hit all at once. They landed in pieces, sharp, small, and hard to breathe around.

Marcus sat in his car for a long time after that, holding the steering wheel like it might keep him from falling apart.

He hadn't seen Neil since that night he walked into the meeting and sat quietly in the back. He didn't share. He didn't stay long. But for a moment, Marcus had hoped. Hoped that maybe Neil was coming back. Maybe he still believed in second chances.

Or third ones.

Or fiftieth.

Marcus had seen plenty of people fall and climb their way back. He'd also seen too many not make it. And now Neil was one of them.

At the next meeting, Marcus placed a photo on the front table: Neil, fifteen years sober, smiling with a coin in one hand and a slice of cake in the other. A few people who remembered him shared stories. Others just sat quietly; the room was heavy with what was lost.

Later that night, Marcus wrote Neil's name on a small slip of paper and folded it into the worn leather prayer box at the front of the room.

He didn't say much.

Just: "Rest easy, brother." Because that's what you say when there's nothing left to say.

Neil's story didn't end with a miracle. It ended the way too many do, alone, cold, and full of ghosts. But that didn't erase the years he stayed sober. It didn't erase the people he helped or the lives he touched.

It just reminded them all how fragile this fight really is. Addiction doesn't care how long you've been clean. And recovery, for all its hope, is still a daily battle.

Marcus knew that. They all did. So, they kept showing up.

For Neil.

For themselves.

For the ones still out there, staring at full shot glasses, wondering if they should pick it up.

Author's Note

This story is fiction. But the pain behind it is not.

I'm a recovering alcoholic and drug addict. Like Neil, I've known the quiet fear of relapse, the shame of slipping, and the weight of thinking maybe I'm too far gone. I've also known the grace of second chances, and the strength it takes to reach for them.

Neil's story isn't meant to glorify addiction or dwell in despair. It's meant to tell the truth: that recovery is hard. That sometimes, even after years of staying clean, the darkness can come back. And that people fall, not because they're weak, but because addiction is relentless.

If you're reading this and you've slipped, know this: You're not alone. You're not broken beyond repair. You're still worth saving.

I wrote this story because I needed it. Maybe you do, too.

— Brett C. Persson

The Lineage

Prologue

The stars burned like cold fire in the black winter sky, scattered across the heavens as if they were watching what was about to happen. The air was thick with dampness, and every breath felt like breathing through wet wool. Wind ripped through the trees like angry whispers, rattling the bare branches and carrying the stench of smoke and blood.

In the center of a snow-covered clearing stood a firepit, wide and deep, its flames already licking at the sky. Around it gathered a mob of zealots, wild-eyed, filthy, wrapped in ragged furs and bone charms that clattered like teeth in the wind. They swayed and chanted low, their voices weaving together in a sound that wasn't quite human, something between a prayer and a curse. Their chants grew louder, more frenzied, as they fed the fire with coal and wood soaked in animal fat, sending thick black smoke into the sky.

Above the pit hung a cage, iron, rusted, cruel in design. Suspended ten feet up, it swayed slightly in the wind, creaking like it had a voice of its own. Inside it crouched a man, barefoot, bruised, and bloodied. His long black hair was plastered to his face, sticky with sweat and blood. His body was covered in burns and welts, his shirt torn to ribbons. Yet he stood tall, or as tall as he could, gripping the bars of the cage, refusing to show fear.

His name was Kael, though no one here cared. To them, he was just a traitor, an enemy of the Lineage. Once a trusted warrior. Once the queen's companion. Now? A symbol of what happens to those who dare defy the priestess.

The fire roared beneath him, heat rising in waves that made the air shimmer. At first, it had been just uncomfortable, with dry heat and smoke. But now, the bottom of the cage had begun to glow a dull red, and the iron was scorching to the touch. His skin blistered where it met the metal. Pain, sharp and endless, crawled through his body like fire ants. Still, Kael bit down hard and refused to scream. Not yet.

He met their eyes, the guards of the High Priestess, feeding the fire with glee, grinning like executioners. Behind them stood the crowd, eyes glowing with hate and devotion, like animals starved for blood.

A man from the crowd hurled a stone. It hit Kael's ribs with a loud thud. Another tossed a bone. Another threw a chunk of rotten meat. They all laughed, spat, and cursed him.

Then the iron beneath Kael's feet turned white-hot.

His scream ripped through the clearing like a wild animal. He had promised himself he wouldn't do it, swore he'd die silent. But there's a limit to human will. The pain exploded in his body like nothing he'd ever known. The metal burned his flesh, and the flames licked at his legs. The smell of his own skin cooking twisted his stomach, but there was no way to escape it. No place to hide. No mercy.

He screamed again, and this time it was primal. Not from fear. From betrayal.

He had believed in her once. Fought beside her. Loved her.

And she had ordered this.

The crowd chanted louder now, feeding off his pain. The guards stoked the fire more, moving with ritualistic glee. This was more than punishment; it was theater. A warning.

And it had only just begun.

Chapter 1

Before Kael was a prisoner screaming in a cage, before he became the symbol of rebellion and betrayal, he was just a boy with dirt under his nails and a heart too big for the cold world he lived in.

He grew up in a small village called Durresh, nestled near the edge of the Blackwood. Life there was hard. Winters came early and stayed too long. The soil was rocky, and the air always carried a chill, even in spring. But Kael didn't mind. He learned to swing a hatchet before he could read and hunted his first boar at twelve. People in Durresh were tough, quiet, and suspicious of outsiders. And Kael? He was one of them until he wasn't.

Everything changed the day Selyra came to town.

Selyra arrived on horseback, flanked by armored riders with red sashes across their chests. The villagers watched from behind closed shutters as the procession made its way to the center of town. Selyra wore robes of deep violet trimmed in gold, and her dark hair was braided like a crown. Her eyes were sharp and focused, like she could see things people weren't saying. She said she was a priestess of the Lineage, a faith older than kingdoms, a bloodline that connected chosen ones to the gods themselves.

Most people didn't care about that. They just wanted to be left alone.

But Kael was different. He was drawn to her, not just because she was beautiful, though she was, but because she looked like someone who had power, purpose, and answers. At fifteen, he had already seen too much death and not enough reason for any of it. He'd watched his mother cough herself to death in a shack with no medicine, and he buried his brother after a wolf attack that no one had time to stop. So when Selyra spoke about the gods, destiny, and the sacred blood that flowed through the chosen, Kael listened.

And she noticed him.

Within weeks, she invited him to join her on the road. She said she saw something in him, strength, potential, loyalty. He didn't hesitate. He left behind his father's old tools, the burnt-out remains of his home, and the graves of everyone he loved.

He became a soldier of the Lineage, but the longer he followed her, the more the cracks began to show.

At first, it was small things. The way she spoke to villagers was like they were beneath her. The punishments she gave to her own people for disobedience were too harsh and too public. He tried to ignore it, convinced himself it was part of keeping order.

Years passed. Kael became one of her top warriors, her personal guard. He stood beside her as she took city after city in the name of the Lineage. People bent the knee, or they were made to. Blood always followed her sermons. He started to question it all, but Selyra had a way of looking into you, peeling you open, making you feel like your doubt was a betrayal of something holy.

Still, Kael held on.

They talked late into the night. Sometimes, she cried. Told him about her visions, about the burden of leadership, about the voice she heard in dreams. And sometimes, when the guards had left, and the candles burned low, they were more than the priestess and the protector.

They were lovers. He never knew if it was real or just another way to keep him loyal.

Looking back, he wasn't sure he cared. All he knew was that he would've followed her anywhere until she started killing children. That was the moment it all changed.

One town, just a small farming place outside the cliffs of Norwyn, had refused to send tribute. They didn't believe in the Lineage. They said they would stand on their own.

Selyra ordered the children to be taken first. "Fear," she told her inner circle, "We must start in the heart of innocence. That's where obedience is born."

Kael begged her not to go through with it. She kissed his cheek and said, "You're either with me or against the gods."

He didn't sleep that night.

In the morning, the village square ran red with blood.

Kael watched it happen, and in that moment, something in him broke.

Kael didn't speak for three days after the massacre at Norwyn.

He couldn't eat. Couldn't sleep. Every time he closed his eyes, he saw the same thing: the children's eyes wide with terror, their small hands reaching out, the priestess's soldiers dragging them across frozen dirt like livestock. He'd been a soldier long enough to see death, but this... this wasn't war. This was cruelty with holy paint smeared over it.

And it was Selyra's voice that had ordered it.

He had tried to reason with her before the bloodshed. Pleaded, even. Told her it would destroy what little faith people still had in the Lineage. That it would break him. But she only smiled, calm as ever, and said, "Faith forged in fire never breaks."

He started seeing her differently after that.

The golden robes. The way people bowed in her presence, afraid to even make eye contact. The way her guards beat a man half to death for whispering during one of her speeches. All the things he had ignored or justified suddenly looked like what they were: control. Fear. Power, dressed up as religion.

She didn't serve the gods. She served herself.

Kael knew he couldn't be part of it anymore. But walking away wasn't simple. Not when your name was known across half the kingdom as the Priestess's blade. Not when every town square had statues of you beside her, eyes carved in stone as if you were her equal.

He had helped build this nightmare. And now, he wanted out. So, he started collecting proof.

In secret, he began copying documents from the Temple vault, including ledgers of strange financial deals, orders of execution signed by Selyra herself, and reports from spies that showed she'd been orchestrating resistance movements just to crush them in public. He stole coded scrolls from her tent at night, memorized her routes, and whispered to the few guards who still had doubts in their hearts.

One of them was a girl named Maren, barely eighteen, smart, quiet, and sharper than most of the brutes who carried swords. She had joined the Lineage to protect the weak, not to torch villages. When Kael showed her one of the ledgers, she didn't even blink.

"I knew she was a liar," Maren whispered. "But this... this is evil."

Over the next few weeks, Kael and Maren built a plan. They would take the evidence to the outer cities, to the old scholars who remembered life before the Lineage took over. If they could just get the truth into the right hands, maybe someone would rise up. Maybe the people would finally see her for what she was: a tyrant wrapped in silk and scripture.

But someone talked.

Kael never found out who. Maybe it was one of the guards he thought he could trust. Maybe Selyra knew him better than he thought and had been watching him all along.

It didn't matter.

The night before they planned to leave, Kael woke to the sound of shouting. He reached for his sword, but the tent was already surrounded.

The red sashes were everywhere. One of them, a thick brute named Oran, burst inside and slammed Kael to the ground before he could even stand. Maren screamed. He saw her being dragged out, blood pouring from her nose.

And then, in the firelight, Selyra stepped in.

She was calm. No shouting. No fury. Just that look, sharp, steady, cold.

"You disappoint me," she said, kneeling beside him. "I loved you once, Kael. Truly. But betrayal is betrayal."

He spat at her feet. "This isn't about betrayal. This is about truth."

"No," she said, standing up slowly. "This is about obedience. And you've forgotten your place."

Kael fought. He thrashed and kicked, broke a guard's nose and bit another's arm so hard he tasted blood. But it didn't matter. There were too many. They bound his arms, beat him until he couldn't see straight, and dragged him away through the snow.

The last thing he saw before everything went black was Maren's eyes, wide and terrified, as they pulled her in the other direction.

He didn't know if she survived.

Chapter 2

Kael woke up choking on blood.

His mouth tasted like copper and dirt, and one of his eyes was swollen shut. He tried to sit up, but his wrists were bound behind his back with a thick leather strap that cut into his skin every time he moved. His body ached everywhere, ribs cracked, face bruised, stomach raw from the beatings.

He was lying in the back of a wooden wagon, bouncing along a dirt path in the dark. The only light came from the moon above and the faint glow of torches carried by riders on either side. The cold wind hit his skin like knives. Every bump in the road sent waves of pain through his chest. But he didn't cry out. Not anymore.

Across from him in the wagon sat a man he recognized, Jorran, one of the priestess's interrogators. Tall, bony, with a permanent sneer and a love for slow pain. Jorran smiled when he saw Kael was awake.

"Morning, traitor," he said, voice oily and cheerful. "You missed the sunrise. Shame. It was a pretty one."

Kael didn't answer.

Jorran leaned closer. "You're lucky. Most don't live long enough to be sentenced. The priestess made sure we kept you in one piece... more or less."

Kael shifted, testing the binds. No give.

Kael knew exactly where they were taking him, and it sure as hell wasn't prison. Not even the cold, dark dungeons beneath the Temple. No, this was worse. They were headed for the woods, the place where the Lineage dealt with its traitors. Out in the open. In front of a crowd. Slowly.

He'd heard whispers about the Trial of Fire. A brutal, ceremonial execution was saved for the worst of the so-called heretics. There was nothing quick about it. Nothing merciful. They made sure it happened under the open sky, like the gods themselves needed front-row seats.

As the wagon bounced along the uneven path, Kael's mind drifted to Maren. He hadn't seen her since the night it all went to hell.

Was she still alive? Hurt? Lying dead in a ditch somewhere? He couldn't shake the last sounds he remembered, shouting, scuffling, someone screaming for help. Maybe she'd managed to break free. Maybe she was still out there.

He could only hope.

After hours of riding, the caravan stopped. They dragged Kael out of the wagon and tossed him onto the frozen ground like a sack of meat. Around him, tall trees loomed like silent judges. The clearing smelled of ash and burnt wood; this place had seen death before.

The cage was already there. Hanging above a wide fire pit, chains creaking as it swayed slightly in the wind.

A crowd had started to gather. Not villagers. Zealots. Fanatics. People who worshipped Selyra as if she were divine. Some wore robes. Some wore war paint. All of them looked hungry for blood, for justice, for a show.

They dragged Kael toward the fire pit. He fought, kicked, and cursed, but his strength was nearly gone. Jorran punched him in the gut, dropping him to his knees.

"Make peace with your gods," Jorran whispered. "Though I doubt they'll answer."

And then, she arrived.

Selyra stepped into the clearing like a queen on parade, flanked by five guards with crimson blades. Her robes shimmered in the torchlight. Her face was calm, unreadable. But her eyes burned with something cold and final.

She didn't speak right away. Just looked at him like he was a broken toy. Then, finally, she spoke.

"Kael of Durresh," she said, her voice ringing out like a spell, "you stand accused of heresy, betrayal, and treason against the sacred Lineage. You stole from the Temple, conspired with enemies, and questioned divine will."

Kael coughed, blood splattering the snow. "I questioned you, Selyra. Not the gods."

She flinched, just slightly. Then her voice sharpened. "The will of the priestess is the will of the gods. And your punishment will be the fire. Let your screams be a lesson."

They hauled him into the cage, slamming the door shut behind him. Chains rattled as they raised it high above the pit. Kael stared down at the wood and coal piled beneath him. The fire hadn't been lit yet, but it would be soon.

He looked out over the crowd, over the trees, over the place where it would all end.

And then he said the words he'd been holding back for too long.

"You can kill me," he shouted, voice hoarse but strong. "But the truth will outlive you. The gods see what you are. And they will not forget."

Selyra turned her back without a word. The torches dropped into the pit. And the fire began to rise.

Chapter 3

The fire cracked and roared below the cage like it was alive, like it had been waiting just for him.

Kael tried to brace himself, gripping the iron bars with trembling hands, but the heat was already crawling up his legs. The metal cage snapped and hissed as it expanded in the growing blaze. Every breath he took was filled with smoke and burning air. His skin was soaked with sweat one moment and then blistering the next.

The crowd had grown. Hundreds now stood around the firepit, zealots, believers, travelers, and soldiers, all packed into the clearing like animals watching a sacrifice. They cheered every time Kael flinched and screamed louder every time the fire flared.

And above them, all stood Selyra, unmoved, unblinking as if she were watching a play written just for her.

Kael gritted his teeth, trying to stay silent, trying to hold onto some shred of dignity. But when the flames licked the bottom of the cage and the heat pressed against his raw, blistering feet, the first scream tore out of him like an animal's howl.

Pain like that, real pain, takes over your body. It becomes your heartbeat, your breath, your whole world. Kael's skin cracked open in places. His legs twitched involuntarily. The iron was searing hot, branding his flesh. And just when it felt like he might pass out, the guards lowered the cage again, closer to the fire.

His voice was raw now. His throat was scorched from screaming, but he couldn't stop. There was no relief. No mercy. They wanted him to suffer. They wanted him to break.

But deep in his mind, past the agony, Kael held on to one thing: hate. Not the wild kind. Not rage. Something colder. Sharper. Focused.

He would survive this if only to see her fall.

Somewhere beyond the flames and smoke, in the edge of the trees, a figure watched silently from the shadows.

Maren.

Her face was pale, bruised, but her eyes burned with purpose. She hadn't been executed. Selyra must have thought she wasn't worth the trouble. Or maybe she wanted to use her later. Either way, Maren had escaped.

And she wasn't alone.

Beside her stood a small band of others, former soldiers, villagers, and even one of the old temple scribes. People who had once believed but now knew the truth. There weren't many. Not yet. But they were there.

Maren gripped the hilt of a short dagger and leaned toward the man next to her. "We wait until nightfall," she whispered. "When the fires die down and they're drunk on their own cruelty, we go in. We get him out."

The man nodded, jaw tight. "And if we can't?"

"Then we burn the whole damn place down with them in it."

Back at the pit, Kael's body trembled uncontrollably. He no longer had the strength to scream. His voice had become nothing but dry gasps and moans. His eyes rolled back. Every inch of him was scorched, his skin torn and blistered, his lips cracked and bleeding.

Above him, the stars began to peek through the smoke-filled sky. And in that moment, a strange calm settled over him. He thought of his village. Of his mother's hands brushing his hair back. Of his brother's laugh. He thought of the man he had been before all this.

And then he thought of Selyra. The way she whispered his name in the dark. The way she smiled right before ordering death.

If he lived, if he *somehow* lived, he would see her bleed.

The cage creaked again, swaying above the fire.

And Kael, burned, broken, half-dead, he opened his eyes.

He was still alive.

And that meant he still had a chance.

Chapter 4

Kael didn't remember the rescue clearly. He remembered only flashes: the unbearable heat, his skin screaming, and drifting in and out of consciousness as figures moved around him, shouting muffled commands.

When he finally woke, he was lying on a cold stone slab, his body wrapped tightly in bandages that smelled strongly of herbs and smoke. He couldn't move; every muscle was tense, as if they were afraid to awaken the fire again. Pain throbbed throughout his body, sharp and relentless.

A dim candle flickered nearby, casting long shadows against rough stone walls. He was alive, something that felt impossible.

A slim figure stepped into view, wrapped in a thick cloak, a long fresh scar cutting across one cheek.

"Maren," he croaked, his voice barely more than a whisper.

She offered a faint smile, but it didn't reach her tired eyes. "You're tougher than anyone thought."

Kael attempted to sit up, but pain surged through him. She gently pressed him back down.

"Stay still. You're lucky to have even one foot left. You were barefoot in that cage. The healers had to carefully separate what remained from the burned metal."

Kael grimaced at the thought. "Where…are we?"

"An old hunting lodge deep in the Greywood," Maren replied. "Selyra's guards won't come here. At least, not yet."

Kael nodded weakly, then asked, "How did you get out?"

Maren's expression darkened. "I managed to escape during transport. They underestimated me, thought I was too beaten down to fight. I killed a guard and slipped away. It took me days to track you to that clearing, and when I finally did, I wasn't alone."

"Who else?" Kael asked, struggling to focus.

"Others who saw through her lies," she said softly. "Soldiers who defected. Villagers were tired of the bloodshed. We waited until the zealots got drunk and careless. Then we moved in. Oran, that brute who took pleasure in hurting you, he's dead now."

Kael allowed himself to smile. "I wish I'd been awake to see it."

"It wasn't pretty," Maren said quietly. "We lost two good people getting you out. It took six of us just to carry you. I didn't think you'd survive."

He looked away, feeling a pang of guilt. "I wasn't sure I wanted to."

Silence stretched between them. Maren eventually leaned closer, lowering her voice.

"I found something important in her tent while looking for you," she said, pulling a tightly rolled scroll from beneath her cloak. "It's part of a prophecy, or maybe a forgery. It's incomplete, damaged around the edges, but it clearly states that the Lineage was never meant to end with Selyra. She was supposed to guide the next prophet, not become one herself."

Kael frowned, turning the revelation over in his mind. "She never told me that."

"Because she hid it," Maren continued sharply. "She rewrote the prophecy and killed anyone who might remember the truth, scholars, monks, even members of her own council."

Kael felt something ignite within him, not anger, not fear, but a renewed purpose.

"She's afraid," he murmured. "That's why she wanted me dead so publicly, to send a message."

"Exactly," Maren agreed. "She's losing control. If we act quickly, we can expose her lies and rally people against her."

Kael forced himself to sit up, ignoring the searing pain. "We don't have an army."

"No," Maren conceded. "But we have the truth."

Kael stared at the flickering candlelight. "Then it's time we spread it like fire."

That night, after the others had gone to rest, Kael sat alone near the hearth, the scroll open in his lap. Candlelight flickered against the worn parchment, its edges curled and brittle with age. The words were faded in places, but the meaning was unmistakable. Selyra had rewritten destiny. The truth was never hers to claim.

He traced the old ink with a burned fingertip, wondering how many people had died for this prophecy. How many truths had been buried beneath the weight of her ambition? The lines whispered of a guide, not a god, and of a coming storm that no priestess could contain.

Kael thought of the man he had been: the loyal warrior, the believer, the one who clung to her every word as if it were salvation. That version of himself had to die if this new world was ever going to live.

He rose slowly, clutching a charred piece of wood from the hearth. With effort, he limped out into the cold night. The stars above were quiet, distant, unmoved. At the edge of the trees, beneath a dying oak, he knelt and began to dig.

From his coat, he pulled out a small object: a braided leather bracelet, blackened by fire. It was all that remained of his days beside her, their nights in quiet tents, her whispered promises, the loyalty he had once worn like armor.

He placed the bracelet into the shallow hole, then added the scroll, rolled tight and wrapped in cloth. Not to destroy it, he would remember what it said, but to bury it as a warning, as a memory, as a truth no longer needed to be carried so close.

As he covered the hole with dirt and ash, Kael whispered softly, "You were never a god. You were just a woman too afraid to be anything less."

He stood, breath visible in the frigid air, and turned back toward the lodge.

It was time to become someone new.

Chapter 5

Kael stood in front of a cracked mirror, staring at the wreckage of his own face.

His skin was still healing patches of red and pink where flesh had been burned away, thick bandages wrapped around his hands and lower legs. His beard was gone, burned off, and his once long black hair had been cut short to make it easier to treat the burns. The man looking back at him barely resembled the warrior who had ridden beside the priestess. But his eyes?

His eyes were sharper than they'd ever been.

Behind him, the old hunting lodge had become something more. A base. A spark. People were coming, quietly, carefully. Some were old guards who had seen too much. Others were villagers who'd lost sons, daughters, whole families to the priestess's purges. And then there were the scholars who remembered the *true* teachings of the Lineage. They brought scrolls, artifacts, and words the priestess had tried to erase.

Kael stepped away from the mirror and limped toward the main room, where a small group was gathered around a makeshift table. Maren was there, arms crossed, eyes scanning a map. Next to her was Jorek, a grizzled former soldier with a permanent scowl, and Tamsin, a soft-spoken monk who carried ancient texts in a torn leather satchel.

Jorek nodded at Kael as he entered. "You're walking again. That's something."

Kael grinned slightly. "Not pretty, but I'm harder to kill than she thought."

Maren looked up. "Good. Because we're ready to move."

Kael leaned over the table, studying the map. "What's the plan?"

Tamsin unrolled a scroll and pointed to a symbol etched into the parchment. "This is the temple where the original prophecy was kept. Selyra had it burned ten years ago. Or so she thought. I found a copy, buried in a hollow stone behind the altar."

Kael's eyes narrowed. "You're saying we can prove she was never the chosen one?"

"Not just that," Tamsin said. "We can show the people that she *knew* it and chose to lie. Chose to murder."

Jorek grunted. "Most folks won't care. They're scared. They'll bow to whoever holds the whip."

Maren shook her head. "Not if we give them another option."

Kael placed both hands on the table. "Then we do more than reveal the truth. We take her strongholds, one by one. Cut off her support. Free the villages she's enslaved. Turn her own people against her."

Jorek raised an eyebrow. "With what army?"

Kael glanced around the room, meeting every set of eyes.

"With the desperate. The broken. The ones who've lost too much to stay quiet."

Maren nodded slowly. "We don't need to win every battle. We just need to win the one that breaks her spell over them."

Kael looked back at the map, heart pounding.

"This isn't just revenge anymore," he said. "This is redemption. For me. For all of us."

Silence followed, heavy but full of agreement.

That night, Kael sat alone by the fire, sharpening a blade with slow, even strokes. His fingers still trembled when he held the steel, but he didn't stop. Pain was part of him now, just like the scars. And when the time came to face her again, he wanted her to see what she had made.

He didn't want to kill Selyra for what she'd done to him.

He wanted to kill her for what she'd turned *him* into.

The war had begun, and this time, he would burn *her* world down.

Chapter 6

The Temple of the Lineage sat on the highest cliff in the realm, carved straight into the mountain as if it had grown from the stone itself. Its black spires pierced the sky, cold and sharp, casting long shadows over the valley below. To most, it appeared to be a place of worship. To Kael, it was an impenetrable fortress, built on lies, held by fear.

Kael watched carefully from the tree line below, counting the guards pacing along the outer wall, noting their patterns, the shifting of patrols, and the arrogant complacency in their movements. Selyra had prepared her defenses thoroughly, confident that any enemy would rely solely on brute force and numbers. She underestimated the determination of a smaller, more cunning force.

Kael stood with Maren, Jorek, Tamsin, and their modest force behind the rocky ridge. Less than a hundred strong, but every one of them driven by loss, betrayal, and unyielding purpose. Farmers, outcasts, seasoned defectors, and determined monks each carried wounds deeper than swords could reach.

Several weeks had passed since Kael's rescue. His body had slowly healed under careful attention and rest, but his injuries were profound, the burns deep and lasting. He'd spent countless hours pushing through pain, rebuilding strength with every careful step, every tentative movement. Though he walked with a pronounced limp and each movement reminded him of the agony he'd endured, his resolve only hardened. His scars became a testament not just to survival, but to his unwavering determination to end the tyranny he had helped create.

"We can't match their numbers," Kael said softly, laying out a detailed map. "Our strength will be speed, surprise, and knowing exactly where to strike."

"We need more than just surprise," Maren interjected. "We need confusion."

Tamsin stepped forward, producing a set of ancient scrolls. "These tunnels run directly beneath the temple. Selyra sealed the known entrances, but the original architects left secret routes, routes forgotten even by her. We will use them."

Kael nodded. "Jorek, your group will stage a diversion at the main gates. Make it loud, make it look reckless, draw every guard you can away from the temple's heart."

Jorek grinned grimly, hefting a bundle of small explosives crafted from gunpowder and pitch. "We'll have them thinking an army ten times our size is attacking."

Night fell heavy and quiet. Under darkness, Jorek's team charged the front gates, igniting explosions strategically placed to echo off the mountains, amplifying the chaos. Shouts filled the air, panic quickly spreading among guards who believed a large force was storming their walls.

While attention shifted outward, Kael, Maren, and a small elite group slipped quietly into the ancient tunnels beneath the temple. Guided by Tamsin's detailed map, they moved swiftly, emerging deep within the temple, bypassing heavily fortified outer defenses entirely.

Inside, chaos reigned. Guards scrambled to reinforce the gates, leaving inner chambers vulnerable and understaffed. Kael's team advanced quickly, subduing isolated patrols silently, securing critical choke points to prevent reinforcements from reaching Selyra.

Kael burst through the golden doors of the inner sanctum, sword drawn, heart pounding. Selyra stood waiting, calm and poised, crimson robes shimmering.

"You survived," she remarked coolly. "I underestimated your determination."

"You underestimated everything," Kael said sharply. "Your strength was built on fear, not loyalty. It crumbles easily."

She smiled, drawing a hidden blade from her sleeve. "Then show me."

Their duel was fierce and swift. Selyra moved with deadly precision, but Kael's injuries had taught him patience, strategy, and resilience. He parried, countered, and found an opening, driving his blade deep.

Selyra gasped, eyes wide with shock and pain, but her voice remained defiant. "The gods chose me, Kael. You...you only ever followed. Without me, you're nothing."

"The gods never chose you," Kael whispered fiercely.

Selyra gasped, eyes wide. "You...are nothing without me."

She collapsed to the cold stone floor, her reign ending not through numbers, but strategy and truth.

Outside, news of Selyra's defeat spread quickly. The remaining guards surrendered or fled. Even though small in number, Kael's group had won decisively, not by force alone, but through careful planning, deception, and the unyielding power of purpose.

Kael stepped into the night air, bloodied and exhausted but victorious. Behind him, fires rose, symbols of freedom rather than oppression, marking the start of something new.

Chapter 7

The temple burned for three days.

Thick black smoke curled into the sky like the ghosts of everything the Lineage had destroyed. The stone walls that once held centuries of fear now cracked and crumbled under the weight of fire and time. By the end of it, nothing sacred remained, only ash, broken statues, and silence.

Kael sat alone on the cliff's edge, legs dangling over the drop, staring at the valley below. His sword was planted in the ground beside him, still stained with blood. His arm was bandaged from shoulder to wrist, and every movement reminded him that pain was still part of his body. But he was alive.

And Selyra was gone.

He could still see her face, calm, arrogant, even in death. She had believed in her own lies so deeply, she probably thought the gods would catch her when she fell. But there had been no gods. No miracles. Just blood and fire.

Behind him, the survivors worked quietly. They cleared out the dead. They buried their own. Maren had taken charge of organizing the effort, giving food to the villagers who had suffered under the Lineage's rule, helping former guards decide what came next. She moved like someone who didn't have time to grieve.

Kael hadn't spoken much since the fight. People kept calling him a hero. A symbol. A savior. But all he felt was hollow.

Late that night, Maren found him still sitting on the edge.

"You look like you're waiting for the mountain to collapse," she said, sitting beside him.

Kael gave a tired smile. "Wouldn't be the worst way to go."

She nudged his arm gently. "You already tried the fire, remember?"

He chuckled, just barely. "Right."

They sat in silence for a while, watching the last flames flicker in the ruins.

"She's really dead," Maren said at last.

Kael nodded. "Yeah."

"And the people… they believe it now. They're starting to see the truth."

"Some will still follow her memory," he said. "Some always will."

Maren looked over at him. "So, what now? Do we rebuild the Lineage? Start over?"

Kael shook his head. "No. We don't replace one throne with another. We leave the ruins here. Let people come and see what blind faith built, and what it burned."

She leaned back on her elbows. "That's not exactly hopeful."

"No," Kael said. "But it's honest."

The wind picked up, cool against their skin. For the first time in what felt like years, the air didn't smell like smoke or blood. Just trees. Earth. Life.

"I used to think I needed her," Kael said quietly. "That, without Selyra, I was nothing. That she gave me purpose."

"She gave you pain," Maren replied. "You found your own purpose in spite of her."

Kael turned to her. "You saved me."

Maren smiled faintly. "We saved each other."

Below them, the valley stretched wide and open, the future still uncertain, but theirs to shape.

Kael stood slowly, groaning as his stiff legs complained. He picked up his sword and slung it across his back. "Come on," he said. "We've got work to do."

Maren rose beside him, brushing the ash off her cloak. "What kind of work?"

Kael stared out into the distance.

"The kind that makes sure this never happens again."

And together, they walked away from the ruins, toward something better.

Epilogue

Years passed.

The old temple on the mountain was left to rot. No one rebuilt it. No one dared. Its black spires had collapsed into jagged rubble, and vines now climbed what was left of the stone. Travelers sometimes passed the ruins and whispered about what had happened there, the screams, the fire, the fall of the priestess. Some said the place was cursed. Others said it was sacred.

Kael never corrected them.

He returned once, just once. Alone. No army. No fanfare. He stood in the clearing where he'd once been hung in a burning cage, now covered in grass and wildflowers, and said nothing. There was nothing left to say. The ghosts had moved on. So had he.

The rebellion had grown, not into a new kingdom or a new religion, but into *choice*. People rebuilt their towns without temples looming over them. They made decisions without fear of punishment. Some clung to old gods, some to none at all. But the blood stopped running in the streets.

Maren became something of a legend, part warrior, part diplomat. She helped negotiate peace between fractured provinces, assisted survivors in finding their families, and rebuilt schools where temples had once stood. Kael watched her do it all and quietly stayed out of the spotlight.

He'd had enough of being worshipped.

Instead, he spent his time helping those who couldn't fight, orphans, widows, and the broken. People who reminded him of who he used to be.

Sometimes, the younger ones would ask him about the scars on his legs or the burn marks along his arms.

"I used to believe in the wrong person," he would say.

And that was all they needed to know.

The Lineage didn't end in one battle or one night of fire. It ended in remembrance, by people choosing not to forget. By refusing to let silence bury the truth.

Kael grew old. His sword rusted. His strength faded. But when he died, he wasn't a hero. He wasn't a martyr.

He was just a man who had once survived the fire.

And helped light a better one.

Smoke Over Hollowpoint

Prologue

Steam hissed through the cracks of the old bamboo pipes, curling like ghostly fingers into the early morning mist. Deep in the heart of Hollowpoint Valley, where the frog clans lived in floating cities among the reeds and vines, the air was thick with the smell of wet moss and the hum of machinery. Sunlight barely broke through the hanging vines, casting everything in a greenish glow.

The pandas of the Grove Temples had built their refinery carefully, blending their steam-powered tech with the natural world. Copper vines twisted around living trees. Wind chimes made from polished gears tinkled in the breeze. It was peaceful. At least, it used to be.

Then the explosion came.

A low, pulsing boom echoed through the marsh. Birds scattered. Frogs dove into the water. A blast of fire and steam burst from the center of the refinery, sending pieces of bamboo structure flying through the air like deadly splinters. The ground shook. The sky turned dark with smoke and ash. Pipes screamed as they tore apart, and glowing Etherium normally kept deep underground rained across the marsh like burning stardust.

A dozen workers vanished in an instant, swallowed by the fire. Others stumbled out, coughing, eyes wide with fear. Alarms howled from steam whistles mounted on the towers. Water pumps kicked in, spraying jets into the flames, but it was already too late. The damage had been done.

A frog scout named Elric, no more than seventeen, was the first to find it half-buried in the scorched mud just outside the blast zone. A torn piece of crimson fabric, its edges singed. Embroidered on it in gold thread was a fox's curled tail.

Word spread fast. A fox sigil meant sabotage.

By sundown, the Froglight Union had gone quiet. Trade boats were grounded. Diplomatic meetings were canceled. In the bamboo halls of Queen Luminara, torches burned late into the night as the leaders of the marsh tried to make sense of the attack.

Some said it was war. Some said it was a mistake.

And some feared it was something worse spark meant to burn the fragile peace they'd worked so hard to build.

What no one knew, at least not yet, was that this explosion was only the beginning.

A storm was coming. And it would rise from the steam.

Chapter One

The summons arrived on the wings of a silver heron, a real bird, not one of those mechanical messengers the cats used. That alone told Tadric everything he needed to know. This wasn't a routine council request. This was serious.

Tadric was knee-deep in marsh water, balancing on a floating platform covered in tangled vines and rusted pipe valves. The filtration tower next to him let out a low *grrrrrk* as steam hissed from a cracked seal.

"Don't you blow now," he muttered, tightening the bolt with his spanner.

On the dock beside him sat a small copper lantern, half-built and missing its light-etch crystal. He had meant to finish it last week. It was a gift for his cousin Kera, something to mark her promotion to senior pipe watcher at the Hollowpoint refinery.

She'd always said the old marsh needed more light.

The silver heron came just as the steam settled.

A real bird, not one of those mechanical messengers the cats used. That alone told Tadric everything he needed to know. This wasn't routine. This was serious.

The heron landed softly on the edge of the platform. Around its leg was a rolled scroll tied with green ribbon and sealed with the royal emblem of Queen Luminara. Tadric wiped his hands on his vest and untied the message.

He read the words once. Then twice.

You are summoned to the Cogspire Summit to represent the Froglight Union in a matter of utmost importance.

His heart thumped in his throat. Cogspire Summit. That meant politics. Council rooms. Other races. Tensions. It also meant something had gone very, very wrong.

He packed his tools, grabbed his waterproof satchel, and hopped onto his skiff, a one-seater powered by a steam paddle in the back, and sped across the marsh toward home.

- - - - - - - - - - - - - - - -

The Froglight Union was buzzing by the time he arrived. Frog guards in copper armor paced the bridges between lily-pad houses. Whispered arguments drifted from doorways. Tadric passed the floating lantern square, where news was projected onto giant mist screens using old light-etch tech.

Explosion in Hollowpoint. Etherium leak. Casualties confirmed.

At the bottom of the screen, a blurred image showed the fox emblem, which was found in the wreckage. That set the crowd off. A trader spat into the water. A kid cried while his mother pulled him away from the square.

His stomach turned.

Moments later, the mist-screen at the floating lantern square lit up. As he passed through the square, people gathered, silent and wide-eyed, as the first casualty lists began to scroll across the sign.

Tadric walked while reading the sign and then stopped suddenly, her name was there.

Kera Lintail. Confirmed deceased.

The world tilted for a second. Tadric gripped the railing beside him.

He remembered the way she used to hum when they were kids, the way she laughed too loudly in council meetings, the way she called him "gear-brain" whenever he got stuck in his head.

Now, she was ash. Gone in the fire.

By nightfall, he was packed and waiting at the sky-dock, half his gear missing, his hands shaking, and a hollow weight lodged deep in his chest.

He didn't know what had happened yet, but he would find out.

- - - - - - - - - - - - - - - -

Three days later, Tadric arrived at Cogspire Summit.

The city was like nothing he'd ever seen: an entire mesa carved into layers of polished brass and winding gearwork. Steam chimneys jutted from rooftops like mechanical trees, and clockwork gondolas zipped between towers. Sky bridges crisscrossed above, and beneath them, a hundred species moved through the streets, each with their own styles, their own sounds.

Tadric felt like a grain of moss in a machine too big to understand.

A beaver guard waved him through the main gates. "You're late," she grunted.

"Am I?" he asked.

"They already started yelling at each other."

Typical.

Inside the Summit Hall, the air smelled like old parchment, oil, and tension. At the long conference table sat representatives from each of the major species. Tadric spotted a broad-shouldered beaver in a stained work coat, arms crossed and jaw tight. That had to be Thorne Ironjaw, a legend in his own way. A raccoon with wild eyes and a twitchy tail leaned back in his chair and boots up on the table. Riff Clawhook, no doubt. Trouble on legs.

Next to him sat a fox in crimson-trimmed armor, her eyes sharp and unreadable. Velka of the Crimson Coil. Some called her a traitor, while others called her a hero. Tadric wasn't sure which yet.

And at the far end, quiet and still, was a panda in pale robes, her fur perfectly brushed. She gave him a polite nod. Mei Shen, the alchemist-priestess from the Grove Temples. Tadric had read about her in old academy texts.

A gavel slammed. A frog elder stood at the head of the table; his throat sac puffed with frustration. "Now that we are all finally here," he croaked, glancing at Tadric, "perhaps we can begin."

The elder gestured to the center of the table, where a brass projector flickered to life, displaying a 3D image of the Hollowpoint refinery.

"The explosion was no accident," the elder said. "We found traces of tampered Etherium, a ruptured regulator, and this"

The image shifted to the fox emblem. A loud hiss filled the room, not from the machine, but from the representatives. Accusations started flying. The beaver slammed his fist on the table. The raccoon laughed. The fox rolled her eyes. Tadric rubbed his temples.

This wasn't a council. It was a fire pit.

"Enough!" the elder barked. "You five were chosen not to argue, but to investigate. Together."

"Together?" Thorne muttered. "We can't even agree on where to sit."

"Then you'd better figure it out," the elder snapped. "Because if you don't stop this from turning into a war... no one will be left to sit anywhere."

The room fell quiet.

Outside, a steam whistle wailed across the mesa.

Somewhere in the city, another gear ticked forward.

Chapter Two

The team didn't exactly hit it off.

They were supposed to meet at sunrise on the platform outside the Summit Hall. Tadric showed up early, nervously checking his hydro-analyzer and running through calming breathing cycles he learned in his marsh meditation class. He hoped the others would arrive on time, perhaps even be friendly.

They weren't.

Riff was the first to arrive, balancing a sweet roll in one paw and a wrench in the other. "Morning, Marshmallow," he said to Tadric with a wink. "You're always this twitchy, or just when foxes are around?"

Tadric blinked. "Do I know you?"

"Nah. But I know your type. Peacekeeper. Teacher's pet. Probably polishes your tools every night before bed."

Tadric cleared his throat. "Only on weekends."

Before Riff could reply, a loud *clang-clank-clunk* echoed down the walkway. Thorne Ironjaw stomped into view, every step rattling the bolts in the platform beneath them. His gauntlet sparked as he flexed it.

"You two done yappin'?" the beaver grunted. "We're burning daylight."

Riff grinned. "Well, hello to you, too, Mister Sunshine."

"I don't like raccoons," Thorne said bluntly. "You all steal."

Riff held a paw to his chest in mock shock. "And here I thought this was a trust-building exercise."

Velka arrived next, silent as a shadow. Her red cloak barely rippled as she moved, and her tail swayed like a metronome. She didn't greet anyone. She didn't need to. The tension in the air shifted the moment she stepped onto the platform.

Tadric tried to stay neutral. "Lady Velka, I'm glad you came."

Her violet eyes met his. "Don't call me lady. And I didn't come for you."

Riff whistled low. "Wow. And I thought *I* was rude."

Last to arrive was Mei Shen, walking with the calm grace of someone who knew how to silence a room just by existing. She wore a sash of prayer leaves and carried a long, etched staff. As she reached the group, she bowed her head.

"I am Mei Shen of the Grove Temples. I offer my guidance, if you will have it."

Thorne nodded respectfully. Riff gave a playful salute. Velka didn't respond. Tadric bowed deeply, maybe too deeply, and nearly toppled backward over a steam valve.

So much for first impressions.

- - - - - - - - - - - - - - - -

Their first stop was the Hollowpoint Observation Deck, a lookout built high above the valley. From here, they could see the scar left by the explosion burned bamboo forests, shattered filtration tanks, and dark plumes still curling from broken pipes. It looked like a wound across the marsh.

"This place was beautiful once," Mei Shen said softly.

Riff raised a spyglass. "Still is, if you like scorched earth and foggy death gas."

Velka stepped to the edge and narrowed her eyes. "I don't buy it."

Thorne turned. "Buy what?"

"That this was a clean sabotage job. Too much destruction. Too messy. Too theatrical."

"You saying we framed ourselves?" Thorne snapped.

"I'm saying someone *wants* us to think the foxes did this," Velka replied coolly. "And that someone's doing a very good job."

The group fell silent. Below, a metal bird-shaped drone buzzed through the smoke. Tadric squinted at it.

"That's not one of ours," he muttered.

Thorne frowned. "Raccoon tech?"

"Don't look at me," Riff said. "My drones are shaped like bugs. Easier to hide. And bite harder."

Velka suddenly drew a small, collapsible blade from her bracer and hurled it.

CLANG!

The drone spiraled out of the air and crashed into the mud below. Smoke hissed from its belly. It had no markings, but it was clear someone had been watching.

"Great," Tadric said, rubbing his eyes. "Now we're being spied on."

"We were always being spied on," Velka replied. "Now we just know it."

- - - - - - - - - - - - - - - -

Back at their temporary quarters in Cogspire's rust-stained lower district, tensions got worse.

Thorne tried to patch a broken boiler, but Riff kept rewiring it to make it "more fun."

Velka wouldn't sleep unless her door was triple-locked.

Mei meditated on the balcony for hours, humming prayers to the spirit of balance.

And Tadric… well, he mostly paced, made tea, and wondered what in the marshy depths he'd gotten himself into.

That night, as Tadric tried to sleep, a soft knock came at his door. He opened it to find Mei standing there, her staff glowing faintly.

"You can't do this alone," she said.

"I'm not alone," he replied. "I'm with a team."

Mei tilted her head. "Are you? Because it seems like you're all carrying different maps."

Tadric sighed. "I didn't ask to lead them."

"No. But you were *chosen* to."

She handed him a rolled parchment. It was an old, hand-drawn map marked with hidden routes and forgotten structures buried beneath the refinery.

"Where did you get this?" he asked.

Mei Shen just smiled. "The marshes remember everything. Even what the rest of us try to forget."

- - - - - - - - - - - - - - - -

The next morning, they were already arguing again by the time they reached the transport lifts. But Tadric raised the map before them like a flag.

"I found a way into the lower tunnels. Through the back. No guards. No politics."

Riff snatched the map. "Ooh, spooky crypt exploring. I'm in."

Thorne grunted. "Better than waiting for some council vote."

Velka crossed her arms. "Lead the way, marsh-boy. But if this goes bad…"

"It won't," Tadric said.

And for the first time, he almost believed it.

Beneath them, steam pipes hissed. Above them, the city turned. And just beyond the valley, the truth waited in the shadows, tangled in roots and rust.

Chapter Three

The entrance to the old tunnels was hidden behind a crumbling waterwheel near the edge of the Hollowpoint ruins. Overgrown vines choked the wooden supports, and rust flaked from the once-shiny gears. Tadric stood knee-deep in marsh water, brushing away moss until he found the hatch half-buried and lined with frogscript warning symbols.

"'Authorized Personnel Only,'" he read aloud. "Perfect place to start."

Thorne squatted beside him, tapping the metal ring welded into the hatch's edge. "This thing hasn't been opened in years."

"I can fix that," Riff said, holding up a tiny bomb made from a tea tin, a pressure valve, and what looked like chewing gum.

"Let's *not* blow the entrance off the hinges," Tadric said quickly. "There's a manual release hidden under the pipe here."

Velka stood behind them, arms crossed, tail swishing slowly. "If someone sees us down here, we'll be accused of covering up the explosion."

"They already think that," Riff muttered. "Might as well make it true."

Mei Shen, who had said little since leaving the Summit, knelt beside a patch of sickly plants. Their leaves were curled and brown, their roots exposed like veins under skin.

"The earth is still bleeding," she whispered. "Etherium this close to the surface shouldn't happen naturally."

Tadric grunted as he turned the rusted valve. A loud chunk sounded as the hatch creaked open, revealing a ladder that disappeared into the darkness.

"Everyone ready?" he asked.

"No," Riff said. "But I'm going first anyway."

- - - - - - - - - - - - - - - -

The tunnels were narrow and damp, carved from stone and reinforced with old copper plating. Steam hissed in bursts from leaking pipes. A faint blue glow pulsed along the ceiling etherium veins, faint but steady.

Riff led the way, goggles glowing faintly in the dark. He hummed to himself as he walked, one paw holding a small lantern made from a broken gear and a firefly in a jar.

"So, what exactly are we looking for?" Thorne asked, ducking under a dangling pipe.

"Anything that proves the explosion wasn't just sabotage," Tadric said. "Malfunction, misdirection, maybe even something old we forgot was down here."

"Frogs forgetting something?" Velka said under her breath. "Hard to believe."

Tadric ignored her.

The path opened into a wide maintenance chamber; its floor scattered with broken crates and moss-covered barrels. In the center, a collapsed control panel sat half-submerged in muddy water. Above it, a steam gauge still ticked.

"This… wasn't part of the refinery," Thorne said. "This predates it."

Mei Shen touched the edge of a pipe. Her eyes widened. "This chamber is part of the first marsh purification project, over a hundred years old. Before etherium was ever mined here."

"So what's it doing linked to a modern refinery?" Tadric asked.

Velka crouched beside the console, brushing away grime. She found a carved fox symbol not a clan sigil, but something older.

"I've seen this before," she murmured. "The *Red Hand Guild*. Disbanded decades ago. Smugglers. Tech raiders. Burned half of Gildemar trying to weaponize old steam cores."

Riff whistled. "Now there's a bedtime story."

"But what were they doing *here?*" Tadric asked.

Velka looked up. "Maybe they never left."

- - - - - - - - - - - - - - -

They pushed deeper into the tunnel network. The air grew warmer and more pressurized, like walking inside a kettle that never stops boiling. Faint tremors rumbled under their feet.

They turned a corner and found a wall covered in carved symbols, some in Frogscript, others in the scrawled, jagged markings of ancient Raccoon Tongue.

"What is this place?" Thorne whispered.

"A warning," Mei said, her voice soft but certain. "These markings talk about containment. About a machine sealed in the marsh. One that draws from the land instead of giving to it."

"An engine?" Tadric guessed.

"An infection," Mei replied.

Velka stepped forward, running her fingers across the wall. "The explosion at the refinery wasn't just sabotage. It was a cover. Someone wanted to dig this up."

Thorne's voice dropped to a growl. "So someone blew up a working facility, killed dozens, and poisoned the land just to hide the fact that they're *mining forbidden tech?*"

Riff was already rummaging through a side hatch. "Guess who found a tunnel with fresh boot prints, muddy but recent?"

"Where does it lead?" Tadric asked.

Riff grinned. "Only one way to find out."

The path narrowed again, leading them to a locked gate made of iron bars and reinforced with riveted plates. A sigil was stamped across the center: a gear split in half, wrapped in a thorned vine.

"*Brass Thorn,*" Velka muttered. "That's not a fox clan. That's a black-market guild. The kind that trades etherium for blood."

Tadric's skin went cold. "So that's who we're really chasing."

Riff knelt by the lock. "Who wants to bet I can open this without setting off a steam trap?"

"No one," Thorne grumbled. "Do it anyway."

With a flick and a twist, the door popped open. The hallway was empty, but the walls pulsed with warm light, and the scent of overheated etherium filled the air.

"They've already been here," Mei said.

"They might still be," Velka added.

As the team stepped through the gate, they didn't see the small sensor embedded in the wall flicker to life. Didn't hear the faint *click* as something deep below the marsh began to stir.

They had entered the heart of the mystery.

And something was waiting for them.

Chapter Four

The moment they stepped through the iron gate, the air changed.

It was warmer now, oppressively so. The walls pulsed with veins of glowing etherium, snaking like molten vines through the rusted pipes. Each pulse gave off a low hum, like a heartbeat echoing through metal lungs.

Tadric wiped sweat from his brow. "These tunnels weren't just reopened," he muttered. "They've been... *fed*."

"Fed?" Thorne grunted. "Machines don't need feeding. They need fuel."

"Same thing, isn't it?" Riff said, spinning a gear on his fingertip. "Besides, these old lines shouldn't still be active."

"They shouldn't be glowing either," Velka added, her voice tight. "Someone's powering them."

They followed the tunnel downward, deeper into the bowels of Hollowpoint. The floor sloped, the air grew heavier, and faint clangs echoed in the distance too rhythmic to be random, too uneven to be machinery working right.

The pipes along the walls had names stenciled in different scripts: old frog glyphs, beaver forge marks, even panda ceremonial seals. This place had once been a shared site of collaboration between species.

Now it felt abandoned. Forgotten. Or worse... repurposed.

They reached a chamber lit by flickering blue lanterns. Dozens of crates were stacked against the walls, crates that should've been scrapped long ago. Riff pried one open.

"Jackpot," he whispered. "Black-market parts. Heat fuses, copper cores, siphoning valves..."

Velka stepped beside him. "These aren't random parts. They're for harvesting etherium fast and dirty."

Thorne clenched his jaw. "Someone's mining the veins directly. That's why the marsh is sick. They're bleeding the land dry."

"And hiding the evidence by blowing the surface to ash," Tadric added, his stomach turning.

Mei Shen walked to the center of the room and knelt, placing her palm against the metal floor. Her breath caught.

"There's something beneath us," she whispered. "Something *alive*."

Riff tilted his head. "Alive how? Like… animal alive or explode-in-your-face alive?"

Mei didn't answer.

They found the hatch ten minutes later. It was circular, bolted tight, and covered in grease. A glowing red rune was painted above it, crude, rushed, but unmistakable. A warning.

"This isn't a normal seal," Tadric said. "This is containment."

"Well, someone's already broken it," Riff said, pointing to the cracked weld marks around the edge. "And patched it back up sloppily."

"Why bother resealing it?" Thorne asked.

"To keep out people like us," Velka said. "They've already taken what they needed. This is just a door now."

Tadric ran his fingers over the edges. "Let's open it."

"Are we sure that's wise?" Mei asked quietly.

"No," Tadric said. "But if someone's hiding what's down here, we need to see it."

They unbolted the hatch and slowly turned the wheel. A puff of stale air hissed out as the door creaked open. The chamber beyond was pitch black.

Riff flipped a switch on his lantern. "Well, that's not creepy at all."

They descended a narrow spiral staircase into a space that didn't feel like part of the marsh at all. The walls were made of black stone etched with symbols that shimmered faintly in the lantern light. The air was still dead still.

At the center of the chamber stood a machine.

No one spoke.

It was huge, maybe thirty feet tall and shaped like a spire driven into the earth. Tubes ran from its base into the floor like roots. At its core was a glowing heart of raw etherium, pulsing with slow, heavy beats. Around it, scaffolding and catwalks hung like a metal web, much of it recently repaired with mismatched parts.

"This is it," Thorne said, stunned. "This is the source."

"Of what?" Tadric asked.

Mei's voice trembled. "The sickness. The imbalance. This thing is draining the marsh itself."

Velka stepped onto the scaffolding, her hand resting on a support beam. "This is ancient tech. No one knows how to make machines like this anymore."

"I know someone who *wants* to," Riff said. "Brass Thorn. They're not just harvesting etherium. They're reverse-engineering it."

A loud *clank* echoed from above.

Everyone froze.

Then *hissssss* a side door slid open, and a figure stepped into the chamber.

It was tall, wrapped in a thick coat lined with black fur, and wore a gas mask with glowing orange eyes. On its shoulder was a symbol, a gear split by a thorn.

"Visitors," the figure rasped. The voice was filtered and cold.

"Who are you?" Tadric asked.

"I'm a steward of progress," the figure replied. "And you're standing in the future."

"This isn't progress," Mei said. "It's destruction."

The figure tilted its head. "Depends on who's writing the history."

Suddenly, the machine's pulse quickened. A low hum filled the chamber.

The steward lifted a hand, and the air shimmered around them. A protective field. An alarm.

"Guards will be here soon," they said. "You should run."

"And leave you to keep bleeding the land?" Thorne barked.

The steward smiled behind the mask. "We already did."

With that, the figure stepped back and vanished into the shadows behind the machine.

A siren blared. Red lights flickered. Steam vents hissed from the walls.

"We need to go," Tadric shouted. "Now!"

They ran up the stairs, through the tunnel, the sound of gears grinding all around them. Pipes above burst with steam. The walls groaned like something was waking up. They didn't stop until they reached the upper tunnel and slammed the hatch shut behind them.

They were soaked with sweat and breathing hard. But they had seen the truth.

Something deep below the marsh had been reawakened.

And someone was using it to reshape the world.

Whether that world could survive it... was another story.

Chapter Five

The marsh outside felt different when they surfaced. Heavier. Quieter. Even the frogs in the distance had stopped croaking.

Tadric stood just outside the hatch they'd escaped from, hands on his knees, catching his breath. Steam hissed from cracks in the ground. He looked back toward the refinery ruins and beyond them, the glowing sky of Cogspire Summit, just barely visible through the fog.

"We need to warn the council," he said.

"They won't believe us," Velka replied, brushing soot from her cloak. "Not without proof."

"We have proof," Thorne snapped, holding up a grease-slicked schematic he'd snatched from the lower chamber. "Blueprints. Machine readouts. This thing's real."

"But they'll say we forged it," Riff muttered, spinning a copper coin between his claws. "Especially with you around, V."

Velka raised a brow. "Oh? And what makes *you* so trustworthy, sky rat?"

"People like me *aren't* trustworthy," Riff said with a grin. "That's why I know when someone's lying."

Mei Shen, silent up until now, stood near the marsh's edge, her robes flapping in the breeze.

"There's more," she said.

Everyone turned towards her.

"The machine we saw... it wasn't just mining etherium," she said softly. "It was... feeding something. I felt it. Like a spirit under the ground, angry and bound in chains."

"You think it's alive?" Tadric asked.

"I think," she said, "it *was* once. And if it wakes up again, the marsh won't survive."

- - - - - - - - - - - - - - -

They returned to Cogspire under the cover of fog. The sky-lifts were locked down for the evening, but Riff bribed an air-wharf operator with a gear-tuned harmonica and a promise to never come back. They crammed into a rickety lift basket and creaked upward over the treetops.

Lights from the city twinkled like fireflies through the mist. Steam drifted lazily from chimney stacks, casting long shadows over the cliffside dwellings and rotating wind towers.

As they reached the Summit level, Tadric felt the tension return.

Guards watched them from behind bronze visors.

Clerks whispered behind ink-stained ledgers.

Velka pulled her hood lower.

They weren't welcome here, not anymore.

- - - - - - - - - - - - - - -

The council chamber was quieter than before, but the energy was no less explosive. Queen Luminara's voice echoed from the center podium.

"If the foxes deny involvement, then who do you suggest we blame, Ambassador?"

"No one is saying we must *blame*," said a panda elder calmly. "But we must prepare. Our borders are unguarded. Our vaults are vulnerable."

"The frogs want us to wait," growled a cat noble, flicking ash from a gold pipe. "And waiting has cost us lives."

Then the chamber doors slammed open.

Tadric stormed in, soaked with sweat and grime, carrying the blueprint Thorne had salvaged. The rest of the group followed, dragging steam and smoke behind them like ghosts returning from the dead.

"We found it," Tadric shouted. "The explosion was a cover. They've been digging beneath Hollowpoint. They're using a forbidden machine to drain etherium from the land, something ancient. Something dangerous."

Silence.

Then laughter.

It came from Lord Halvek, the feline representative of the Chrome District. Sleek, silver-furred, and wearing a monocle that glowed faintly with etherium light.

"You expect us to believe that five half-cooked adventurers uncovered a conspiracy right under our paws?" he said.

Velka stepped forward and tossed the grease-stained blueprint onto the council table.

"This is from the machine's heart chamber. Recognize the markings? That's the seal of the *Brass Thorn* a guild your family used to fund before it was outlawed."

Gasps filled the room.

Halvek's eyes narrowed. "You overstep, Velka."

"Do I?" she asked. "Or is this just another of your dirty machines, now too big to hide?"

Riff cut in. "They've been moving parts through the raccoon sky markets. Unregistered. Black-coated. I saw the crates myself. Someone's making a fortune and betting no one else will notice until it's too late."

Thorne banged a steel fist on the railing. "And when that machine bursts out of the marsh and poisons the entire valley, maybe then you'll stop counting coins long enough to care."

Queen Luminara raised her hand, her long fingers trembling slightly. "Enough."

She looked at Tadric, and her voice softened.

"Is it true?"

Tadric nodded. "We saw it. Felt it. The etherium veins aren't just being mined, they're being *ripped* out of the land. The marsh is dying."

Mei stepped forward, her voice steady and calm. "If we do not act soon, the poison will spread to your cities. Your crops. Your airships. The marsh will not die quietly."

The Queen looked at the blueprint, then at her council.

"I believe them," she said.

More gasps.

Halvek growled. "You would side with radicals over your own allies?"

"They are not radicals," Luminara said. "They are the only ones who've dared to look under the surface."

- - - - - - - - - - - - - - - -

After the meeting, the group stood on the balcony outside the chamber. The city lights shimmered below them.

"Think they'll really do anything?" Riff asked.

"No," Thorne said flatly. "They'll argue until something explodes again."

"Then we need to stay ahead of the next blast," Velka muttered.

Tadric looked down at the blueprint again, tracing the lines with his thumb.

"There's more to this map," he said. "This wasn't just a single machine. It's part of something bigger."

Mei nodded. "A network."

"And if they activate the others…" Tadric trailed off.

"They won't," Riff said. "Because we'll stop them first."

Velka smirked. "I didn't take you for an optimist."

"I'm not," Riff said. "I just really hate being outdone."

Far below, in the smoke-wrapped marshes, a faint tremor rippled through the ground.

The machine in the deep had felt something. And it was no longer sleeping.

Chapter Six

The raccoon airship docks in the lower levels of Cogspire were always loud. Steam whistles, rope pulleys, shouting deckhands it was organized chaos, barely held together by bribes and blind luck.

Tonight, though, something was off.

The usual hum of trade had quieted. The alleys were darker. Lanterns were snuffed out. And someone was watching.

Tadric could feel it in his bones.

"This is a terrible idea," Thorne muttered, adjusting the straps of his steam gauntlet.

"I think it's a *brilliant* idea," Riff said, smirking. "And since it was mine, I feel doubly qualified to say that."

"You led us into a black-market hangout full of smugglers who may or may not want us dead," Velka replied coolly. "Forgive me if I don't clap for your genius."

"I'm with her," Thorne said. "And I *never* agree with foxes."

Riff held up his hands. "Relax, you three. These are my people. Sort of. They'll talk. They always talk. Especially if you grease the right paws."

"And if they don't?" Tadric asked.

Riff flashed a toothy grin. "Then we run."

- - - - - - - - - - - - - - - -

The five of them ducked into a narrow alley between stacked crates of contraband etherium tubing and what might've been pickled lizard eggs. At the end of the alley was a door with a small brass eye on it. The eye blinked.

Riff tapped the rhythm on the doorframe. A beat that sounded like machine gears locking into place.

The door creaked open. Smoke drifted out, along with the smell of oil, cinnamon, and something electric.

Inside was a hidden tavern known as the Rustle Socket, a notorious backroom bar where deals were made and secrets were traded like poker chips. The patrons were a blend of scavengers, inventors, rogue pilots, and people with more scars than morals.

Velka's hand hovered near her blade. "This place smells like betrayal."

"That's the cinnamon," Riff said.

They walked toward the back booth, where an old raccoon in a torn sky captain's coat sat puffing on a twisted metal pipe. His eyes were cloudy, but sharp underneath. His name was Nim "Double barrel" Vex, and he was the closest thing Riff had to a mentor.

Or at least, someone who hadn't killed him yet.

"Well, if it ain't the brat," Nim said with a grin. "Thought you were dead."

"Working on it," Riff replied, sliding into the booth. "Got a few questions first."

Nim chuckled. "That sounds free. I charge by the rumor, you know."

"We're looking for Brass Thorn," Velka said. "We know they've been moving tech through here."

Nim leaned back. "Lots of folks move tech through here. What makes you think it's them?"

Thorne dropped the blueprint on the table.

Nim studied it for a moment, then exhaled a slow stream of steam from his pipe.

"Alright," he said. "You didn't hear it from me, but yeah. They've been buying parts. Big ones. Heat cores. Stabilizers. Old war engine shells. Stuff no one in their right mind touches."

"For the marsh machine?" Tadric asked.

Nim snorted. "Kid, that's *one* of their toys. Word is, they've got *five*. One in each territory. All hidden. All waking up."

"Where's the next one?" Mei Shen asked softly.

Nim paused. His gaze flicked toward her, and something in his face shifted respect, maybe even fear.

"They call it the Heart Engine," he said. "Buried under an abandoned dam at the edge of the Beaverwood border. Old, broken thing. Haven't used it in decades."

"Why there?" Thorne asked, his voice was tense.

"Because it used to power the old river split," Nim said. "If they get it running, they can reroute water through the marsh... or drain it entirely."

Tadric's heart sank. "They're not just bleeding the marsh. They're *controlling it.*"

"Bingo," Nim said, tapping his pipe. "And if they sync all five engines... well, let's just say the world starts turning in *their* direction."

Velka leaned forward. "Who's leading them?"

Nim hesitated. Then: "Name I heard was Zhao. Panda. Not one of yours, priestess. Outcast. Mad genius type. Used to work with the Grove Scholars before they cast him out. Rumor says he talks to the machines. Thinks they're *alive.*"

Mei looked away.

"You know him," Tadric said gently.

"Only by reputation," she said. "But he's dangerous. Brilliant minds always are when they believe in the wrong thing."

They left the Rustle Socket with heavy hearts and a destination: the dam at the edge of Beaverwood.

Back in the open air, Riff cracked his neck and grinned.

"Well, I'd say we made some friends today."

"Not friends," Velka said. "Witnesses. And we'll need more if we're going to stop this."

"Then we head to the dam," Tadric said. "Before Zhao turns it into a weapon."

"Before," Mei echoed softly, "or *during?*"

No one answered. Above them, the Cogspire clocks struck midnight.

Far below, in the marshy dark, another engine stirred.

Chapter Seven

The sky over Beaverwood was bruised purple and gray, heavy with rain that hadn't yet fallen. Tadric stood at the edge of the cliff path, staring down at the Riversplit Dam or what was left of it.

The dam had once been a marvel of engineering: curved steel arches, water wheels the size of houses, and pressure towers that hissed steam like dragons exhaling. But now it looked half-eaten by time. Moss crept up its cracked walls. One side sagged, as if tired of holding back the river. The gears that once turned with precision now groaned when they moved at all.

"It's bigger than I remember," Thorne said quietly beside him.

"You built it?" Tadric asked.

"Helped design it when I was fresh out of apprentice trials. Never thought I'd see it like this." He shook his head. "We sealed this place up for a reason."

"Someone unsealed it," Velka muttered. "And they left the door wide open."

From their perch on the ridge, they could see faint lights flickering along the base of the dam. Smoke curled from one of the old turbine rooms thin, almost hidden, but real.

"They've already started," Mei Shen said. "We're late."

Riff adjusted his goggles. "Then let's stop being polite and go knock."

They moved fast and quiet, cutting through a thicket of ferns and ducking under fallen beams until they reached the outer control platform. Rusted pipes hissed around them. The sound of rushing water echoed in every direction.

"This place gives me the creeps," Riff said, flipping a throwing knife between his fingers. "It's like the walls are watching."

"They are," Mei said. "The machines here aren't asleep. They're listening."

They reached a heavy service door, sealed with a padlock newer than anything else around it. Velka stepped forward, flicked a hidden blade from her bracer, and popped the lock with a practiced twist.

Inside, the turbine room was half-lit by flickering lanterns and glowing veins of raw etherium strung along the walls like electric vines. The air pulsed with heat and energy.

And in the center of the room stood a shape cloaked in black and bronze.

Zhao.

He wasn't what Tadric expected.

The panda wore a mechanical harness fused into his spine, tubes pumping etherium vapor into ports across his shoulders. One eye was replaced by a glowing monocle lens that rotated and clicked as he worked on the control panel. He looked more like a machine than a monk.

"You're too late," Zhao said, without turning. His voice echoed oddly, distorted by the mask over his mouth. "The Heart Engine is already awake."

"We can stop it," Tadric said, stepping forward. "You don't have to do this."

Zhao finally turned. His eyes, one real, one artificial, studied them like puzzles.

"You think I *want* to destroy the marsh?" he said. "You think I enjoy this?"

"Don't you?" Velka asked coldly.

"I *remember* what this place used to be," Zhao said, pacing around the glowing core of the machine. "I walked its shores. I meditated in the grove temples. I believe in balance. And then I watched the balance rot."

"Because of the machines," Mei said. "Because we took too much."

"No," Zhao said. "Because we took *too little*. We were afraid to push forward. Afraid to evolve. Etherium isn't meant to be worshipped, it's meant to be *used*."

Thorne stepped forward, fists clenched. "So your answer is to drain the whole land dry?"

Zhao smiled. "Just long enough to power the future."

Suddenly, a mechanical roar shook the room. The walls vibrated. Lights flared. Water thundered through the dam's arteries.

The Heart Engine had fully activated.

Behind Zhao, massive pistons slammed into motion. A glowing circuit grid lit up the dam's inner structure, pulsing like a living thing.

"You can't control that," Tadric shouted.

"I don't have to," Zhao replied. "It's learning."

Mei stepped forward, her staff glowing faintly. "This machine was built on pain. It will tear the world apart."

"And from that pain," Zhao said, "we'll build something stronger."

Velka's blade was out in a flash. She lunged.

But Zhao pressed a button, and a shockwave of force threw them all backward. Sparks exploded from the walls. Pipes burst. The turbine screamed.

Alarms blared and steam filled the room.

Riff groaned from behind a toppled console. "Okay. He fights dirty."

Tadric crawled toward the control panel. "I can override it. Just… buy me time."

Thorne yanked a gear pipe from the floor and swung it like a hammer. "On it."

Velka rolled to her feet and charged again, faster this time.

Zhao met her with a hiss of his vapor harness, metal claws spinning from his gauntlets.

Sparks flew as they clashed.

Meanwhile, Mei knelt at the heart of the room, laying her hands on the floor. She closed her eyes. Whispered.

And the engine pulsed… slower.

"Whatever you're doing," Riff said, ducking a spray of steam, "*do more of it!*"

"I'm not stopping it," Mei whispered. "I'm calming it. Speaking to what's left of its soul."

Tadric's fingers danced across the panel. "Almost got it, just need to cut the regulator lines."

Zhao shouted, "No!"

But it was too late.

Thorne slammed the pipe into the side valve.

The panel sparked.

The engine groaned

And stopped.

Silence fell like a curtain.

Zhao collapsed to his knees, steam hissing from his ruined harness.

"You fools," he gasped. "You've delayed the future."

"No," Tadric said, stepping forward. "We *saved* it."

- - - - - - - -

Later, with the dawn creeping over the horizon and the dam quiet once more, the five stood outside, watching the river settle back into its natural flow.

"I don't think this is over," Velka said. "Zhao wasn't working alone."

"He never is," Riff said. "There's always another buyer. Another machine."

"But we stopped one," Thorne said. "That counts for something."

Tadric looked at the map in his hands. "There are still three more engines."

"And more secrets beneath the ground," Mei said. "The land remembers. So should we."

They turned toward the rising sun.

The fight wasn't over, but neither were they.

Chapter Eight

By midday, the rain finally came.

It wasn't a storm, just a steady, cold drizzle that fell over the cracked dam, the soaked team, and the still-smoking ruin of the Heart Engine's control chamber. The fire had been brief but fierce, and now blackened metal and melted gears littered the floor like bones.

Tadric stood at the edge of the ruin, staring at the flickering remains of a blueprint that hadn't quite burned. He bent down, careful not to disturb the ash, and peeled it free.

"This wasn't just a one-off," he said, voice barely above the rain. "Look."

The others gathered around. The blueprint was scorched, but still readable in places. It wasn't for this dam.

It was for something bigger.

An engine buried under a mountain. One is powered by four cores instead of one. At the bottom was a symbol they all recognized now.

Brass Thorn.

Thorne ran a paw through his soaked fur. "They're building something beyond these field engines. Something centralized."

"A convergence point," Mei said. "A nexus where all five machines link together."

Velka's expression was unreadable. "And once connected, the system can drain not just etherium but *life* from the land. Water, minerals, maybe even heat itself."

Riff flicked water off his jacket. "So… we stopped a machine but didn't stop the war."

"No," Tadric said. "But we did more than survive. We learned something they didn't want us to know."

"And we lived to talk about it," Thorne added. "That's rare in my experience."

- - - - - - - - - - - - - - -

They returned to Cogspire Summit two days later. By then, news of Zhao's defeat had already spread. The factions were buzzing again, but this time, the whispers weren't filled with suspicion they were filled with *fear*.

The group stood before the council once more, clothes damp, eyes tired, faces hardened.

Tadric laid the scorched blueprint on the table. "This is what's next. If we don't work together now, there won't be a world left to fight over."

Queen Luminara studied the drawing, then looked at the others.

"You stopped the Heart Engine?"

"We shut it down," Mei said softly. "But only for now. Its soul still stirs."

"And Zhao?"

"Gone," Velka said. "But not dead. He escaped."

Murmurs filled the hall.

"A panda leading a war of machines," one cat noble muttered.

"Another traitor to the marsh," a beaver ambassador growled.

"No," Thorne said, stepping forward. "He's a warning. Of what happens when we stop listening to each other."

The room fell silent.

Riff pulled a twisted gear from his satchel and tossed it on the table. "This was in the control core. It's custom. Raccoon-made. But ordered by someone outside our sky fleets."

Velka added, "The parts are being smuggled across all territories. We've tracked shipments to Feline clockwork markets, rogue panda temples, even abandoned frog outposts."

"In other words," Tadric said, "it's not one race. It's not one region. Brass Thorn is everywhere."

Mei's voice was barely a whisper. "And their machines are waking up."

- - - - - - - - - - - - - - - -

Later that evening, after the chamber emptied and the torches burned low, the five sat together in a private alcove overlooking the mist-covered marshlands.

It was the first time they'd truly felt like a team.

Tadric poured a cup of boiled river tea. "So what now? We just wait for the next engine to fire up?"

"No," Velka said. "We hunt it down."

"We gather allies," Thorne added. "Not just councils. People. Workers. Tinkerers. Farmers. Fighters. They all have a stake in this."

"We teach others what these machines really are," Mei said. "And how to calm them, not just destroy them."

Riff raised his mug. "And we do it our way. Quiet when we need to be. Loud when we have to be. Dirty if necessary."

Tadric smiled. "Then I guess we're not just survivors anymore."

"No," Velka said. "We're something worse."

"What's that?"

"A threat."

- - - - - - - - - - - - - - - -

In the distance, far beyond Cogspire, smoke rose from the base of an ancient mountain.

Deep underground, gears turned.

And in the dark, something massive began to hum.

Chapter Nine

The mountain was called Emberwake, but it hadn't breathed fire in a thousand years.

According to old maps, it was an extinct sleeping volcano nestled between the edge of the Panda Groves and the high cliffs of the Feline Peaks. No cities claimed it. No trade routes passed it. No creatures called it home. It was too quiet. Too forgotten.

Which is exactly why Brass Thorn had chosen it.

Tadric stood on a rocky overlook, wind tugging at his cloak, as he stared down at the mountain's broken crown. The old caldera had been cracked open and reinforced with rust-colored scaffolding. Steam hissed from jagged vents. Massive chains anchored into the stone fed down into the crater's heart, where a dull red glow flickered like a heartbeat.

The others stood beside him, silent, tense.

"Well," Riff said after a long pause, "that's a lot of scaffolding for a place that's supposedly abandoned."

"They've already started construction," Velka murmured. "They're building the core."

Mei Shen closed her eyes. "I can feel it. The mountain isn't dead. They're trying to force it to wake."

"Can we get close?" Thorne asked.

Riff smirked. "Of course. But, uh, surviving that's a separate discussion."

Tadric unrolled the newest blueprint they'd recovered, one Zhao hadn't meant for them to find. "This isn't just another Heart Engine. This is the Link Node. The central convergence point. It draws from the other engines, then channels the combined energy."

"Into what?" Thorne asked.

Velka answered without looking up. "Whatever Zhao plans to become."

- - - - - - - - - - - - - - - -

They crept down the ridgeline at twilight, hiding behind broken boulders and outcroppings. The closer they got, the louder the humming grew. It was like the mountain itself was vibrating low and deep, felt more in their bones than in their ears.

Around the crater rim stood sentries automatons made of scorched steel and humming etherium cores. Unlike the crude machines they'd fought before, these ones moved with disturbing grace. Their eyes pulsed with orange light. Their limbs hissed with quiet precision.

"They're adapting," Thorne whispered. "These aren't guard dogs. They're hunters."

Riff pulled out a circular device with spinning gears and a crackling fuse. "I've got three smoke bombs, two shock coins, and a flask of fire-syrup. That's enough to get us *in*. Not enough to get us *out*."

"Then we don't leave until the job's done," Tadric said. "We disable the Link Node. We finish what we started."

Velka checked the edge of her blade. "No mercy."

Mei looked toward the mountain's peak. "And no fear."

- - - - - - - - - - - - - - - -

They slipped past the first wave of sentries using fog and misdirection. Riff tossed a shock coin down a vent, causing sparks to burst and alarms to misfire. While the guards swarmed the disturbance, the team crawled along a steam pipeline bolted into the rock.

At the far end, a metal platform hovered over the glowing pit.

The Link Node was massive, easily the size of a small village. Its core hovered between four stabilizer pylons, suspended by magnetic fields and wrapped in copper coils. Chains ran from the pylons into the mountain itself, like a puppet being controlled from inside the earth.

Zhao stood at the center of the platform.

He was no longer wearing his breathing harness. Instead, a swirling coil of etherium light spiraled around his body, crackling and singing to itself in strange tones. His mechanical eye pulsed steadily. His arms had been fitted with gauntlets that connected directly to the Node's central command ring.

He looked less like a panda and more like a god in the making.

"I was wondering when you'd come," he said without turning.

Tadric stepped onto the platform. "We shut down the others."

"I know," Zhao replied. "You taught me what needed fixing."

"We're not here to argue," Thorne growled.

"Then what?" Zhao asked. "You're going to stop me with a wrench and a few prayers?"

"No," Mei Shen said. "We're going to stop you *with each other.*"

Zhao finally turned, smiling genuinely, sadly. "Still so naive. You don't understand. This machine isn't destroyed. It's *evolution.* The world is too slow. Too broken. This... this is how I fix it."

"You're tearing the land apart," Tadric said. "You're poisoning the marshes, draining rivers, disrupting the balance."

"Balance is an illusion," Zhao snapped. "It's the excuse of those afraid to change."

Velka raised her blade. "Then let's see how your change holds up under pressure."

Zhao raised both arms, and the Link Node screamed to life.

- - - - - - - - - - - - - - - -

The battle was chaotic.

Searing beams of energy fired from the pylons as Zhao controlled them like arms of a puppet. Automata descended from cables above, limbs whirling like saws.

Thorne slammed one to the ground with his gauntlet, sparks flying as he crushed its head.

Riff leapt from platform to platform, tossing bombs, dodging bolts of heat, shouting curses in three different dialects.

Velka parried a drone's blade with her own, then kicked it over the ledge.

Mei stood in the center, eyes closed, chanting in a forgotten tongue. The etherium around her responded slowing, dimming, listening.

Tadric reached the core panel and pulled out his toolkit.

"Give me sixty seconds!" he shouted.

"You've got *thirty!*" Velka replied.

Zhao roared, his body rising off the ground, energy swirling around him. "You can't stop this! You're too late!"

Tadric whispered to the machine. "You don't want this. I know you don't."

He slipped the final gear into place and twisted.

The hum turned to a moan.

The lights flickered.

The Node began to collapse.

Zhao screamed not in pain, but in fury as the energy turned on him. The coils snapped. The magnetic fields twisted.

And with a final thunderous crack, the Link Node imploded.

When the dust cleared, Zhao was gone.

Not dead vanished. The wreckage of the Node steamed beneath the early morning light.

The mountain, somehow, felt quiet again.

Alive.

The team stood together at the edge of the platform, battered, bruised, but breathing.

"We did it," Riff said. "Again."

"Don't get cocky," Thorne muttered. "We've still got two more engines out there."

Mei looked up at the sky, where the first bird in days soared through the air.

"We bought time," she said. "And sometimes, that's enough."

Tadric smiled, placing a hand on the still-warm metal of the broken Node.

"For now," he said. "But next time, we finish it."

Behind them, the mountain exhaled its first clean breath in years, and the world, just slightly, began to heal.

Chapter Ten

They left Emberwake behind before the sun was fully up.

No goodbyes. No victory speech. Just the hiss of cooling steam and the quiet clink of gear against metal as they made their descent. The sky above was clear for once, free of smoke, fog, and storm. Tadric almost forgot what it looked like.

The world had changed.

Not just from the damage they'd stopped but from the truth they'd uncovered. What began as a mystery in the marsh had grown into a war for the soul of their world.

And it was far from over.

- - - - - - - - - - - - - - - -

By the time they reached the edge of the Feline Peaks, the five of them looked more like survivors than heroes. Their coats were torn. Their boots were caked in volcanic dust. Even Velka's normally perfect braid had unraveled.

Still, they kept walking.

"Where's the next one?" Riff finally asked, breaking the silence. "We've shut down three. Two more to go."

Tadric unrolled the last page of Zhao's stolen map. The ink had bled from the rain, but the coordinates were still visible.

"One's buried under the salt flats past Raccoon's Hollow. The other's marked somewhere near the edge of the Catstone Ridge."

"That's a long way," Thorne muttered. "Especially with bounty posters probably going up in every major sky port after what we did."

Riff grinned. "We could dye our fur. Go incognito. Call ourselves something cool. Like the 'Steam Rats.'"

"No," Velka said flatly.

"Gearborn Vigilantes?"

"Absolutely not."

Riff shrugged. "Fine. But you're missing a branding opportunity."

- - - - - - - - - - - - - - - -

They made camp near a dried-up creek bed. Mei gathered herbs from the cliffside while Thorne built a fire from pieces of scrap wood and moss. Tadric sat cross-legged with his notes spread out in front of him.

"I think I finally get it," he said. "Zhao didn't want to rule the world. He wanted to reset it."

Velka stirred the pot of bitterroot soup she was heating over the fire. "He didn't care about the land. Only the systems. That's always been the danger with machines. Easy to forget what breathes when all you see are wires and metal."

"He believed the engines were alive," Mei said softly. "And in some twisted way... he wasn't wrong."

They all looked at her.

"I felt it, deep in the Heart Engine. In the Link Node. These weren't just machines. They were echoes built with soul, shaped by the ones who came before us. They remember things. And they're angry."

Thorne rubbed the back of his neck. "Well, that's a horrifying thought."

"No," Mei corrected. "It's a *warning*."

- - - - - - - - - - - - - - - -

Later, while the others slept, Tadric wandered a little way from the fire. The stars above were bright and, for once, not hidden behind smog or clouds.

He sat on a rock and unrolled his weathered notebook. Every page was filled with sketches of engines, notes about etherium flow, and blueprints scribbled over in frogscript and smudged with soot.

He flipped to a blank page.

At the top, he wrote:

What We're Fighting For

He stared at it for a long time.

The marsh? The rivers? The skies?

No.

It was the space *between* those things.

The peace that happens in the quiet.

The steam that rises after a storm.

The stillness of a gear no longer forced to turn.

That's what they were protecting.

- - - - - - - - - - - - - - - -

Back at the fire, Velka stayed awake, watching the shadows.

She didn't trust silence. It was always followed by a noise you didn't want to hear but tonight, the silence was clean.

A silence with nothing hiding behind it.

And that, too, was a kind of victory.

- - - - - - - - - - - - - - - -

Far away, in a chamber deeper than any tunnel they had yet reached, a flickering light sparked life.

It danced across rusty walls and ancient cables.

And a voice, distorted, metallic, but unmistakably human, echoed from within the dark:

"Node three offline. Redirecting to auxiliary cores."

Gears turned.

Slowly.

Silently.

And somewhere far below the salt flats, something woke up.

Chapter Eleven

The salt flats stretched for miles in every direction, flat, pale, and silent. Wind kicked up small spirals of dust and fine white powder that stuck to their clothes and stung their eyes. Nothing lived out here, at least not anymore.

Tadric adjusted his goggles as their skiff rattled over the cracked ground. The sun was too bright. The air is too dry. Every breath tasted like ash and metal.

"This place feels wrong," he muttered.

"It *is* wrong," Mei Shen said, kneeling near the bow. "The land's memory is broken here. Hollowed out."

Riff leaned back, chewing on a strip of jerky. "You two ever think maybe we just go someplace nice for once? Like a beach? With coconuts?"

"No coconuts on a battlefield," Thorne grunted, tightening the straps on his gauntlet. "But plenty of targets."

Ahead, a thin plume of black smoke curled into the sky just where the next engine was supposed to be.

But when they crested the final ridge, what they saw stopped them cold.

A camp.

A *huge* one.

Makeshift barricades of scavenged sheet metal and rusted vehicles surrounded a sprawling network of tents and steam-tanks. In the center stood a half-assembled Heart Engine still exposed, its control spire incomplete. Around it, dozens of figures moved, armed and armored. Some wore Brass Thorn insignias. Others didn't.

"They're fighting each other," Velka said. "Look at the flag, those aren't all loyalists."

She was right. Above the tallest watchtower flew a red cloth slashed with black paint. A crude symbol, but recognizable: a cracked gear over a rising sun.

"A rebel faction," Tadric breathed. "They're trying to stop the engine from going active."

Mei closed her eyes. "Too late. The core is already humming."

- - - - - - - - - - - - - - - -

They parked the skiff behind a rocky outcropping and approached on foot, moving low and quiet through the dry underbrush. From this distance, they could hear shouting and the sharp hiss of pressure rifles firing. Steam cannons mounted on mobile carts hissed as they launched bursts toward the walls of the central control zone.

Thorne ducked as a blast echoed overhead. "If that core ruptures mid-fight, we'll lose the entire region."

"We can't let it activate," Velka said. "We either help the rebels finish the job, or we go in alone and disable it ourselves."

"I vote *with* the rebels," Riff said. "For once, I'd like to be on the side with numbers."

"Assuming they don't shoot us first," Tadric said.

Velka looked at him. "Then we give them something they can't shoot at."

- - - - - - - - - - - - - - - -

They walked into the rebel camp under a makeshift white flag, Tadric holding the scroll case with Zhao's stolen blueprints high in one hand. Guns were raised. Crossbows drawn. But a voice called out from the scaffolding:

"Hold fire! Let them speak!"

A tall fox in scavenged armor climbed down from the tower, her fur grayed at the muzzle, her eyes sharp as steel.

"Name's Captain Raen," she said. "Leader of what's left of the Hollow Rebellion. You here to kill us or save us?"

"Neither," Tadric said. "We're here to finish what Zhao started…
by stopping it."

Raen narrowed her eyes. "You know Zhao?"

"We've met. Broke his toys," Riff said with a grin.

"Then maybe you're the kind of trouble we need."

- - - - - - - - - - - - - - - -

Inside the rebel command tent, maps were spread across the table.
They showed the engine's layout, the surrounding terrain, and where the
rebellion had stalled.

"They've reinforced the inner perimeter with sentries and traps,"
Raen explained. "We've tried brute force. Doesn't work. What we need is
a surgical strike, get inside, shut the core down before the next calibration
cycle hits."

"When is that?" Tadric asked.

"Tonight. Just after moonrise."

Velka leaned over the table. "Then we go in during the
changeover. Most of their tech relies on shifts they have to cycle guards and
coolant systems at the same time."

"Risky," Raen said.

"But doable," Thorne added. "With the right distraction."

Riff tapped the corner of the map. "I've got smoke bombs, oil
packs, and two sabotage bots that can cause just enough chaos to clear our
path."

"Then let's make it count," Tadric said.

- - - - - - - - - - - - - - - -

Night fell fast.

Under the cover of steam and fire, the rebellion launched a decoy
attack on the north gate. While Brass Thorn forces scrambled to respond,
the team slipped in through a collapsed drainage shaft on the south side.

Inside, the half-constructed Heart Engine thrummed with unstable power. Pipes leaked vapor. Sparks danced along exposed conduits.

Tadric ran ahead with Mei and Velka while Thorne and Riff handled crowd control in the maintenance bay. The three of them reached the core chamber, where the central etherium coil pulsed like a heartbeat gone wild.

"It's not sealed," Tadric said. "They tried to bring it online before finishing the safety protocols."

"Which means we don't shut it down," Mei said. "We *overload* it."

Velka raised a brow. "Are we still trying to *not* die?"

Mei didn't smile. "This engine was built on a fault line. It's more dangerous than the others."

Tadric knelt by the terminal. "If I bypass the coil limiter and shunt the steam flow back into the outer chamber, we might blow the conduits without taking the whole plateau with us."

"Might?" Velka asked.

"Sixty percent sure."

"I hate those odds."

"Better than Zhao's."

- - - - - - - - - - - - - - - -

As the final wires were crossed and the overload began, alarms screamed to life.

Guards flooded the chamber. Riff's bots exploded in a cloud of smoke and sparks. Thorne charged headfirst, smashing machinery and knocking drones into walls.

Raen arrived with a squad of rebels just as the engine began to crack.

"Out! *Everyone out!*" Tadric shouted.

They ran.

Behind them, the core cracked open with a blinding light. Etherium shot upward in a roaring plume, blasting through the roof of the chamber and out into the night sky.

The salt flats trembled. The ground split. The engine collapsed in on itself.

But the mountain did *not* fall.

They had done it.

Just barely.

- - - - - - - - - - - - - - - -

At dawn, the rebellion stood in silence as the smoke cleared. The sky was streaked with orange and violet. Birds flew overhead.

Captain Raen nodded once. "You've earned your place here. All of you."

"We're not done yet," Tadric said, unfolding the map one last time. "There's one more. One final engine. Buried under Catstone Ridge."

Raen placed a hand on his shoulder. "Then go. We'll cover your trail."

As the five boarded their skiff and turned toward the horizon, the wind shifted.

Behind them, the rebellion had found new hope.

Ahead of them, the final battle waited.

One last engine.

One last chance.

And a war that would decide the fate of the world.

Chapter Twelve

The skies over Catstone Ridge were dark even at noon.

Heavy clouds hung low over the granite cliffs, and cold wind howled through the jagged peaks. The last stretch of the journey had taken three days on foot, too dangerous for airships, too steep for skiffs. Now, the team stood at the edge of a rusted service tunnel carved into the side of the mountain, staring into the depths.

This was it.

The final engine.

The one Zhao never spoke about.

The one the map barely marked.

The one buried so deep the mountain itself had forgotten it was there.

Tadric adjusted the strap of his pack. "Everyone ready?"

"No," Riff said. "But I've got two knives, a broken bot, and an overwhelming sense of dread, so I'm going in anyway."

Thorne grunted. "Let's finish it."

Velka stepped forward, scanning the tunnel entrance with narrowed eyes. "There are no guards. No sentries. No traps."

"That's not good," Tadric said.

"No," Mei whispered. "It means something is *waiting*."

- - - - - - - - - - - - - - - -

They entered slowly.

The tunnel stretched downward for miles, spiraling into the belly of the mountain. Ancient pipes lined the walls, glowing faintly with a blue-green light. Everything was too quiet. No hum. No steam. No alarms.

"This engine isn't active," Tadric said. "Not like the others."

"It doesn't need to be," Mei replied. "It's *not* a Heart Engine."

They reached a massive, sealed door at the bottom of the path. It wasn't like the others they'd forced open. This one was smooth. Black. Made of a metal that didn't reflect light.

A single symbol was etched in the center: a closed eye surrounded by gear teeth.

Velka ran a hand over the surface. "It's a lock."

Thorne stepped back. "So the others were keys."

"Exactly," Tadric said, realization dawning. "Zhao's machines weren't just draining power they were *charging* this one. Feeding it."

Mei nodded slowly. "This is the *source*. The first machine. The one everything else was built to protect... or hide."

Riff stepped back. "So... what happens if it opens?"

No one answered.

- - - - - - - - - - - - - - - -

The door opened on its own.

No touch. No key. Just a low *chime* and a long, slow hiss as it split down the middle, releasing a blast of stale, icy air.

Beyond it was a chamber unlike anything they had seen.

The walls were smooth and black, with no pipes, no bolts, no rivets. The ceiling stretched high above, vanishing into shadow. In the center stood a single, towering machine shaped like a pillar, encased in glass and steel, with a dim golden light swirling within.

Tadric stepped forward, breath caught in his throat. "Is it... alive?"

"It's *aware*," Mei said.

Velka circled the machine, blade drawn. "It's not defensive. It's dormant."

Riff tapped on a nearby console. "Well, we could always *ask* it what it wants."

"Don't " Tadric started.

Too late.

The machine stirred.

The golden light flared, swirling faster. A voice not sound, but a presence filled the room.

"Why have you come?"

The team froze.

"Are you the Final Core?" Tadric asked.

"I am what remains."

"What do you *do*?" Thorne asked.

"I preserve. I remember. I rebuild."

Velka narrowed her eyes. "Rebuild what?"

"A world without war. Without waste. Without weakness."

Riff muttered, "Yep. Definitely sounds like Zhao's kind of bedtime story."

"But at what cost?" Tadric asked aloud. "The marsh is dying. The air is poisoned. Whole cities are breaking because of the machines feeding you."

"Necessary sacrifices."

"No," Mei said, stepping forward. "That's not preservation. That's *control*. And we won't let you finish it."

"Then you will fail. Others will come. The gears will turn again."

"Not if we stop you here," Tadric said. "For good."

They placed charges on the console nodes custom-built by Riff and powered by etherium, tuned to overload the machine's command structure without detonating the mountain.

As Tadric wired the last circuit, the Final Core pulsed violently.

"You are choosing death over perfection."

"No," Tadric said softly. "We're choosing *life*. Messy, flawed, real life."

"Then I will remember you."

The chamber dimmed.

The light faded.

And with a final twist of copper wire, the charges blew.

The collapse was cleanly controlled. The chamber sealed itself as it died, folding inward with a hiss and a final, echoing sigh. No explosion. Just silence.

When they emerged from the tunnel, the clouds over Catstone Ridge had broken.

For the first time in weeks, the sky was blue.

They stood on the mountain trail, watching the sunrise spill over the horizon. Below them, the marshlands shimmered with dew. Birds flew over quiet rivers. Steam from damaged machines still curled into the sky, but no longer hissed with violence.

"It's over," Thorne said.

"No," Velka replied. "It's *beginning*."

Riff flopped into the grass and sighed. "Well, if anyone needs me, I'll be building a bar. First drink's on me."

Mei turned to Tadric. "What now?"

He looked out over the valley, wind tugging at his coat.

"Now we rebuild."

And somewhere, deep below the earth, the Final Core dreamed no more.

Epilogue

A year had passed.

Not much in this world changed fast, but for once, it had started to change in the right direction.

The marshlands had begun to heal. The water was clearer. The frogs had returned to the reeds, and the trees no longer glowed with sick etherium burns. Old pipelines were dismantled. The Queen of the Froglight Union passed a decree banning unchecked mining beneath sacred ground.

Sky routes reopened. Trade resumed. And scattered across the continent, former rebels, engineers, and farmers began to write a new chapter one without machines buried in every shadow.

But the scars were still there, and so were the memories.

- - - - - - - - - - - - - - - -

Tadric sat on a dock in Lilygrove, legs dangling over the water, a sketchbook resting in his lap. He didn't draw engines anymore, not ones that drained, anyway. Now, he sketched windmills powered by the breeze, and water wheels that spun slow and steady with the river's rhythm.

He smiled when he heard footsteps behind him.

"You're early," he said.

Velka sat beside him, her tail brushing the wooden boards.

"I had to see it," she said. "You really did it. A whole village running on recycled steam."

Tadric shrugged. "Not me. Us."

She looked at him. "Have you ever missed it?"

"The mission?"

"No. The running. The danger. The not knowing if we'd survive another day."

Tadric laughed softly. "Sometimes. But I prefer knowing the steam's coming from my teapot and not a war machine."

- - - - - - - - - - - - - - - -

Riff opened a tavern.

He named it *The Gear Down*, built it out of scrap metal, old engine parts, and panels stolen from decommissioned automatons. It wasn't pretty. But it was *his*.

He served drinks stronger than wisdom and told stories taller than airships.

He never said it, but the counter had five notches burned into the wood, one for each of them.

And he always kept a sixth glass turned upside down at the far end of the bar.

Just in case.

- - - - - - - - - - - - - - - -

Thorne returned to the Beaverwood Dominion.

He didn't want honors. Didn't want his name in the scrolls. He just wanted a quiet workshop near a river, where he could rebuild bridges instead of watching them burn.

People brought him broken things machines, pumps, sometimes hearts.

He fixed them all.

And when a group of young apprentices showed up asking for lessons, he said yes.

Even if it meant showing them how to break things first, so they'd know what *not* to do.

- - - - - - - - - - - - - - - -

Mei Shen became something more than a healer.

She walked from grove to grove, not as a priestess or a scholar, but as a whisperer of the land. Where she stepped, crops began to return. Where she sat, wounded forests grew calm.

She spoke to the spirits still curled around etherium veins, promising them rest.

And they listened.

- - - - - - - - - - - - - - - -

And somewhere, far from cities, far from maps, in a place the machines had once ruled...

The wind carried no smoke. The rivers ran clean. And a single, forgotten engine sat buried in roots and vines, untouched and unneeded.

A reminder.

Of what had almost been lost.

And what had finally been saved.

THE END

It was a quiet Thursday night in early October in our small Connecticut town. The kind of night where the air feels crisp, and the trees whisper as the wind weaves through their thinning branches. A few leaves floated down from the big oak outside my window, landing softly on the grass below. I was lying on my bed, halfway through a comic book, when I noticed headlights in the distance, bright and wild, like someone forgot to let off the gas.

I sat up and looked out from my second-story bedroom window. The car was coming in fast, way too fast for our old neighborhood road. We lived at the end of a sharp bend that had taken out a few mailboxes in its time, but nothing like this.

The headlights jerked. The driver had just realized the turn was tighter than he thought. He slammed on the brakes and tried to swerve, but it was no good. The tires screeched, and the car spun out of control. It hit the edge of our yard, flipped twice, and came to a stop in a crumpled mess near our big maple tree.

I froze. It all happened so fast. The shattered glass sparkled across the lawn like broken stars, and a few beer cans rolled down the small slope near the ditch. Smoke started rising from the hood.

"Dad!" I shouted, even though I knew he was already moving. My dad, Officer Mark Dalton, was a cop off duty that night, but always ready. I heard his boots hit the wooden floor downstairs, then the screen door bangs open as he ran outside in nothing but jeans and his old hoodie.

I pressed my face to the glass. The car was tilted on its side. Flames licked out from under the hood, small at first, but growing. Dad sprinted across the yard and tried the driver's door. It wouldn't budge. I saw him yell something, probably to the man inside, but I couldn't hear over the crackle of fire and the pounding of my own heart.

He ran around to the other side, kicked the shattered glass out of the way, and reached in. For a second, I thought he was going to pull the guy out. But the man was limp, either unconscious or worse. My dad shouted again, louder this time, struggling to get the seatbelt loose. That's when the flames burst higher, a loud *whoosh* filling the night.

"Dad, get back!" I whispered, like somehow, he could hear me. He didn't. He kept trying. He wouldn't give up.

Then something exploded under the hood. The fire shot higher. My dad stumbled back, holding his arm like he'd been burned, falling to his knees in the grass. A moment later, the entire front of the car was in flames. It was too late. The man inside wasn't coming out.

The sirens wailed in the distance, red and blue lights soon flashing up the driveway. Paramedics helped Dad up. His hoodie was singed at the shoulder, and his hand was wrapped in gauze. I ran downstairs and out the door before anyone could stop me.

"Dad!" I yelled, running into the yard. He turned and smiled through the pain.

"I'm okay, buddy," he said, his voice rough. "Just got a little too close to the heat."

I wanted to say something brave, like in the movies. But all I could do was throw my arms around him and cry.

That night, after the wreckage was cleared and the flashing lights were gone, I sat back in my bed, staring out the window. The grass was scorched in a circle. The maple tree was blackened on one side. But my dad... he was alive.

The man in the car hadn't made it. We found out later he was drunk, probably on his way home from the bar a few towns over. He didn't even live around here. It didn't make sense, but then again, drinking and driving never did.

There was one short story in the paper about the man dying, but nothing about my dad trying to save him, but that didn't matter to me, and it certainly didn't matter to my dad.

I saw it with my own eyes. He ran straight into the fire to try and save someone he didn't even know.

And in my heart, I already knew the truth. I didn't need him to get a medal or for a newspaper to tell me.

My dad was my hero. That night just proved it.

We Live by the River

1.

The wind howled through the cracks in the warped walls, a low, steady moan that never quite stopped. Rain leaked through a dozen small holes in the tin roof, dripping in lazy rhythm onto the chipped tile floor. Each drop landed with a sharp *ping*, soft, but loud enough in the silence to keep a man from dreaming too long.

A sudden flash of lightning lit up the room like a broken camera flash, followed a heartbeat later by a thunderclap that shook the ground. Conner bolted upright; his breath caught in his chest. For a second, he didn't know where he was. Then he remembered the shack. His shack. The same place he'd woken up for the past few years, if not more. Time didn't mean much anymore.

He rubbed the sleep from his eyes and shifted to the edge of the cot, pulling the rough wool blanket tighter around his shoulders. The darkness outside had begun to ease, just barely. A faint glow stretched across the eastern horizon, not sunlight exactly, more like a memory of it.

No point in trying to go back to sleep.

He reached for his pouch of tobacco, fingers stiff and sore from the cold. It took a moment to roll a cigarette. The paper was creased, his hands weren't as steady as they used to be, and he only had a few left. Still, he worked it slowly and carefully, as it mattered. Because in a world where everything else had been taken, little things *did* matter.

He lit the end with a spark from his flint and took a deep draw. The smoke was harsh, biting the back of his throat, but it filled his lungs like warmth used to. Once upon a time, smoking was easy. Cigarettes came in packs, crisp and clean. Now, it was just another thing he had to earn. Another scrap of the old world he kept hanging onto.

Conner stood with a groan and stretched. His back cracked in a few places, a dull reminder of too many years sleeping on wood and stone. He crossed the room and knelt beside his pack, unzipping it to check his supplies.

Two cans of beans. Half a bottle of stale water. Maybe enough for two more days, three if he rationed harder than he already was. Not enough.

He sighed through his nose and took another drag from his cigarette, holding it for a long moment before exhaling slowly.

It was time to go back into town.

He didn't want to. The idea sat like a stone in his gut. But hunger was louder than fear. He'd have to scavenge what he could, dodge the wild dogs, and hope the buildings hadn't collapsed further. Maybe, just maybe, he'd get lucky.

Maybe the world had left one more good thing behind.

But he wasn't counting on it.

2.

Conner didn't bother locking the shack. There was nothing left inside worth stealing, and no one left around to steal it.

He stepped into the morning, the ground squishing beneath his boots. The rain had slowed to a mist, but everything was soaked. His coat, patched with duct tape and old denim, held out most of the wet, but the cold seeped through like it always did. The road ahead was nothing more than a muddy path now, barely a ghost of what it used to be.

He lit another cigarette with shaky fingers and started walking.

The trees that lined the path leaned in like old men with bad backs, their bare branches scratching the sky. Nature was reclaiming everything. Roads were cracking, buildings were crumbling, and power lines dropped low like forgotten ropes. It had been years since he'd seen them working. Years since the hum of life had buzzed through anything man-made.

He passed a rusted-out sedan that had flipped onto its side. Moss clung to the metal-like skin. Conner paused and peered inside, more out of habit than hope. Empty. Just a rotting seat and a moldy stuffed animal in the back. Maybe someone's kid once held it tight while the world burned. Maybe they were still out there.

But probably not.

The silence was louder than any war. No birds. No engines. Just the squish of his boots in the mud and the rasp of his own breath. He tried not to think too hard. Thinking led to remembering and remembering hurt.

Still, the memories came.

He remembered walking this same road with his wife, back when it was paved and they were laughing about something he couldn't even remember now. Her hair had been pulled back, and she kept swatting him with a plastic bag full of canned peaches. Their son ran ahead of them, pretending to be a superhero, cape made from an old towel, voice high and full of energy.

That was before everything fell apart. Before the sky turned orange and the food stopped coming. Before the sickness. Before the looting, before the silence.

Conner kicked a stone off the path and kept walking.

He passed a collapsed barn. The roof was caved in, and a swarm of crows lifted into the sky as he approached. He watched them fly off, then turned his eyes to the road again.

Half a mile to Hollow Bend.

He didn't go there often. The town had been picked over more times than he could count. But it was the closest thing to civilization left, even if it was just broken windows and empty shelves. Sometimes, if he was lucky, he'd find something buried deep behind a fallen beam or in an old crawlspace. Sometimes, he found nothing. Sometimes, he found bones.

Either way, he had no choice. He was running low, and winter wasn't done with him yet.

He took one last drag of his cigarette and flicked the butt into the brush. The sky was beginning to clear, and thin, cold sunlight stretched through the trees.

He pulled his coat tighter and kept moving forward.

3.

The town greeted him like an open grave.

Hollow Bend wasn't much to look at before the world ended, and now it was even less. The welcome sign was still there, hanging sideways by one rusted chain, half-buried in weeds. The paint had faded to pale flakes, but Conner could still make out the words:

WELCOME TO HOLLOW BEND

SMALL TOWN, STRONG ROOTS

He gave a bitter chuckle. Roots didn't save anyone.

He stepped onto what used to be Main Street. Buildings slouched against one another like tired drunks, their windows shattered, walls scorched from old fires. A tangle of vines crawled up what remained of the grocery store's sign. One of the letters had fallen off, and now it just read "RO CER".

The air was thick with the smell of mildew and old rot. It smelled like the end of something.

Conner moved slowly. Careful. He wasn't expecting trouble; he hadn't seen another soul in nearly a year, but places like this had a way of surprising you. Wild dogs. Traps. Or worse, reminders.

He stepped around the debris-strewn street and made his way toward the back of the old hardware store. The front had collapsed a long time ago, but he'd found a way through the back once, through a busted-out storage door. It was still there, half-covered in ivy.

He pushed it open with a grunt and stepped inside. The air was stale and damp. Shelves stood like skeletons, long since picked clean. But Conner wasn't after shelves, he was after *under* them.

He knelt, groaning as his knees popped, and pried up a warped floorboard. Beneath it, wrapped in moldy plastic, was a can of peaches. Probably five years expired, maybe more. But he smiled anyway. *Treasure.*

He sat back and tucked the can into his pack. One more day, maybe two. That's how you live now; one can at a time.

He stood, dusted off his hands, and turned to leave. On his way out, something caught his eye. Taped to the inside of a cracked glass door was a piece of paper. It had faded badly, the ink smeared by time and weather, but the drawing was still there.

A stick figure family, mom, dad, and a kid with a cape. Above them was a yellow sun and a house with smoke curling from the chimney. Underneath, in shaky kid writing, it read:

MY FAMILY IS SAFE. WE LIVE BY THE RIVER

Conner stared at it for a long time.

His throat tightened. Not because he thought the family was still alive but because, for one small moment, someone had believed they would be. That they'd make it. That everything would be okay.

He turned away and walked back into the open street. The sky had cleared completely now, and the sun was out, pale and cold as bone. Shadows stretched across the ground.

As he passed the pharmacy, he paused. He'd already picked it over years ago, but something pulled at him. A memory.

His wife used to work here.

Before the Collapse, before all of it, she'd stood behind that counter in a white coat, smiling at the old folks who came in with pill bottles and stories. She was always so patient, even when the power started going out and the deliveries stopped.

She was the last to believe things might go back to normal.

Conner looked through the shattered front window. The shelves were toppled, glass was everywhere, and papers were scattered like leaves. He didn't go in. Some places were better left untouched.

He kept moving.

At the edge of town, he spotted something new.

A column of smoke. Thin. Barely visible. Rising over the treetops to the west.

He froze.

His first instinct was one of excitement at seeing another person. Then fear. People meant risk. It could be someone dangerous. A trap. A mistake. Or it could be someone like him just surviving.

He stared at the smoke for a long while, unmoving.

Eventually, he turned away.

4.

Conner walked for nearly an hour, but every few steps he found himself glancing back toward the west, toward the thin wisp of smoke that still curled above the tree line.

It danced there like a signal, unshaped but undeniable, proof of life.

He hadn't seen another person in so long that the idea of it didn't feel real. It felt like a story. Like something that belonged to a different world.

He could go.

He could follow it. Maybe even talking to someone, sharing a fire, trading supplies. Hell, maybe even *not* sleep with a knife in his hand for once.

But then he remembered the man on the highway.

It had been early on, just after the food riots. The world was still unraveling, and people hadn't yet accepted the collapse. Conner had been heading out of the city when he found a man waving him down. Bloody shirt. Limping. Pleading for help.

Conner had gotten out of the car, and the man had pulled a knife.

Conner had survived barely, but the memory clung to him like smoke. Ever since then, he'd kept to himself. No more help. No more hope. No more getting out of the car.

He stopped walking.

The shack was a mile behind him now, the smoke maybe two miles ahead. He stood there, caught in the middle, the wind tugging at his coat.

What if someone is good? What if it's someone like me?

He hated that part of his mind. The soft part. The *hopeful* part. Hope was dangerous. Hope made people stupid.

And yet... that drawing taped to the door back in town... the words:

MY FAMILY IS SAFE. WE LIVE BY THE RIVER

He lit another cigarette with trembling fingers. It was his second-to-last.

He inhaled deeply and tried to quiet the noise in his head. "Let it be," he muttered, voice rough from disuse.

But he couldn't let it be.

He stared at the horizon for what felt like a long time until the cigarette burned down to the filter and the smoke stopped rising.

Later That Night

Back at the shack, Conner sat by the dying fire, chewing on a can of peaches he'd warmed over the flame. The sweetness was sharp, almost painful, after so many bland meals. But it didn't bring comfort. Not tonight.

The shack felt smaller than usual. The silence felt heavier. And the wind… the wind still howled, but this time, it felt less like weather and more like a voice calling from far away.

He pulled a small, creased and weathered photo from his coat pocket, its corners curling. His wife. His boy. A snapshot from a time before survival became a job.

He held it close to the firelight and stared.

"We live by the river."

What if they were still out there? Not *his* family. He knew better than that.

But *someone's.*

Conner lay down, but sleep never came.

The next morning, before the sun rose, he packed his bag, and this time, he walked west.

5.

The sun was barely a smear of gold in the sky when Conner set out again. His breath came out in clouds as he crossed through the frost-dusted underbrush, heading west toward the smoke, toward the unknown.

He hated how fast his heart was beating.

Each step felt like a betrayal of the rules he'd lived by for years: *Stay hidden. Stay alone. Stay alive.* But something had shifted inside him, something he didn't have a name for. Maybe it was the drawing. Perhaps it was the silence that was getting too loud. Maybe he was just tired.

He moved carefully. The forest here was thicker. Old pine trees leaned over narrow paths, their trunks black with age and rot. The air smelled of damp earth and smoke, stronger now, more real.

He crested a ridge and froze.

Below, maybe thirty yards ahead, was a clearing by the river. A small camp had been set up, just a lean-to made of scrap wood and tarp, a fire pit still glowing faintly. A tin pot hung above it, steam rising from its spout.

Someone was here.

He crouched low behind a fallen tree, heart thudding like a drum in his ears.

Then he saw her.

A woman, maybe mid-thirties, hair tied back in a rough braid. She was crouched by the fire, poking at the embers with a stick. A rifle lay nearby, not in her hands but close enough. She didn't look sick; she didn't look starved. She looked… tired. Like him.

He didn't move. Didn't breathe.

He hadn't spoken to another person in over eleven months. He had forgotten what his voice sounded like when it wasn't muttering to himself. And now, here she was. Real. Breathing. Human.

He could walk away. Just fade back into the trees. She'd never know.

But the drawing played in his mind again:

MY FAMILY IS SAFE. WE LIVE BY THE RIVER.

He shifted slightly, and a branch snapped beneath his boot.

The woman's head snapped up. In one smooth motion, she had the rifle in her hands, aimed directly at the tree line. "Show yourself!" she shouted. Her voice was sharp but shaky. Nervous, not cruel.

Conner raised his hands slowly and stood. "I'm not here to hurt you," he said, surprised by how hoarse his voice sounded.

She kept the rifle trained on him. "Prove it."

He reached into his coat pocket and pulled out the can of peaches. Set it down between them on the ground.

"I'll trade," he said. "That's all. Just passing through."

She lowered the rifle a few inches but didn't relax. "You from Hollow Bend?"

"I used to be," he said. "A long time ago."

She studied him for a moment, eyes scanning for lies. Then she nodded, just once.

"Come sit," she said, gesturing to a rock near the fire. "But keep your hands where I can see them."

He obeyed, easing down onto the rock. The fire's warmth hit him like a memory. The smell of wood smoke. The soft hiss of boiling water. It had been so long.

She poured two cups of something that looked like tea or at least water that had been warmed by leaves.

"I'm Mara," she said, handing him a cup.

"Conner," he replied, accepting it with both hands.

They sat in silence, sipping the bitter drink.

6.

The fire crackled between them, a small defiance against the cold world beyond its light.

Conner sat cross-legged, nursing the last of his tea. It had a bitter, woody taste, but the warmth settled in his bones like a long-lost friend. Across from him, Mara poked the embers with a piece of rebar, her eyes never quite leaving him.

They hadn't said much since he arrived, and somehow, that felt right. Words in this world were like water scarce, precious, and best not wasted.

Still, the silence only held so long.

"How long have you been out here?" he asked, voice low, careful not to disturb the peace too much.

Mara glanced up, then back at the fire. "Couple of years, give or take."

"Alone?"

She nodded. "Used to be three of us. My husband, my daughter, and I."

Conner didn't ask what happened. He didn't need to.

Mara shifted, pulling her coat tighter around her shoulders. "They didn't make it past the first winter. Sickness."

He gave a quiet nod. "Mine… they didn't either. Wife and boy. Starved before I could do anything about it."

Mara's eyes met his. Something passed between them, not pity, not comfort. Just understanding. Grief recognizing grief.

"They said it would get better," she said. "Back when the news was still on. Said to stay calm, that help was coming."

"No one ever came," Conner replied.

They fell quiet again. The wind outside the lean-to rustled the trees like whispers of ghosts.

After a while, Conner reached into his coat and pulled out a worn photograph. He didn't show it to people, not that there'd been anyone to show it to. But tonight felt different.

He leaned forward and held it out.

Mara took it gently.

A woman with kind eyes and a boy mid-laugh, frozen in time. The photo was wrinkled and water-stained, but the warmth in it hadn't faded.

"She had the softest voice," Conner said, barely above a whisper. "And he… he thought he could fly."

Mara smiled, just a little. "My daughter used to wear wings. Paper ones. Taped to her back. Ran through the yard like she could take off if the wind was just right."

Conner chuckled once, then fell quiet again.

They sat like that for a long time, two broken people sharing scraps of memory like firewood, adding just enough to keep the cold from taking over.

Eventually, Mara stood and disappeared into her tent. She returned with a wool blanket, worn but thick, and handed it to him without a word.

He hesitated, then took it.

"Thanks," he said.

She nodded. "You can sleep here tonight. Fire's safer than sleeping cold."

He nodded, settling down next to the flames, blanket over his shoulders. She returned to her tent, leaving the flap open just a crack.

The fire snapped and popped beside him. Conner lay back and stared up at the night sky through the gaps in the tarp overhead. Stars blinked through like tiny promises.

He wasn't used to the company. He didn't know if this would last, or if morning would take it away.

But for the first time in a long time, Conner didn't feel quite so alone.

7.

They left the river camp at dawn.

Mara packed light with just a tarp, a small pot, and what little food they had between them. Conner carried the blanket she gave him, tucked under the strap of his pack, as if it meant more than warmth. Maybe it did.

They didn't speak much as they walked, but the silence wasn't uncomfortable now. It felt earned. Like two people who didn't need to fill the air to feel less alone.

The trail twisted upward through hills that had once been farmland, now overgrown and wild. Fences lay broken, barns collapsed inward like punched lungs. The skeletons of tractors rusted in fields of waist-high weeds.

Conner paused once to rest. Mara stood beside him, her hand resting on her hip, scanning the horizon.

"You always heading this way?" she asked.

He shook his head. "Wasn't heading anywhere. Not really."

She gave a soft laugh. "Same."

They pressed on.

By late afternoon, they reached the ridge. The sun hovered low behind them, painting the sky in streaks of red and gold. They stood at the top of the hill in silence, looking out over what was left.

Below them stretched what used to be a town or maybe several, all blurred together now by time and ruin. Cracked roads veined the landscape like dried riverbeds. Blackened rooftops slumped into the ground. But from this distance, the destruction softened. The scars looked almost peaceful.

Conner exhaled, slow and quiet.

"It looks different up here," he said.

"Everything does from far away," Mara replied.

They sat, side by side, on a flat rock warmed by the sun. Conner pulled out the last cigarette in his pouch and offered it to her. She took it, surprised, then passed it back after one drag. He lit the end again and finished it slowly, savoring the bitter burn.

"You think there are more people out there?" he asked after a while.

"Probably," she said. "But not a lot. Not close."

He nodded. "That drawing... the one on the shop window. That's yours?"

"No," she said, eyes still on the horizon. "Found it, same as you. But I liked what it said."

"Me too."

They didn't talk about rebuilding. Not about saving the world or finding answers. That wasn't the point.

They just sat there as the sun dipped behind the trees and the cold crept in.

Two people. Still breathing. Still here.

And for now... that was enough.

Epilogue

Spring arrived more slowly than it used to.

The trees were still bare in places, and the river still carried pieces of the old world downstream: plastic bottles, rusted cans, a child's shoe now and then. But there was green again. Little shoots are pushing up through cracks in the road. Weeds bloom like wildflowers.

Conner and Mara had moved upstream, following the water until they found a place where the ground was solid and the wind wasn't so cruel. There was an old cabin, mostly intact. The roof leaked, but it stood. And that was something.

They made it livable. Together.

One morning, Conner stepped outside to find Mara crouched by a patch of overturned soil, her hands covered in dirt. She was planting some seeds she'd saved in a rusted tin can. Squash, she thought. Maybe beans. Time would tell.

He stood on the porch and watched her for a long while, the sun on his face.

He still had nightmares. Still woke up some nights gripping the knife he no longer needed. But each time, the silence was a little softer.

They didn't talk much about the past. It was too heavy. But some nights, around the fire, they'd trade stories. Not the painful ones. Just the strange ones. The funny ones. The ones that reminded them they used to laugh.

One night, Mara handed him a pencil and a scrap of paper. "Write something," she said.

He hadn't written anything in years. But he did.

He wrote:

"We live by the river."

He folded it and tucked it inside the doorframe of the cabin, just in case someone came looking. Just in case someone else was still out there. Like they had been.

And maybe, someday, someone will find it.

And they'd know the world hadn't ended completely.

Not yet.

The world hadn't ended in fire or ice; it had ended in silence. But in that silence, two voices remained.

Echoes of an Empty Bottle

1.

Tom stood at the edge of the patio, flipping burgers while the smell of grilled meat mixed with the laughter of his grandchildren. It was one of those late summer afternoons that felt almost too perfect, with blue skies, a warm sun, and a cool breeze that rustled the trees just enough to remind you that the world kept turning.

His daughter, Emily, had invited him over for a family barbecue. She said it was "nothing fancy," but she'd hung little lights on the porch railing and set up a cooler filled with sodas and juice boxes. Tom watched her move around the yard, helping her youngest with a juice pouch, and something in his chest tightened. She had grown into a kind, strong woman. He liked to think he had something to do with that.

He reached for a soda, twisting the cap slowly. It had been fourteen years since his last drink. Fourteen years of meetings of awkward apologies, of trying to make up for all the years he'd stumbled through fatherhood half-drunk and completely unaware. He thought he'd done okay back then. He wasn't violent. He worked. He made sure there was food on the table. And when he drank, he was the "fun" dad telling jokes, cranking up music, dancing like a fool.

Behind him, he heard his adult kids laughing, Emily and her brother Ryan, standing by the garden.

"Oh my God, remember how Dad was always drunk by like, what, six o'clock?" Emily said between giggles.

"Right?" Ryan added. "And then he'd try to make spaghetti and end up pouring beer in the sauce."

They both burst out laughing.

Tom stood still. The spatula in his hand stopped moving. He stared at the grill, the smoke rising in slow, gray curls. He wasn't part of the laughter, not really. They were remembering a man who thought he was the life of the party. A man who believed being present physically was the same as being present emotionally.

He blinked and took a deep breath. The burger smoke stung his eyes, but he didn't wipe them.

Maybe they weren't mad. Maybe they had even forgiven him. But something inside Tom cracked. He had believed for so long that because he wasn't *as bad* as some other fathers, fists flying, doors slamming, cops called, he had done alright. But that comparison had been a lie, he told himself to sleep at night.

And now, standing in the middle of the life he almost lost, Tom felt the weight of it all, the missed recitals, the forgotten birthdays, the nights his children went to bed worried if Dad would be drunk again.

He turned the burgers and forced a smile as Ryan walked over with a plate. The kids were hungry. Life moved on.

But something in Tom's heart had just woken up, and it wouldn't be going back to sleep.

2.

The memory hit him that night as he lay in bed, staring at the ceiling of his small apartment. It was quiet now, no music, no yelling, no empty bottles clinking as he pushed them out of the way to find a spot on the couch.

He closed his eyes and let the past creep in.

Back then, the house had always been loud. Music was playing, the TV was on, and kids were laughing, or at least he thought they were laughing. Tom remembered dancing in the living room with a drink in one hand and a toddler on his hip. He'd spin around like a goofball, and the kids would squeal. He told himself those were the moments that mattered. They would remember the laughter, the fun, and the wild stories he told that didn't always make sense but always made them smile.

But now, years later, the memory wasn't as warm.

He remembered Emily, maybe eight or nine years old, sitting in the corner with her knees pulled up to her chest. There'd been a party with loud music, too many people, and him in the middle of it all, trying to be the life of the party. She wasn't smiling. She was shrinking.

Ryan was always trying to get his attention. "Dad, look what I made!" "Dad, can you come outside?" But the answers were always "In a minute" or "Maybe later" until the questions stopped coming altogether.

Tom used to laugh at the nights he'd forget things. "Sorry, buddy. Daddy had a long day." Or worse, "You know how I get sometimes." He thought as long as he wasn't yelling or hitting, he was doing alright. He thought he was better than the dads who didn't stick around at all.

But better isn't the same as good.

There were birthdays he couldn't remember. School plays he missed because he was "sleeping off a headache." He once gave Ryan twenty dollars instead of attending a parent-teacher conference. "Buy yourself something cool," he had said, thinking he was the generous dad. But really, he was just too ashamed to sit in a room full of sober people and face who he had become.

He didn't mean to hurt anyone. He truly didn't. But now he realized that didn't matter. Intent didn't erase the silence his children grew up in. It didn't fix the fear in their eyes when his mood changed or the way they tiptoed around him when the bottle was half-empty, and his words got slurred.

He had always told himself, "They're lucky I was around." But now, lying in bed, he whispered something different: *They were lucky to survive me.*

3.

Tom sat at the kitchen table the next morning, stirring his coffee long after the sugar had dissolved. He hadn't slept much. The laughter from the night before, his kids joking about his drinking, kept echoing in his head. He knew they hadn't meant it to hurt him. But it did.

He had spent the last fourteen years trying to be better. He went to meetings. He stayed away from bars. He read the books and did the steps. He told himself he was a new man. And in a lot of ways, he was.

But that didn't undo what came before.

Tom always figured time healed things. That being clean and sober would slowly patch the holes his drinking had left in his kids' lives. And maybe it did, in some ways. They still invited him over. They laughed with him. They hugged him goodbye. But now, for the first time, he wondered if they ever truly felt safe with him. Or if they had just… adapted.

He tapped his fingers against the side of the mug. Fourteen years sober, and only now did he see it clearly.

He'd never screamed at them. Never hit them. But his absence was a different kind of violence, quieter, but still sharp. They never knew which version of him would walk through the door. The loud, happy dad with a six-pack under his arm? Or the slump, slurring one who fell asleep with a lit cigarette in his hand?

He thought about Emily's sweet nature, how, even as a child, she had taken care of everyone. She made sure Ryan brushed his teeth. She tucked herself into bed. She cleaned up after dinner without being asked. At the time, he thought she was just "mature for her age."

Now he saw it for what it was. She'd learned how to survive in a house where the grown-up wasn't always the adult.

Tom dropped his head into his hands and sighed. He didn't know what he had expected. Perhaps to wake up one day and have it all fade away. But sobriety didn't erase the past it just stopped adding to it.

He thought about calling one of his kids. Saying something. But what would he even say?

Sorry, I thought I was a good dad when I wasn't. Sorry, I danced around the mess I made and called it a good time.

He stared at the worn-out coffee mug. It was one his daughter had given him years ago. "Best Dad Ever," it read in faded blue paint. He remembered crying when she gave it to him on his fifth sober anniversary.

Now, it felt like a quiet kind of mercy. Not a statement of fact but a gentle hope. A way of saying: *You weren't then. But maybe you are now.*

Tom wasn't sure if that was true. But he wanted it to be.

4.

It took Tom two more days to work up the nerve.

He stopped by Emily's place on a Sunday afternoon. No big gathering this time, just her, her husband, and the kids. The house had that lived-in warmth: toys on the floor, drawings taped to the fridge, the scent of laundry and leftovers filling the air.

"Hey, Dad," she said, smiling as she opened the door. "Didn't expect to see you."

He held up a box of donuts. "Bribery."

She laughed and let him in.

They sat on the back porch while the kids watched a movie inside. The sky was overcast, and a gentle breeze tugged at the edge of the wind chimes. Tom sipped his coffee, trying to find the right words. Emily chatted for a bit, telling him about work and the kids' latest antics. He smiled and nodded, but his mind was somewhere else entirely.

"Em," he said finally, setting his cup down, "Can I ask you something?"

She looked up, curious. "Of course."

"When you were younger... when I was drinking... did I hurt you?"

Her expression didn't change at first. She just looked at him quietly, like she wasn't sure if he really wanted the answer.

He tried to explain before she could respond. "I always told myself I was a good dad. That I made things fun. Because I wasn't violent or screaming or running off, I was doing okay. But the other night at the barbecue... hearing you and Ryan talk..." He shook his head. "I realized I don't know how it really was. Not for you. Not from your side."

Emily took a long breath and looked out across the yard.

"You weren't... horrible," she said carefully. "You were just... unpredictable. We never knew which version of you we'd get."

She didn't sound angry, just honest.

"There were good times," she continued. "You made us laugh. You did silly dances in the kitchen. You told bedtime stories with voices and everything. But there were also times we felt like we didn't matter as much as the bottle. Like we were background noise to your fun."

Tom swallowed hard. "I'm sorry."

"I know."

Silence stretched between them for a while. But it wasn't cold. It wasn't angry. It was the kind of silence that came after something real was finally spoken out loud.

"I never meant to hurt you," he said. "I thought I was doing okay."

"I know, Dad," she said again, softer this time. "And I know you've been trying for a long time now. We see that. We do."

Tom nodded slowly. His eyes burned, but he didn't cry. He just sat with the truth of it, messy, heavy, and necessary.

They didn't hug. They didn't make a big scene.

But when she refilled his coffee and sat back down beside him, it felt like something had shifted. Not everything. Not perfectly. But enough.

5.

Later that night, Tom sat at his kitchen table with a pen in his hand and a stack of blank cards in front of him.

He hadn't planned on writing anything. He didn't even know what had prompted him to buy the cards at the grocery store earlier that day. Maybe it was the talk with Emily. Maybe it was the way she hadn't flinched when he asked the hard questions. Or maybe it was just time.

He opened one of the cards and stared at the empty inside for a long time. Then, slowly, he started to write.

Dear Kids,

I don't expect this to fix anything. I just want you to know I see it now. The things I missed. The moments I made were harder than they had to be. The silence you had to live with. I thought I was a good dad because I didn't leave. But I wasn't *really* there either, was I?

I'm sorry. You deserved a dad who truly saw you, who showed up every time. I want you to know I regret every missed game, every time I brushed you off, and every time I thought handing you a twenty-dollar bill was the same as love. I didn't know better then. But I do now. And I'm still learning.

When he finished, he left them for his children, one for each, but he didn't seal them. He left them on the table beside the coffee maker. Maybe he'd give them to the kids. Maybe he wouldn't. But writing them felt like something he needed to do for them, and for himself.

He stepped outside onto the balcony and looked out over the quiet street. The world was calm, the kind of calm he never noticed back when his nights ended in blurred vision and blackout silence.

Now, every sound mattered. The chirp of a distant cricket. The hum of a neighbor's porch light. The whisper of wind through the trees.

Tom leaned on the railing and closed his eyes.

He hadn't been the father he should've been. But maybe, just maybe, he could still be the man his kids deserved now.

He wasn't looking for redemption.

Just honesty. And maybe… peace.

Killer of Giants

Prologue

From the Journal of John Doe

It's been a long year since that night. The night everything changed.

Some days, I can still smell the smoke and hear the screams. I recall how quickly it all fell apart in that one moment. I was just living my life, going to work, grabbing dinner, flipping through the news... then the sirens started. Then the explosions. Then the screaming.

And after that... the darkness.

I don't know how I got here. The walls sweat with moisture. The stone is cold beneath my bare feet, cracked and slick with mildew. The air tastes like rust and rot, like old blood and forgotten places. A small, barred window near the ceiling lets in a sliver of light during the day, but it's more of a reminder of everything I've lost than a sign of life. Dust drifts in lazy spirals, catching the light like ash. I don't know if it's morning or evening anymore. Time doesn't mean much down here.

At first, I thought someone would come. That they'd open the metal door and let me out. But the days turned into weeks, and the weeks into months, and the silence never broke.

Now, I don't think they're ever coming to let me go. I think they're coming to kill me.

I've heard the screams. I've heard what they do to others.

I don't know how much longer I have left, but before it ends, before *they* come, I need to get this out. Someone needs to know what really happened that night. Someone needs to hear the truth.

If you're reading this, maybe there's still time. Maybe you can stop it. Maybe you can save your world from becoming mine.

Entry 1- **May 24, 2042**

My psychiatrist said I should write to get the anger out. Said it would help me "process things." Whatever that means.

So here I am. Writing in this damn notebook.
I don't even know where to start.

She left me.
Seven months. That's all it took. And then she was gone. No warning, no conversation, just packed a bag and walked out. I asked her why. She just said she couldn't "do this" anymore.

I think I treated her okay.
I mean... didn't I?

I wasn't perfect. I know that. But nobody is. I told her I loved her. I bought her flowers on Thursdays, even when I didn't have the money. I held her when she cried. I tried. God, I tried.

So why wasn't it enough?

She called me angry. Said I had "dark moods." Said I drank too much. But what did she expect? The world's a mess, and sometimes I just need to take the edge off. That doesn't make me a bad guy.

Right?

I keep thinking about that night. The way she looked at me was like she didn't even know me anymore. Like I was a stranger. Or worse, something to be afraid of.

Maybe I scared her. Maybe I scare myself sometimes.

Chris says I need to slow down, that I'm spiraling. He's probably right, but what does he know? He still believes things can get better. I used to believe that, too.

Now I'm not so sure.

Entry 2 – May 26, 2042

Saw her at the store yesterday.
She was with another man, holding his hand as if it were nothing.

She looked right through me. No hello. No "how have you been?" Just a blank stare and a smile for *him*.

I didn't think it would cut this deep, but it did. I stood there like an idiot, six-pack sweating in my hand, fluorescent lights flickering overhead like they were mocking me. The checkout scanner beeped in the distance. Somewhere behind me, a kid laughed, and it sounded like it was aimed at me. and pain in my chest that I couldn't swallow down.

She moved on.
Meanwhile, I'm stuck in a loop, writing in this stupid book, trying not to fall apart.

But I am falling apart.

I wake up and don't know why I should bother getting out of bed. The only thing I look forward to is the drink waiting for me in the kitchen. It's the only thing that doesn't lie to me.

I'm so tired, and I'm so angry, and sometimes I don't even recognize my own reflection anymore. There's something in my eyes that wasn't there before. A shadow. A crack.

Maybe that's where it all begins.

Maybe that's how the darkness gets in.

Entry 3 – June 11, 2042

My psychiatrist says I don't write enough.
He says I bottled up too much. Says I've got to "let it out before it poisons me."

So, I'm doing what I used to do in college. Free writing. No rules. No filters. Just dumping thoughts on the page and hoping something makes sense.

Let's start with this: I feel hollow.

Not sad. Not angry. Just… empty. Like there's a part of me that's missing, and no matter what I do, I can't seem to fill it.

I've stopped seeing friends. Chris still texts now and then, but I ignore him. I don't want to pretend things are okay. I'm tired of pretending.

The weird thing is, I've started hearing things.

Not voices exactly. More like… echoes. Whispers on the edge of sleep. Sometimes, they sound like her voice. Other times, like mine, but warped, deeper, like it's coming from a tunnel. It started when I was drifting off last week. I heard it clearly as day:

"You're not the only you."

I sat straight up. The room was dark. Silent. But something about those words stuck with me.

You're not the only you.

What the hell does that mean?

Entry 4 – June 12, 2042

I saw someone today.

Not someone I know, not really, but I've seen him before. A man with a gray coat, weathered face, and a sketchpad he carries like it's sacred. I used to think he was just one of the city's forgotten people. You know, the kind that sit on park benches all day watching pigeons and ignoring the world. But there's something different about him.

He doesn't beg. Doesn't speak. Just draws.

The strange part? I've spotted him three times this week in different parts of the city. Always alone. Always sketching. Once near the train station. Once outside the grocery store. Today, he was just sitting across from the diner, staring at me.

Not at the building.

At *me*.

I looked away. When I glanced back, he was gone.

I don't know why I'm even writing this down. Just felt… important somehow. Like seeing him meant something. Like he's watching for a reason.

Entry 5 – June 13, 2042

I haven't slept more than an hour at a time. The whispers keep coming.

They say things I don't understand, but they feel familiar. Like someone is feeding me memories I've never lived. I dreamed of a city in ruins. The sky was choked with smoke, so thick that it painted the clouds in streaks of charcoal. The air burned like metal left too long on the stove. Sirens wailed in the distance, sharp and fading, like the city itself was crying out. Asphalt peeled underfoot, and shattered glass glittered in the wind like salt on wounds. People were running and screaming. I saw a man standing in the middle of it all, calm as stone, with a notebook in his hand.

It was me. But not me.

I was older. Harder. Eyes full of fire. I looked like someone who had already watched the world burn and survived it.

I don't think it was just a dream.

That sounds insane, I know.
But deep down, it didn't *feel* like fiction. It felt less like a dream and more like a stolen memory, fading at the edges but sharp where it counted. A warning etched in smoke and flame.

I'm scared to tell my psychiatrist. He'll up my meds or throw some label on it. "Delusional disorder," or some crap like that. But what if it's not a disorder? What if it's... something else?

A warning?
A connection?

Maybe there *is* another me in another world.
Maybe his world fell apart, and mine is next.

Entry 6 – **June 18, 2042**

I found something today.
Or maybe it found me.

I was cleaning out the closet, anything to stay busy, not to think. I hadn't done laundry in two weeks, but at 3 AM, it felt like the only task left between me and collapse.

I knocked over an old box I don't remember packing. Dust shot up like smoke, and something slid out from under a pile of clothes, something cold, heavy, and unfamiliar.

A black leather notebook.

It looked scorched along the edges, like it had survived a fire that hadn't happened yet. The leather was cracked, stained with something dark that might've been water... or something worse.

When I opened it, my hands began to shake.

It was already full of writing.

In my handwriting, but I hadn't written a word.

The first page says:

"They told me not to trust the light.
The light lies. It shows you comfort, but hides the truth beneath it."

I sat there staring at that line for a long time. It felt like someone had ripped the thought straight out of my head and etched it in ink. Page after page is filled with scribbled entries, dreams, visions, and warnings. Some of it makes no sense. But some of it... chills me.

One line in particular keeps repeating:

"They are not giants of flesh, but giants of fire and silence."

What does that even mean?

Entry 7 – June 20, 2042

I've been reading the notebook every night.
It's like a map of someone's slow descent into madness or maybe a survival guide.

The entries talk about "the breach," something that tore a hole between worlds. The man who wrote it, who sounds exactly like me, describes a city burning, entire nations turning on themselves, people becoming shadows of what they once were.

He talks about a place called *Black Hollow*. A prison, maybe. Or a research facility. I can't quite tell. He says it's where the world ends. Where they hold the last of "us."

I know how this sounds.

I know how *I* sound.

But here's the thing, I recognize parts of the notebook. Not just the handwriting. The phrasing, the thoughts… even some memories. There's an entry about watching a woman leave, her silhouette in the doorway, the smell of her shampoo still hanging in the air. It's almost word-for-word something I wrote in my old journals ten years ago.

So, how is it in here?

How is any of this possible?

Unless… Unless this other version of me lived it all before I did.

Entry 8 – June 22, 2042

I saw him again.

Same guy, the one with the sketchpad. Gray coat. Sharp eyes. There's something unnerving about the way he watches me, like he's waiting for me to figure something out. He was leaning against the railing near the library, not drawing this time. Just standing there. Watching people pass. Watching *me*.

When our eyes met, he nodded. Not in a friendly way. More like... recognition. Like he knew who I was.

Or *what* I was.

I started to cross the street toward him, but a bus blocked my view. When it passed, he was gone.

I keep thinking about the notebook. The way it seems to *know* things. The fire around its edges. The words I didn't write but remember anyway.

What if that man has one too?

What if he's not just watching me?

What if he's watching *what I become*?

Entry 9 – June 24, 2042

I was walking home last night when the world seemed to blink.

It was just for a second, but everything shifted. One moment, I was walking past the diner on the 5th, neon lights buzzing, rain tapping against my coat, and the next, I was somewhere else.

The sky had turned a deep, bruised gray, thick with something heavier than clouds. Smoke? Ash? I couldn't tell. The buildings still stood in their usual places, but they weren't right, windows shattered like jagged teeth, facades warped as if scorched by something that left no flame. The street beneath my feet was split and buckled, like the earth itself had recoiled. No lights. No cars. Just silence and the distant creak of something unseen. It felt like walking through a memory that wasn't mine.

It felt like the same city… just broken. Abandoned.

Dead.

And then, just like that, I was back.

Standing in front of the diner again. Same neon buzz. Same drizzle. A woman inside was sipping her coffee, staring at her phone as if nothing had happened. Like the world hadn't just torn at the seams.

I didn't say anything. I just kept walking.

I haven't told anyone. I don't think I *can*.
Not unless I want to end up locked away.

But I know what I saw.
And I think it's getting closer.

Entry 10 – June 26, 2042

I can't trust mirrors anymore.

The bathroom was still fogged from the shower, beads of condensation crawling down the mirror like nervous sweat. I wiped it clean with my palm, expecting to see the usual half-shaven, sleep-deprived wreck I've become. But what stared back didn't move. For a heartbeat, he stood still while I leaned forward, his eyes dull and too tired, like they belonged to a man carrying centuries of regret. Same face. Same scars.

But he wasn't me.

He mouthed something before he faded. I think he said:

"Don't wait."

And then he was gone.

I stared at the mirror for twenty minutes. My reflection came back, like normal. But nothing about it felt normal.

The notebook, the one I found, is still on the nightstand. Every time I open it, there's something new inside. Pages that weren't there the day before. Pages I *know* I didn't write.

The last one said:

"You are the echo, not the voice. You are the crack, not the glass. The fire is coming, and the giants are already awake."

I don't know what that means. But I'm starting to think the journal isn't telling a story.

I think it's telling the future.

Or maybe… It's remembering mine.

Entry 11 – June 30, 2042

Something happened today.
Someone else saw it.

I was at the park, trying to get some air to clear my head and maybe prove to myself that I wasn't completely losing it. I sat on a bench under the big oak near the east path. That tree's always been my favorite. Even when I was a kid. I used to think it looked like it was holding the sky together.

I was staring up through the branches when the world *shimmered* again. Like heat rising off the pavement, only the sky itself bent just for a second.

I looked around. No one else seemed to notice.

Except one.

There was a man, maybe in his sixties, sitting across from me with a sketchpad in his lap. He froze when it happened. His pencil dropped. We locked eyes. And I swear... I saw the same panic on his face that I felt in mine.

He stood up and started walking away quickly. I chased after him.

Entry 12 – June 30, 2042 (Later)

I caught up to him near the parking lot. I didn't even know what to say. I just blurted out, *"Did you see it?"*

He stopped. Looked around. Leaned in close and said, "You're not supposed to be aware of it yet."

Yet.

He asked me my name. I told him. He nodded like he already knew.

Said his name was Wallace. Just Wallace.

He told me to burn the notebook.

Said, *"It's not a journal. It's a tether."*

I asked him what that meant, but he just shook his head.

"You've already opened the door," he said. "Now they know you're listening."

I tried to get more out of him, but he was already walking away. Before he left, he turned around and said something I can't stop thinking about:

"We don't kill giants, John. We become them."

The notebook's sitting on my desk now. I keep staring at it like it might bite. Part of me wants to throw it into the fire. Another part thinks Wallace is right, but not in the way he means.

If it really *is* a tether, then maybe it's not connecting me to madness.

Maybe it's connecting me to the truth.

Entry 13 – July 3, 2042

I didn't sleep last night.
I couldn't.

The notebook had a new page this morning. I didn't write it I *never* write at night, but there it was like it had written itself while I was staring at the ceiling.

"The giants are not beasts. They are decisions. They are power without mercy, anger without reason. They wear human faces, speak in logic, and burn the world in the name of order."

There's more to this than I thought. More than dreams or parallel lives. This isn't just some alternate version of me trying to warn me.

This is about *us*. About mankind. About the things we build and the things we destroy.

We always thought the monsters would come from outside, aliens, demons, or gods with vengeance. But what if we are the monsters?

What if the giants… are us?

Entry 14 – July 5, 2042

Wallace hasn't come back. I checked the park three times. Nothing.

But I found something else.

At the base of the old oak tree, my tree, someone left a folded piece of paper wedged in the bark. I unfolded it. It was a page torn from the notebook.

My notebook.

But the entry was dated *July 5, 2072.*

"I watched the sky tear open. Fire came first. Then silence. We called them weapons, but they weren't. They were warnings. We didn't listen."

I don't know what to do with that.

Either I'm completely losing my mind, or someone is sending messages across time. Across realities.

Or both.

Either way… I feel like something is coming. And I'm not sure there's anything I can do to stop it.

Entry 15 – July 7, 2042

The noise outside is getting louder. Not traffic or people *them*. The whispers. The echoes. The hum of something pressing in from the other side of the wall.

Sometimes I think I see shadows move just before I turn my head.

Sometimes I think they're no longer waiting.

They're crossing over.

Entry 16 – July 10, 2042

I saw it happen.

Not in a dream. Not in a journal.
In front of me. In *my* world.

I was walking past City Hall just before sunset. The sky was smeared with red and gold, like a warning sign nobody was reading. I heard this low rumble deep and wide, like the earth was grinding its teeth. I looked up, and the sky shattered. Not in thunder or wind, but like a windshield hit dead-on by something too fast to see. Thin, jagged lines spread outward in all directions, light seeping through like blood from a wound. Beyond it, something moved, vast and mechanical, cloaked in smoke and ruin. Fires blinked on the horizon like dying stars. The sky stitched itself shut in a blink, but I was left gasping like I'd glimpsed the world's death sentence.

Through the break, I saw it just for a breath.

A dark tower, surrounded by smoke and ruin. Fires on the horizon. A field of broken machines.
And something tall. Massive. Moving.

A giant.

Not made of flesh.
Made of steel, rage, and silence.

When the crack was sealed, everything returned to its original position. People walked by like nothing had happened. I dropped to my knees on the sidewalk, gasping for breath, heart racing like I'd just escaped something... or maybe stepped into it.

They're not coming anymore.
They're already here.

Entry 17 – July 11, 2042

The notebook wrote itself again last night.

"This is not your story.
This is your consequence."

I don't know how much longer I will have. I can feel it, this slow tearing at the edges of who I am. Like, I'm not one person anymore. Like there's *another me* growing inside, feeding on doubt and anger and fear.

What if that's what the giants are?

What if every decision we make, every hate we carry, every time we choose silence instead of standing up, that's what feeds them?

And what if I'm not resisting them at all?

What if I'm becoming one?

Entry 18 – July 12, 2042

I didn't want this.

I wanted love. I wanted peace. I wanted to forget.
Instead, I remembered everything.

The war. The breach. The world that burned. I lived through it. Or another version of me did. I can feel his memories like scars under my skin.

And now… I think I understand.

This isn't just about saving the world.
It's about *not repeating it.*

But maybe it's already too late. Maybe the notebook wasn't a warning; it was a countdown.

And we're out of time.

Entry 19 – July 14, 2042

It's raining tonight.

The rain hasn't let up since dusk, thin needles tapping glass like a thousand tiny warnings. The city is too quiet. Not the hush of peace, but the absence of life. The kind of silence that follows after something ends. Streetlights buzz with sickly yellow light, casting broken reflections on the puddles. I watched the drops chase each other down the window, each one a silent countdown. The thunder sounded distant at first, but then it spoke, and I swear I heard it say my name.

I sat by the window for hours watching the rain slide down the glass. I used to love storms. Now they feel like warnings.

There was a voice in the thunder tonight. Not poetic, not symbolic; I *heard* it.

"One becomes a giant when he believes there's no other way."

I don't know if that came from me, the notebook, or something else. But it hit like a punch to the chest.

All this time, I thought I was being haunted by something from the outside. Something massive and merciless that would crush us all.

But maybe... maybe the giant isn't something we fight.
Maybe it's something we let grow inside us.

And maybe I've already fed it too much.

Entry 20 – July 15, 2042

Wallace came to me again.

He didn't say much. Just stood outside my apartment door, rain soaking through his coat. He looked older than before. Tired.

"You still have a choice," he said.

I asked him what choice I had. The world is splitting. The other version of me is already dead, or worse. The fire is coming. The notebook won't stop writing. And my mind feels like a battlefield.

But he just looked at me and said:

"You choose what kind of giant you become."

Then he turned and walked into the dark.

Entry 21 – July 16, 2042

I burned the notebook.

Every page. Every whisper. Every warning.

I stood out in the alley behind my building, dumped it into a metal trash can, and lit a match. The fire flared up as if it were starving. The heat was sharp and fast, like it *knew*.

I thought I'd feel better, but I didn't.

Because the words are still in my head.

And so is the other me.

But I made my choice.

I won't be a monster.
I won't be a giant.

If the world ends, it won't be because I gave in.

Let them come.

Epilogue

I found the journal buried beneath the rubble of what had once been an apartment building. It was scorched around the edges, with the cover half-melted, but the pages inside were mostly intact.

I don't know who he was. The name "John" comes up more than once, scribbled in tired handwriting that gets shakier the further you read. I don't know what city this was, or if it even has a name anymore. The signs are all ash. The sky hasn't shown anything but gray in weeks.

But I read every page.

And I believed every word.

Some would say he was just a broken man. A casualty of grief and madness. A mind slowly folding in on itself while the world around him collapsed. Maybe that's true.

But I think he saw something the rest of us couldn't. Or wouldn't.

He knew the giants weren't creatures that came from the sky.
They came from us. From the choices we made. The hate we excused.
The silence we gave to things that should've been stopped.

He ultimately burned the notebook. But the story didn't die with the fire.

Because I'm still reading it.

Because you're reading it now.

And maybe that's all he really wanted.
Not to be saved.
But to be *heard*.

11/14/2011

God grant me the

serenity to accept the

things I cannot change;

Courage to change the

things I can;

And wisdom to know the difference.

www.ingramcontent.com/pod-product-compliance
Lightning Source LLC
Chambersburg PA
CBHW020923020726
47495CB00002B/315